THE JOURNEY HOME

A Novel by

ZELDA POPKIN

J. B. LIPPINCOTT COMPANY

PHILADELPHIA AND NEW YORK

CHAPTER ONE

Don Corbett went straight to the bar.

The bar was lined with young men in suntans with the orange wings on bright blue, the red-dotted white stars on their sleeves and campaign ribbons over their hearts. They were drinking but without hilarity, indifferently, almost mechanically, as though drinking were merely a species of "busy work," to occupy gullets and hands while minds were working out something important.

Corbett wedged himself in at the end of the bar. A chunky Second Lieutenant who had thought that he had the end pulled in his elbows to give Corbett a few inches more.

The bartender was in the middle of the bar, drawing beer and Corbett's knuckles drummed the mahogany, waiting for him to come down to the end.

The Second Lieutenant noted the knuckles and over the lip of his glass took inventory of the man who was drumming. He saw a tall, lax figure, concave at the belly; a prominent nose and good jaw; a wide, high forehead, with light brown hair, curly, needing a trim. No recruiting poster, but not a bad-looking guy. A sleeve had the wings and the star; collar tabs one silver bar and small silver wings. The Lieutenant was either old—Air Force old, twenty-eight, twenty-nine—or very tired. There were grooves on both sides of his nose, past his mouth and he had the blue-gilled, drained look of someone who hasn't been sleeping. Yet there was a patent excitement about him, an air of expectancy, imminent change, a man going where he wanted to be, in a hurry.

It wasn't entirely that the khaki he wore was new-looking, clean, perfectly creased. On the left breast were the spread silver wings of the bombardier and a rainbow of ribbons. The right had a blue stripe in a frame. The ribbons cut out the need to ask questions. In a shorthand of color and symbol, they told Corbett's story: "European Theatre. Distinguished Flying Cross, Air Medal, two oak leaf clusters; Unit Citation."

The Second Lieutenant wore some of the same on his blouse: the brown and green for Europe and Africa, the oak leaf studded Air Medal orange and blue, but where Corbett wore the D.F.C.'s blue, white and red, he had a violet inch. He asked: "Eighth or Ninth?" and when Corbett said: "Ninth," he nodded companionably, said: "Me, I'm the Eighth" and added "You just got in," not inquiring but stating an obvious fact.

"Today," Corbett said. "And thirsty as hell."

"Take the rum," the Second Lieutenant replied. "Take my advice, take the rum."

Corbett lifted his eyebrows, thinking the guy had his nerve, and when the bartender came down at last, he said: "Scotch."

The Second Lieutenant shrugged, picked up his own glass. "Your funeral, Bud. You were warned."

The bartender held his big paw over the label while he poured Corbett's Scotch. "Soda?" he asked.

"Hell, no," Corbett said.

The bartender ran half a glass of tap water and set it next to the Scotch. Corbett pushed back the water with the scowl of a man who can't bother with trifles. His hand shook when he lifted his whiskey. A few drops spilled on the bar. The bartender mopped it. "Pay when you're served," he said and waited, flicking his rag.

Corbett set down the glass and took out his wallet. He slapped a dollar bill down, then drained his glass. The raw blend was bitter as aloes. He grimaced.

The Second Lieutenant smiled. "What did I tell you? Embalming fluid. After you've been here a while, you'll know better than touch their bar Scotch."

"I'm not staying here," Corbett said. "I'm going on home."

"Your twenty-one days?"

Corbett nodded.

"Got your reservation?"

"I'll get it."

"Oh yeah." The Second Lieutenant raised his shoulders again. He signalled the bartender to mix him another rum collins. "Lieutenant," he said. "You sure have plenty to learn."

The bartender placed a nickel and dime before Corbett and reached back for the bottle of rum. Corbett stared at the coins and said: "Hey!"

The bartender knew what he meant without turning to see. Over his shoulder he tossed: "That's correct."

"That's correct." The Second Lieutenant repeated. "Eighty-five cents for embalming fluid. That's how they welcome us home."

"Hell!" Corbett's nose wrinkled. "Did *you* get any bargains in the E.T.O.? If I'm going to be gypped, I'd rather be gypped by my own."

The Second Lieutenant said "Roger." He raised his glass, mumbled "Short war," and swigged his fresh collins.

Corbett pushed back his glass for a refill. "I'm going to get plastered," he said. "I'm going to get high. I'm going to climb way on top of the flak."

The Second Lieutenant's head wagged. "You're gonna get sick."

Corbett flung an obscenity at him. He threw down a dollar and emptied his glass. None of the liquor had spilled this time. He tried to decide whether the bartender had begun to get stingy or whether his hand was finally steadying. He scooped up the coins and said more amiably than he had spoken before: "Nickels and dimes. I'll need them to call up the girls. Listen, Bud." He half-turned, addressing the Second Lieutenant earnestly as if he had to make something plain. "I'm keeping a promise. I promised myself the minute my heels hit my country, I was going to get stiff. For twenty-one days, if my dough holds out, I won't draw one sober breath."

The Second Lieutenant said "Roger" again and: "Better not call up those girls. You'll just be wasting your time."

Corbett's short laugh held no mirth. "It takes a hell of a lot to put me out." He pushed back his glass, and stood still, knitting his brows, waiting for something to happen.

The Scotch wasn't clicking. Not yet. The length of his frame was a sponge, parched in each fibre, too much to reach, to revive all at once. There was only the driving impatience inside, the nerves straining forward, ready to snap. "Christ!" he considered. "At this rate, it'll take a month's pay for me to get pickled." "Go easy, old boy," he commanded himself. "Take it easy, old kid. You'll make it. Give yourself time."

He set down his empty glass, turned around, bracing his back on the bar.

The place was small. It had a half dozen tables and one shuffling waiter, an old man with a blanched prune face, a sharp, parrot beak. There were girls at the tables.

The room was gray-hazy with smoke and filled to the door stops with Air Force men, at ease in their suntans, with ribbons: the E.T.O. brown and green; the Pacific yellow, the yellow and blue, the purple, the blue, white and red. A saloon full of heroes, of guys who'd been over and up twenty-five, thirty-five, maybe more times.

The thumb of Corbett's right hand sought out his left, pressed it, began to rub, steadily hard. He wasn't aware that he kept rubbing his thumb while he stared at the girls.

The girls were chattering and giggling, as if each of them had to do all the talking and laughing for two. Most of the airmen sat hunched over highballs or beer, dropping only a word here and there, occasionally smiling, quiet, relaxed, as people sit at a fireplace, day-dreaming, sucking in warmth.

One of the men sat with the chain of his dog tag spanning his fingertips, completely immobile, studying his own name and number, to fix it indelibly inside his brain. The girl who was with him reached over, lifted it off and began to play with the trinket. The man didn't protest. He merely looked worried, scared she might break it or keep it or lose it.

A young Sergeant came in and glanced around. A girl yelped: "There's Newt! Hey, Newt, come here," and patted an empty chair seat beside her table. The Sergeant went over and stood, stood minutes long, looking at her and the chair, as though just taking a seat was a problem he had to think through.

Some of the girls were noticing Corbett. He saw them smile, inviting him over. He took a step forward, then stopped. "Nix. No dice," he decided. "I'll find my own." He felt pleased with himself although he knew he had made that decision because the girls weren't special. "Bags," he told himself. "Just bags. I rate better than that."

It was an agreeable surprise to find himself being discriminating. For months, he had been thinking of girls, just thinking, *American Girls,* as though that meant one single person, one face, one body, one voice. And here were the girls. Lots of girls. You could choose. You could say "yes" or "no." You said "no."

Some of these girls were thin; some were plump. They were blonde, they were dark. They wore their hair up in pompadours or down in bobs. They had flowers in their hair. They had bows. They had glittering earrings and combs. They were dressed up for men, in bright colored sports clothes or long evening dresses. They talked with the soft slur of the South, flat Midwestern twangs, Boston A's, nasal Bronx whines. They were all kinds of girls. But not one worth a snatch. "I'll find my own," he concluded. "I'll pick me a dish. I'll look over the town. I'll go where civilians hang out."

"Civilians!" His mind repeated the word, with awe, with an actual hunger.

He knew he was sick of the color of war, the dun brown of khaki. He knew he was fed up with heroes.

He turned back to the bar. "Double," he said, and as if his actions required explanation, he added truculently to whoever was listening: "Suppose I do get stiff. I'm leaving for home first thing tomorrow."

The bartender stopped pouring the Scotch and glanced at

him with a new shade of interest. He rested one elbow on the bar. Offhandedly, with the air of just making small talk, he inquired: "Got your reservation?"

"I'll get one."

"You will, eh?" The bartender's lower lip jutted. "You will?"

"I will," Corbett snapped. His voice rose, waspish with annoyance. "What goes? Have they stopped selling berths out of Miami?"

The Second Lieutenant ducked into the dialogue. "All but," he muttered. "You'll learn, pal. You'll learn."

The bartender, still casual, asked: "How far you going?"

"New York."

"That where you live?" the Second Lieutenant asked.

"Brooklyn, if it makes any difference."

The bartender smiled. Corbett began to feel badgered.

The Second Lieutenant sensed it. "Take it easy," he said. "Brooklyn's as good a place to come from as any, I guess. Me, I'm from Michigan." Then concluding he'd spent enough time on Corbett, he mumbled: "See you," picked up what remained of his collins and meandered off toward the tables.

Corbett paid for his double. The bartender put down the change, but he didn't go down to the beer tap. He rested both arms on the bar. "So you come from Brooklyn and you're going to New York," he mused. He kept his lip out and clucked. "Well, you *could* get on *some* train. Thirty-six hours, if you're lucky. Some folks don't mind sitting on a suitcase fifteen hundred miles to New York. Some folks don't even mind if they have to stand up." He straightened his back, sucked in his lip. "Me, I would mind," he said. He moved down the bar.

Corbett's brows slid together. He cradled his empty glass in his hand, squeezing it hard, as though he intended to crush it. But he didn't look up until the bartender once more was down at his end of the bar. Then he thrust back the glass. The man didn't reach for the bottle this time. Instead he leaned over the bar. "Listen, Bud." He pitched his voice low, just over a whisper. "The waiter might be able to fix you up. He gets cancellations." He looked sideways to make sure that no one was listening. His voice dropped until Corbett had to bend over to hear what he said. "There's a small service charge. Okay with you? I'm telling you so there won't be no squawk."

"Hell, yes," Corbett said. "I have to get going."

The bartender smiled. "I heard that before. Track closed today. If I was you, I'd step on it, Bud, in case he just happens to have—" He winked. "Supply and demand, don't you know?"

"Much obliged," Corbett said.

"Not at all. Always glad to help a serviceman out."

Corbett crossed the room swiftly, tweaked the old waiter's sleeve, leaned down to his ear. "I need a reservation to New York. What you got?"

White eyebrows rose on the parchment face in "Who? Me?" Rheumy eyes sharpened and nostrils twitched.

Corbett tensed with anxiety. He tilted his head toward the bar. "He said you could fix me up."

The waiter darted a furtive glance toward the bar. Corbett saw the bartender nod. He let his breath out in relief.

The old man jerked his thumb toward a door at the rear of the room. "You wait for me. I'll be out."

Beyond the door, was the sensuous Florida night, starry, perfumed, haunted by breezes swept in from the sea. A diluted fragment was penned in an alley, shaded by hissing cocoanut palms, dim-lit by a single-wired caged bulb. Corbett leaned on the white stucco wall of the building. Over the swish of the ocean, he heard the tinkle of glassware and feminine laughter. He inhaled the fetid, warm odors of beer slops and grease. Lassitude spread through him, a feeling of boredom, as with a thing done too often. The place seemed familiar; his own slouch of waiting was almost a habit. "Christ!" he decided. "This is all I've been doing since I went over, waiting in alleys for some buzzard to bring me a bargain. A woman. A bottle. And now a ticket."

The door creaked, slyly opening. The old waiter slid out, went briskly to business. "I got one on the Palm Queen. To-morrer mornin'." With a flourish, he pulled out of his pocket a ribbon of paper and a small scrap of pasteboard, held the little piece up to the light, read: "Seat five. Coach Sixteen." His leer held the pride of man passing miracle.

Corbett's jaw fell. "No sleeper?"

"Listen, Buddy, the President himself couldn't get him a berth out of Miami this week. It's all there is. Last one in town. Some woman decided to stay. She give up her ticket. Bell hop at her hotel, he let me sell it."

Corbett shuffled his shoes indecisively. The palms hissed in his ears, urging him to hurry, make up his mind. At last he stretched out his hand for the ticket.

The old man shook his head. "Take it easy. Don't grab." He mentioned the price.

Corbett gagged. The pulse in his throat throbbed with rage. "You got your gall."

The old man's shoulders rose. "Ain't another ticket in town. Take it or leave it. It's all one to me. I kin sell it a dozen times over." The yellow stumps of his teeth grinned at Corbett. He began to fold up the ticket. "Where you been, Bud? Don't you know there's a war?"

Corbett's hand stiffened. His fingers arched, leaped toward the scrawny old neck.

The man blinked. He backed away but he didn't seem frightened. "That won't get you no place," he said calmly. "It's conditions, Bud. Get wise to yourself." His hand touched the doorknob again. He shook his head, rebuking Corbett. "It's you wants to get home. Not me." He opened the door to the bar and began to go in.

Corbett caught at his sleeve. "I'll take it." He heard a girl's laugh, sudden and brittle, like the breaking of china.

The waiter pushed the door shut. "I thought you looked smart." He tapped Corbett's arm, familiarly. "I thought you wasn't no dope. Bud, you gotta know where you are. Down here in Florida, we just got two crops: tourists and oranges.

We skin 'em both." He cackled, unfolded the ticket, holding it warily until Corbett had opened his wallet.

While Corbett counted the bills, his voice took on a more sociable tone. "Was you out to the track?"

"Hell, no."

"Too bad, Bud, too bad. You mighta got rich. A long shot paid off. Four Freedoms. Seventeen thirty to two. Never saw such a day. The smart dough wouldn't touch it. They laid their money on Sun Again."

CHAPTER TWO

THE PALM QUEEN: THROUGH TRAIN BETWEEN FLOR-IDA, GEORGIA, THE CAROLINAS, VIRGINIA, WASHINGTON AND NEW YORK. SLEEPING CAR, RECLINING COACHES, DINING CAR, SERVING ALL MEALS. LEAVING MIAMI DAILY 8:30 A.M.

Sunday, golden and still, lay over Miami.

The slightest of breezes jostled the palms with fingertip tenderness not to wake up the tourists, exhausted with dancing and drinking and rolling the dice; the natives worn out by selling and serving. A gentle jade sea rocked in the sun, warming a sybarite's bath. In green patios facing the surf, the war-battered, up with the dawn, sauntered in flapping bathrobes, blood-red silhouettes on an azure sky.

Taxis rolled over the Causeway from the white sugar towers at the Beach, through the silent, shut streets of the city. Sleepy, bronzed faces peered through their windows, taking last looks at midsummer in March. Through the mean streets near the train shed, soldiers and sailors plodded, dragging their sacks of clothing and gear.

Silver fox, Persian lamb, mink, filled the station, debouched on the cinders, swarming around hillocks of luggage and golf bags. The soldiers and sailors stayed near the wall of the depot or out next to the track.

A gunner's mate, wearing his whites and ribbons, carried a baby and one big valise out to the edge of the cinders. His wife had a small black suitcase and a blue furlough bag, bulging its canvas. A tiny girl, aged three or four, with a short, red plaid skirt, a red jacket and pigtails tied with red ribbons, clung to two of her fingers. The child carried a battered nude doll, half as big as herself.

The sailor set down his valise. His wife put down hers.

Don Corbett moved a step over to give them more space. He shifted his coat from one arm to the other, put down his own bag. His stomach felt queasy with last night's Scotch, this morning's depot counter coffee and sinkers. His head ached. The pushing inside him was turned to a jittery impatience. The long-dreamed elation of getting home had sunk to the ache of one man in a crowd, with no one to talk to. Everyone else seemed to have someone going along or saying goodbye.

The gunner's mate's wife accidentally nudged him when she reached to take her infant from its father's arms, said, "Oh, excuse me," and Corbett was grateful for that. She was thin, he saw, as service wives are, because they're so young and worry so much and don't eat enough since there's no man coming home for a meal and it's much too much bother to cook for yourself. She had looks, a school-girlish cuteness. Her eyes were bright green. Her mouse-brown long bob looked shiny and soft and well-cared for. She was wearing a topcoat of firemen's red. Nobody would have taken her for the mother of two.

The gunner's mate tightened his grip on the baby. "I'll hold him," he said. "I'll carry him up on the train. You'll have him enough."

The sailor was skinny and freckled. He was wearing practically all of the spectrum. Corbett caught a flash of the blue and white Navy Cross ribbon when the lad shifted the baby. The kid had been wriggling its fat little neck and the strings of its bonnet were coming undone. The gunner's mate tried to tie them with one hand and couldn't. His wife snatched off the bonnet. She said: "He won't need a cap on the train."

The kid had been sweating. His soft golden hairs were damp, stuck together and stood up in a comical point in the middle of his skull. The gunner's mate rolled the point with his fingers to twist in a curl. "He looks like a kewpie," he said. "Remember those dolls?"

"You won one for me down at the Island. I still have it some place."

"Give it to Joanie."

The little girl looked up when her name was mentioned. "I have my dolly," she chirped. "Dolly's going for a ride on the train."

The sailor caressed the top of her hair with his free hand. "It sure was swell to see the kids. Not sorry you made the trip?"

"Sorry?" His wife tossed her head. "Three months in Miami?"

"It was swell," he repeated. "Even the way we were living."

"I'd do it again, if we had to sleep on the Beach." Her face broke of a sudden, went quivery like jelly. She struggled to pull it together before he could notice. Yet when she spoke, her voice gave her away. It was bitter and torn as if her throat hurt. "You'd think they'd have left you here on shore duty. You did enough. Seventeen days on that raft."

He said quickly: "Skip it, Betty. Skip it, old kid." He touched her arm near the elbow. "I had three months here. That's a hell of a lot more than other guys had."

People were crowding around them and they fell suddenly speechless, embarrassed. Corbett glanced down the track, at the switch tower, the palms, the rails shimmering in sunlight. He was glad that the train still wasn't due. For a while more, he wanted to watch the gunner's mate and his wife and to listen to them. He knew that he wanted to hear the simple, deeply-felt words of people who cared for each other. Hearing them say these things to each other was next best to hearing them said to himself. He wanted to see the man kiss her.

After a minute, the sailor said: "Well!" and she answered "Well!" and they gave each other a long, steady look. Then he said: "Well, take good care of my kids."

"Yours and who else's?" she flashed.

He smiled. "Okay. Okay. The baby looks swell."

"I'll say he does. Wonderful. A woman on the Beach yesterday said she wouldn't believe he was only nine months. She said he looked like a year and a half."

"Sure does." He hugged the fat, wriggling mass of body and sweater and rompers against his whites.

"Joanie looks wonderful, too." He yanked the little girl's pigtails.

She cried: "Daddy, don't," without looking up.

"Remember to keep her away from the Good Humor man."

"Who's raising these kids? You or me?"

"All right, you are." He grinned broadly. His grin faded out into a wistful smile. "You know, I can remember the way he used to come down your mama's street every night in the summer, ringing his bell. You and me sitting out on the sunporch, watching the kids running out with their nickels. Which kind did I buy you? I bet you forget."

"Fudge vanilla."

"Nope."

She screwed up her forehead. "Wasn't fudge?"

"Toasted cocoanut, dopey, remember?" He laughed and gave a mock sigh. "I used to dream about that on the raft. Toasted cocoanut ice-cream . . . You keep the kid away from that guy this summer. You know how she is about ice-cream."

The little girl, hearing without seeming to listen, promptly piped: "Mommy, buy me some ice-cream."

"Not now, sweetie-pie." The sailor's wife took the child's hand. "The train's coming soon. We have to get on the train."

The gunner's mate shook his head. "I still don't see how you'll manage with only one seat."

"I've done it before. I suppose we have to be grateful they sold us that one." Her eyes glinted again. She craned her neck to glower at the crowd in the depot. "You'd think *they'd* stay home and give us a chance."

He said: "Take it easy. Just take it easy, old kid."

The signals swung. The sun's gleaming pointer picked up the glass of a headlight far down the track, coming in from the yards. The gunner's mate's wife clutched her child's hand, pulled her back from the rails, reached for her bags.

The snout of a Diesel flashed past. Cars rumbled by as if they never intended to stop. The mob jostled forward. "Easy," the sailor shouted over the din. "Don't shove. There's plenty time—Where's car Sixteen?"

For an instant the couple ran to and fro in the short, frantic lunges of indecision. Corbett put his hand on the man's arm. "These are all Pullmans. Sixteen must be past the diner. I'm in that car. Give me one of your bags."

The couple didn't seem to have heard more than his direction. They ran, dragging their little girl and their luggage. Corbett stayed close behind them and when they got to the car, he scooped up the child and her doll and swung them up to the platform. The child groped back for her mother. He thought she was scared but she wasn't. She smiled at him, asked: "You coming up on my train?"

Her mother said: "Go right in, Joanie. I'm here, darling. Go in the car with the man."

The child's head brushed his hand. Her hair was like silk. He purposely held her close to his side till her mother came into the car and panted: "All right, Joanie, come here, sweet," to her and "Thanks very much, sir," to him.

His seat, number five, was the inside chair next to the window, one back from the entrance. He folded his coat, took off his cap, put them both on the rack, hoisted his bag up beside them, sat down and stretched his long legs to the footrail. He thought, "This is it. Let's get started, get going."

The sailor's family had eight by the window, directly across. The man who had seven, on the aisle, was in his place, already seated. He got up and stood in the passage to let them get settled. The crowd buffeted him. He moved over the aisle and crouched on the arm of the chair next to Corbett. He was stoop-shouldered, pudgy and pale, with a high forehead, a shining bald spot that was fringed by a fuzz of gray hair, and he wore black sunglasses. He stayed on the arm of the chair while the sailor's wife took off her coat and the little girl's jacket, reached for the baby and sat down in the seat, squeezing her thighs together, so that the child and her doll could squat on the edge near the window. Her husband swung the bags to the rack, folded the coats, placed them on top of the valise.

"Want the suitcase down for under your feet?"

"No. It'll be in the way. Just the furlough."

"Be sure the porter puts the bottles on ice."

"Don't worry so much."

"Okay, okay." For a moment the gunner's mate stared at his wife and his kids without speaking. Then he said: "Well, I better get off."

"You better get off."

"Send me a wire when you land."

"Write soon as you can."

"I'll write. All set? Everything under control?"

The young woman's lower lip trembled. "Everything," she began, "excepting . . ."

"Hey, cut that out! It can't be long now."

"It can't be long now," she repeated dully. She drew in her breath as if she was summoning a last ounce of courage. "Joanie, kiss daddy. Give daddy a hug."

The little girl turned reluctantly away from the window, put her doll on the floor. Her green eyes were shining with the excitement of a child going somewhere, seeing not him but far-away places, yet she dutifully flung her thin arms around his neck and squeezed hard. "Such passion!" he laughed. Then he bent over the seat and pressed his lips on his wife's upturned mouth. When he took them away, Corbett saw that the gunner's mate's eyes were as glossy and full as his wife's. He patted her cheek, pressed the baby's curl down, backed into the aisle and let the crowd push him out toward the door.

The man with the sunglasses got up from the arm of seat six and went back to his place. He glanced at the gunner's mate's wife. She was fumbling in her handbag, hunting a handkerchief. She couldn't locate it, apparently, for after a moment, she wiped her eyes with the back of her hand. The man leaned toward her, said something. She looked slightly startled but she managed a smile.

The smile was still on her face when the gunner's mate turned up again. "Say!" He leaned over the pudgy man. "There's another kid in this car. Nice little boy. Name's Chuckie. Comp'ny for Joanie . . . Well, so long, old girl, take good care of my kids." The crowd caught him again and pushed him away.

Joanie had turned from the window at the sound of his voice. "Mommy, why isn't daddy coming with us?"

"Because we're going to grandma. We're going home, dear."

"Can't daddy go home?"

The man in seat seven looked at Joanie and sighed. He asked: "Little girl, would you sit on my lap?"

The child's eyes—bright green like her mother's—grew larger and rounder. She shook her pigtails, backed toward the window, picked up her doll and hugged it tight.

The aisle cleared of people and filled up with luggage.

Two women, one stout, gray-haired, spectacled; one young, thin and sallow, were removing black coats and sombre veiled hats in eleven and twelve, just back of the gunner's mate's family. A middle-aged couple were settling their boxes and parcels in one and two, in front of Corbett. Three held a very old woman, four a blond Marine Corporal.

A man in a tan polo coat came through the passageway and looked down the coach, surveying the crowd and its baggage.

The man looked old though he probably wasn't, old like a rag that has faded in changeable weather. His black hair, slicked down and greasy, had salt sprinkles over the temples. His pupils were coal chips on bloodshot whites. His cheeks bore dark stubble, were hollow and haggard, the flesh almost precisely the shade of the coat turned up around them.

It was the coat, a once costly garment, tightly knotted around a thin middle, now shapeless, bedraggled, and dirty, that stamped him for what he was—a sport on his uppers. He carried no luggage. He came up the aisle to chair six, glanced with quick suspicion at the seat by the window, saw that it held a soldier, relaxed palpably and took off his coat. He folded the garment, set it carefully down on the chair, like a pillow, seated himself, sighed deeply, leaned back, shut his eyes.

*　　*　　*

Few of the passengers bothered to take a last look at the place they were leaving. They were done with Miami. Now this was their home: the Palm Queen, bound for the North, home for a day and a night and a morning and, please God and the railroad, no more.

They busied themselves with arrangement of self and possessions, with ringing for porters, stowing of baggage, hanging up coats, taking off hats—the physical settling that jogs the mind into the station-to-station frame of a journey, that spaces objectives into timetable stops; narrowing all of existence and purpose down to lopping off miles on parallel ribbons of hot, shining steel, to attaining a sign-board, glimpses of roofs, of people less living than figments of dreams, craving none of the thrill of seeing new places but merely brief respite from motion and noise and the comforting thought that for this much of a trip one is safe and continuing home.

In Coach Sixteen, a gaunt, elderly Negro with grizzled hair cropped close to his skull worked like a robot, swinging up bags to the racks over the blue and chrome seats until it was a frieze of black leather, brown cowhide and airplane gray, duffle and furlough bags, tan, blue and white; and bulbous mesh sacks of Florida oranges. At the end of the car, in the small open square in front of seats one and two, valises and golf bags were piled to the edge of the frame of the F.B.I. warning about enemy spies and saboteurs. The aisle was so cluttered with luggage the porter could scarcely get past.

The old woman in three had jammed her hat, Hudson seal coat and half a dozen brown paper parcels and boxes into her seat, so that half of her body hung over the hand rail into the next chair and the Marine had to crouch on the edge to keep out of her way. When the porter swooped down for the old woman's belongings, she grew rigid with terror, clutched at her parcels, whimpered some wordless defiance.

"Leave her be," the Marine said good-naturedly. "I'll move out in a while. I'll give her room."

The middle-aged couple in one and two had opened a lunchbox. The man peeled an orange; the woman uncorked a thermos. She had just filled the cap-cup with coffee when the train suddenly lurched, starting. Coffee spattered her waxpaper wrapped sandwiches. She glared at the porter as if he were to blame.

Down at the end of the car, the long, dark green washroom curtains flapped in farewell.

A procession of women carrying small suitcases marched toward the frosted glass rectangle lettered LADIES at the end of the car and ten minutes later marched back, re-dressed in comfortable slacks.

Right after the Palm Queen got under way, a waiter staggered through the coach, mumbling something that the clairvoyantly gifted could translate to "First and last call for breakfast. Dining car in the rear." A few people got up, stumbling on bags in the aisle. Most of the passengers, however, stayed in their seats, digesting the coffee snatched before traintime, cocooned in the first self-protective withdrawal of travel which regards every fellow traveler as a potential irritant, bore, robber or rapist.

Those in the aisle seats stared at their neighbors, at faces that all looked alike, since none of the words or grimaces that reveal personality had yet passed between them.

Those next to the windows looked out at the view and despised it because it was summer without summer's lushness and prodigal variety—miles of green flat land, sedge grass and sand, clumps of palmetto and scrub pine, sharply erect, geometrically graceless. Swamp waters were gray with mottled brown palm fronds afloat on the surface. Close to the tracks were the places where Negroes and "crackers" resided, the hovels and hutches and lean-tos, shanties and shacks—some painted yellow, some tar paper roofed, most of them raw gray clapboard, dried-out and sagging—the sun-bleached beginnings of a rich continent's fifteen-hundred-mile slum.

Here a fat Negress rocked on a porch, stolidly watching the white man's train flash by; there bougainvillea flamed in a squalid dooryard; horses lolled in a corral under a palm clump; a lone farmer in denims as faded-out gray as the shanty he lived in slouched down a path, carrying pails to his pigsty. A graveyard of tiny white stones sprawled next to a junk yard, where the bones and the carcasses of dead motor cars lay rusting and rotting. Occasionally, silver Texaco tanks brightened the vista, or the belly of planes, swooping low, caught the glint of the sun.

At the yellow Fort Lauderdale depot, a blonde in a silver fox mackinaw got on while a "cracker" in shirtsleeves called after her: "Take keer of yourself, honey. Take keer." At Boca Raton, where army trucks were lined up by dozens beside the track and the roofs of small houses were carnival red, blue and green, a G.I. leaned on the wall of the station with his loneliness spread in his eyes. At West Palm Beach the stop was a long one because a large crowd had to climb into the Pullmans. After West Palm, the conductor, flanked by an M.P. and an S.P. came into the coach, stumbled over the luggage and tore the first strip off the tickets.

By that time the blue mohair chairs had begun to hunt for tender spots in the coccyx and the window watchers to weary of palm and pine, of sun-yellow depots with waiting rooms labelled: "White" and "Colored," to be bored with the scenery and with themselves and eager to find the best listening ears

to which each could confide who he was, the names and estate
of his children, what he did for a living, how much he owned,
and what he would do if he were Roosevelt, MacArthur or God.

* * *

Grandma, in seat three, nudged the Marine. "Maybe you
like a little piece fruit?" She opened one of her brown paper
bags. Her wizened face lit with hospitable zeal.

The Marine shook his head.

She didn't or wouldn't hear his refusal. Painstakingly, she
chose her biggest orange and forced it into his hand. "Take.
It's good."

The Marine's red face got redder. He mumbled "Thanks,"
juggling the globe from one hand to the other.

"You want I should take the skin off for you?"

His blush deepened. "I'll eat it later. I ain't hungry now."

"It's good for you. Eat. My daughter has more. That's my
daughter." Her bony finger pointed across the aisle to the
couple who hadn't stopped eating since they got on. "That's
my son-in-law. I'm the grandma."

"That's nice," the Corporal muttered. "That's fine."

She inched closer to him. "They took me down to Miami.
Now I go home. I live in the Bronx. You live in New York?"

The Corporal shook his head "No," growled "Excuse me,"
clumsily got to his feet. He put the orange down on the chair,
walked back in the coach.

Corbett winked at the Marine when he passed and the Corporal winked back. He was just a kid, a pleasant-faced youngster, fair-haired, with the broad cheekbones of the Slav. He
wore three bronze stars on his Pacific yellow, the red, white
and blue of the Silver Star and the Purple Heart ribbon. A
kid, Corbett realized, a blond kid, with bloody battles behind
him—Tulagi, Guadalcanal, Cape Gloucester, Lord knows
where—places nobody had heard of before that First Division
piled off the boats to print those names large in flame and in
blood. A kid, face still smooth and untroubled.

Abruptly, Corbett turned back to the window. The headache had ebbed, had left in its place a gray vacancy, through which his nerves sent tentative pinpricks.

The green miles were endless, monotonous. On the far horizon were stripings of cloud, trailing off, like the white vapor plumes of the fighters. He felt his spine tensing. He lay back in the seat, closing his eyes, commanding himself to ease up. His eyelids stayed down for less than five minutes. He looked at the landscape again. While he stared, his mind commenced to do tricks, to soar over the fields, swamps and palms, look down through the Plexiglas nose of a B-24 on a far-stretching carpet of green, on cushions of flak, to draw to the infinitesimal hairlines of the bombsight, pin pointing a factory, a bridge, a railyard. A red light clicked on in his brain. He pulled down the shade, turned away from the window and, hopefully craving distraction, looked at his seatmate.

The man in six was asleep, his head rocking gently on the camel's hair coat, clasped hands slumped in his lap. The man's hands were bony as talons, fingers nicotine yellowed, nails bitten and dirty. Above them, the sleeves of his tight-fitting suit —a brown striped with red—were frayed. Yet his alligator belt looked expensive; his cream-colored shirt was silk-finished but wilted and soiled and rubbed at the neckline. His mottled red tie might have been Sulka, long, long ago.

The face, too, showed hard wear in its unhealthy sallow, in the cadaverous tightness of flesh that hadn't softened even in sleep. The narrow, straight nose flared round at the nostrils like the bulb of a scallion. The eyebrows were heavy, as black as his hair. Spaniard? Italian? Greek, Corbett decided. He tried to imagine what the guy did for a living, if any.

The man's torso, shifting position, stretched in serpentine ripples. He threw one skinny leg across the other. His shoes, Corbett saw, were old black and white sport oxfords. The heels were worn down. The sole, upended toward him, had a ragged, round ulcer. Whatever he worked at wasn't producing. That much was clear.

Across the aisle, the gunner's mate's Joanie whimpered: "Mommy, I have to."

"Oh, dear!" Her mother glanced down at the baby. He was sound asleep in the crotch of her arm.

"I have to, Mommy."

The pudgy man took off his sunglasses and looked at them both as if there should be some way he could be helpful. The gunner's mate's wife lifted her infant carefully up toward her shoulder. "Excuse me, please. We'd like to get out."

The gray-haired woman in the chair behind them stood up as if not the stout man, but she had been spoken to. "Please," she said eagerly. "I'll hold your baby while you take care of your little girl."

The young mother's face hardened with the instinctive distrust of a stranger. The woman smiled. She looked kindly and genteel and healthy. A motherly sort, Corbett decided, the kind you'd call a good soul. "Your baby will be all right with me," she said gently. "Don't worry. I've raised my own."

The shoulders of the young woman beside her twitched but her face didn't turn from her window.

"I hate to bother people," the gunner's mate's wife began.

The elderly woman sat down again, smiled coaxingly and stretched her arms for the baby. He squirmed a little when he was shifted, wriggled, exploring the texture of a new lap, yawned without opening his eyes and then slept. The elderly woman beamed down at him. "Look, Elaine, honey," she whispered. "A darling baby. See how he sleeps."

The girl whom she called Elaine pivoted, gave the infant the most fleeting of glances, commenced to say something, bit her lower lip and veered back to the window.

The old woman looked sorry. She shook her head as though she feared she had done something wrong.

Corbett jerked up the shade and drummed on the sill. "This trip's a riot," he thought sourly. "Old women and kids. A goon sleeping off a hangover." His nerves had begun to goad him again, the familiar impatience surging, demanding.

He glanced at his seatmate, this time with distaste so keen it was almost revulsion. The man's eyes opened slowly. They blinked once or twice to brush off the sleep film, and then shifted toward Corbett, examining him with a deliberate, impertinent scrutiny. "As if I were a horse," Corbett thought. "Or a possible touch."

He spoke to the man to break up the stare. "Lousy trip."

"Yeah, Florida stinks," the man growled.

That was putting it thick, yet Corbett nodded a half-hearted agreement. "You been down before?"

"Every year."

"I see." Whatever he came for, it wasn't his health. He looked like God's wrath. "On business?"

The coal chip eyes studied Corbett again. "Hialeah. The track."

"I see," Corbett scowled. He tried to recall a remark that had passed in the night. He remembered. "Have any dough on Four Freedoms?" he asked. He was amused at the other man's snarl. He raised his hand. "Don't say a word." You did simple arithmetic and got your own answers. A bad guess at the track; no luggage. The poor bum was broke, fresh from the cleaners. He paused, then said thoughtfully, "I've met a few other guys who were afraid to take a chance on that nag."

The irony missed, as Corbett knew that it would. The man muttered "A long shot's for suckers," and shrugged. "You go out to the track?"

Corbett shook his head. "Just got in yesterday. On my way home."

The man glanced at the wings and the ribbons. "You a pilot?"

"Bombardier." Corbett's thumbs sought each other.

"Over there?"

Corbett nodded. This was no good. Over there was the day before yesterday. It was sweat and terror and grief. If you could talk, if you would, it wasn't to someone like this.

The man was persistent: "It was tough, huh?"

Anger surged through him. Tough? Sure it was tough. What would this crumb know about tough? And how could you tell him? Why wasn't he personally feeling some of that tough? Why wasn't he in? Hell, he was old; he was broke, on his uppers. The riff raff you always have with you. The frayed fringe. Doesn't do; doesn't count. Just exists. Tell him or not, didn't matter. Just as swiftly as it had risen, his anger flushed out, leaving a kind of numb impotence. "It was rugged," he said. Then he added: "Corbett's my name."

"Pleased to meet you. Kalchis," the other man said. "Benny Kalchis."

As if the naming of names was a period, ending their contact, each man turned away. Kalchis examined his fingers, scowled at them, nipped a pinkie nail between his sharp teeth. Corbett returned to the landscape. He thought: "Greek. I was right," and smiled at the window pane wryly: "Picked a fine seatmate. Oh, what the hell, I'll get out. I'll see if the train has a bar. I'll see if it has any girls." The Marine had been smart, getting out right away. A long train like this must have more than old women and babies and goons. It must have girls. Beautiful girls.

He shifted his haunches, getting ready to rise. "I guess," he said, dropping into what he believed was the man's own vernacular, "I'll step out and case the joint."

The horseplayer's body jerked taut. His pupils contracted. Corbett saw he was shocked; maybe frightened a bit. He laughed. "Christ! Does he think I'm a burglar? An old-time safe-cracker?" He asked: "Was that a fox pass?" The man's attitude made him think of the time he had used the word "bloody" in mixed company in a refined English home. "Case a joint" used to be good American slang. "Maybe it's changed," he decided. "I've been away long. Not even words are the same." He felt that he had to explain. "I'll take me a stroll," he told Kalchis. "Look over the joint. Go see if this train has any booze or good-looking girls."

The horseplayer's face didn't seem quite as belligerent now, though he still looked distrustful. "Sure. Go ahead. Good idea. I might even join you."

He drew up his knees, sitting immobile until Corbett got

out in the aisle. He glanced through the window, his face
screwed up in thought, settling some final detail in his mind.
Then he swung out of his chair and followed the officer through
coach Sixteen.

CHAPTER THREE

You couldn't see legs in the day
coach.

The tilt of the chairs, for visual purposes, sawed all the
women in half.

In car Sixteen, that didn't matter too much, since the females were either too old or too young or too plain or attached.
You didn't require the presence of husbands, drowsing in seats
on the aisle, to tell you that most of the women were wives—
full bosomed, wide hipped wives, in dark dresses and suits
meant to be practical rather than chic, wearing eyeglasses,
pearl button earrings and washboard permanent waves, clutching stuffed handbags in plump, jeweled fingers.

One or two looked up when Corbett lurched past but their
dead-pan expressions made clear that they had even less interest in him than he had in them. Some of the slim young ones
in slacks seemed mildly aware of his passage and he slowed
up to glance at their hands, registering when he saw the band
on fourth finger: "service wife" and when he didn't: "kid sister." There were two cute-looking girls with bobbed hair and
sweaters who even smiled. Both wore the bands. He smiled
back at them and went on.

"It must be a dish," he admonished himself. "While you're
shopping, old boy, get the best."

He yanked the door open, emerged from the cool, air-condi-
tioned coach onto a platform where the clatter and scrape and
creak of sun-heated metal, the grime and oil stench made a

two by six hell. A female was standing out there alone. She was dressed in a turquoise blue slack suit and dangling pink earrings, had bushy, frizzed henna hair. She was smoking. When she saw Corbett she dropped her butt, stepped on it, pulled a fresh cigarette from the pack in her pocket. She smiled up at him, drawled: "Got a match, soldier?"

He went past without answering and crossed into the diner.

The waiters, in brown twos and fours, were having late breakfasts. The white steward was eating alone at the far end of the car.

Corbett stopped at his table, asked: "This train carry a bar?"

Without looking up from his plate, the man mumbled: "No."

"No place where a fellow can buy a drink?"

The steward laid down his fork and looked up. He had the thin, harassed face of a chronic dyspeptic. Red-rimmed, tired eyes studied Corbett, trying to decide about him. Air Force men were usually gentlemen drinkers. It was sailors you had to look out for. They became playful and noisy and the crabbier passengers were apt to complain. The Lieutenant seemed hardly the type that made trouble. And so the steward asked: "What car you in?"

"Sixteen."

"Your porter might be able to round up a pint."

"Thanks, pal."

"You're welcome." The steward picked up his fork, turned back to his breakfast.

Kalchis, edging past, brushed Corbett's shoulder. He tossed Corbett a nod. "Find what you want, Buddy?"

The steward glanced up again, scowled.

Corbett flushed. He regretted that Kalchis had greeted him publicly, aware it had lowered his stock in the steward's eyes. He growled: "Give me time."

"You got plen'y time. This roach cage is running a hour late already."

The steward's frown froze in a glare.

"Gotta expect it," the horseplayer said cheerfully. "Don't

you know there's a war?" He nudged the bombardier's shoulder and moved on.

"Friend of yours?" The steward seemed hostile.

"Oh sure. Bosom chum," he said lamely. "You pick up all kinds on a train." He lingered alongside the table to give Kalchis a start and to fill in the pause, looked down at the steward's breakfast. "Don't tell me civilians eat Spam?"

"What's wrong with Spam?"

"Oh nothing . . . Things must be rugged out here. Worse than I thought . . . You like the stuff?"

"Saying I don't won't get me sirloin."

"If I never eat it again, it'll still be too soon."

The steward paused between mouthfuls. "You just back?" Corbett nodded.

"We doing all right?"

"If you believe what you read in the papers."

"Suits me good enough. Over by Christmas, you think?"

"Cripes, we haven't got started."

"Good gosh. It's got to be over. We can't keep going this way."

Corbett sneered. "See who's talking," he said to himself. "How many missions has that guy been on?" Pretty rugged, he thought, to be a headwaiter on a luxury train, sweat out the war on the Florida run.

The steward was cleaning his plate with a fragment of roll on a fork, mopping it thoroughly to take up every drop of the grease. He swallowed the tidbit, set his knife and fork down together on the rim of the plate and shook his head gloomily. "They work us to death. Isn't a man in this crew that's slept more than six hours in the last forty-eight. The gov'ment keeps begging folks not to travel." He humphed. "You gotta look hard to find any guy who'll give up one single pleasure because his gov'ment asks him."

He waited for Corbett to make some comment but the bombardier merely asked: "Club car that way?"

The steward lifted his coffee cup cautiously so that none of the beverage slopped. "No club car on here. Smoking lounge

next car ahead." He called after Corbett, "No smoking al-
lowed in the coaches."

The rear dining car platform was almost filled up with bundles of used table linen, an open bucket of garbage, a crate of
potatoes. A Negro in greasy, soiled apron was sprawled on
the bundles, asleep. Someone was singing, a rich Negro bari-
tone. He followed the sound to the galley. A fat, chocolate
brown man in a charlotte russe chef's cap and jacket and horn-
rimmed eyeglasses, stood just inside the door to the galley,
holding an enormous cigar, puffing it briefly at the end of each
line of his song.

This was new, this nonchalance of people who worked on
the trains—the waiter asleep on the linens, the chef smoking
and singing, the to-hell-with-it air. "I like it," Corbett decided. "The country's gotten more human. The war makes a
difference."

He crossed the couplings and looked into the lounge.

Two rows of stiff armchairs faced one another. The seats
were all filled, and gray spirals of smoke rose from each
chair, spreading a fog through the car. Shoulders bobbed up
and down to the jounce of the train. At the far end of the
car, a big mirror reflected the ridiculous jiggle.

He stood, hand on the knob, and stared through the glass.
He saw faces he knew. The Marine Corporal was there, looking flushed and uncomfortable, between a stout woman with
a big hat full of flowers and an elderly man who was trying to
read. Benny Kalchis was there, next to a grande dame with
ginger-red hair, a waggling crest of green and black feathers,
and a small Pekinese of the same hue as her hair. Two other
men looked familiar—one with red jowls and raccoon eyebrows; one with a profile and toothbrush gray mustache that
seemed hewed from the same slab of granite as the suit that he
wore. Corbett's brows slid together while he tried to recall
who they were and where he had seen them before. Oh, in
some paper or magazine, probably. This was the part of the
train where you might meet the names in the news.

There was one other woman in a chair near the door, a

blonde in a silver fox jacket. Her legs were crossed high and
were definitely good. And her face wasn't bad. No, not good
enough, not the dish. The lashes were much too long, too
plainly store bought, like the platinum sheen of her hair and
the orange-red bow of her mouth. He looked at her hands: diamonds on fourth finger and a diamond bracelet thrust out
from her jacket. By the self-conscious way she kept shifting
her eyes to her bracelet, he was informed it was new.

It puzzled him at first, that all these strangers looked so
much alike—even the women, although feature by feature,
they certainly weren't. It wasn't merely the sun tan, the
smooth, glowing bronze of the Florida sun. It took him a moment to know why it was. They looked bored. That car-full
of travelers was like all the dull parties he'd ever been on
where strangers sit in a circle waiting for someone to trot out
a drink or a joke that might break the ice.

Resentment stung him. They *dared* to look bored. In
forty-eight hours, he now was aware, he had come a long way,
not merely back from the countries of war, not just from one
world to another, but to a new time and age where people
were so untouched by trouble that they dared to look bored.

It can't all be like this, he assured himself. This is special,
a vacation train . . . But what right have they? He found
himself repeating the words that the gunner's mate had said to
his wife at the depot: "Take it easy, old kid. Take it easy."

He waited one moment more, on the outside to let himself
simmer, cool down, before he opened the door and went into
the lounge. It surprised him a little that some of the men
seemed quite young—young and virile, carefully barbered,
very well dressed, and he caught himself thinking the inevitable question: why aren't they in? Yet he walked down the
carpeted aisle very slowly, taking advantage of the sway of
the train to pause at each seat. He wanted to hear what they
said when they talked, to pick up a phrase, a familiar allusion.
Without being sure why, he knew that he wanted the sense of
belonging with them.

He heard the blonde say: "But you really *must* learn to

rhumba." He heard a man in a sport suit mention his golf score, the man next to him yawn and say he was sleepy. He heard the man with the raccoon eyebrows boom to the stony face next to him: "Margie and Pat will go on to New York. Pick up some new clothes." He heard the woman with the flowers on her hat ask the Marine: "But don't the men pray in the foxholes?" He heard a heavy-set man say: "We're keeping our inventories light, just in case . . ." He heard Kalchis say "Hi!" He heard a young man remark: "Feel I need to get set before *they* get back. I made some fine contacts down there."

"Contacts." That was the word. That was the touchstone that gave you America. That was the word that brought you back home.

He carried it out of the car to the platform and stood, resting his back on the dusty glass of the door, saying the word to himself. *"Contacts."* Not what you knew but whom you knew. Not learning a trade or plying an art but lunching or drinking with people who could help you get on. "When it's over, I'll have to make contacts again." He found the thought frightening. "But I won't speak their language. I won't know their thinking. Nor they mine." He felt the flutter of panic. "We're strangers. I'm a stranger in only two years." He recalled how the horseplayer had stared when he said "case the joint." "I don't know the words or the music." The Second Lieutenant back in the bar had said: "You'll learn, pal, you'll learn." Short refresher course in American ways. Just three weeks. How much to learn in so little time?

He tried to think back to where he'd left off, what they had thought about, cared about then . . . Well, there was Murder, Incorporated. And the Dodgers had won their first pennant. Manville had taken a wife, his fifth or his sixth or his seventh . . . You went to the movies. You listened to Allen or Bergen or Archie or Hope on the radio. On Sunday afternoon there was the Philharmonic . . . Philharmonic—where they halted the music and gave you Pearl Harbor. And then you stopped thinking.

After two years the important thing was to find liquor and girls. To find girls.

He straddled the couplings to get to the Pullman.

The Pullman behind the lounge car was named Loch Lomond.

The conductor had just begun to work the Loch Lomond. He was opening the door to drawing room A. The M.P. and the S.P. who were with him filled up the passage. Corbett halted a moment until they might step aside and let him slip by.

He peered over their shoulders, into the drawing room There were three men in the room. He could see feet of three, profiles of two. One of those profiles, on the settee next to the window, turned around and looked at him squarely. Corbett felt a sharp tweak at his nerves. That was the face that gave you the nightmares, the face you had seen through the Plexiglas nose. The reflex of habit made his hand reach out from his side, grope for a gun that he knew wasn't there. Kill the bastard! Get him before he gets you.

The M.P. asked brusquely: "Feeling sick, sir?"

He shook his head, no. He said: "Just seeing him—"

"Oh him! Don't mind him. He can't do no harm where he is."

On the green mohair seat, he caught the glimmer of metal between two wrists. The handcuffs amazed him. Dangerous criminals traveled this way, not prisoners of war. He asked himself: "What else is this son of a bitch?"

Corbett dawdled a moment, steadying himself, before he went on, past two open doors of compartments where restless kids clambered over the laps of their mothers.

So high were the backs of its seats that at first the Pullman seemed empty. People were reading or conversing quietly. The car had a living room coziness and when Corbett came down its aisle, one or two people glanced up and gave him that challenging stare of resentment you offer to strangers who have strayed into your parlor.

The women who traveled in Pullmans, he saw, were differ-

ent from those in the coaches, yet like one another. They
seemed to be cut of one piece of cloth with a single sharp snip
of the shears. They were tanned, lean, shellacked, and dressed
to the eyes. Their hair had the slickness of curried race horses.
Their nails and their mouths were dipped in fresh blood. At
each pair of ears, baubles hung, twists of copper or gold or
clusters of stones. Their bosoms were little, their kneecaps
dark through transparent hose. High heels and a criss-cross of
leather hung from each leg. They stared at him boldly as if
they wouldn't mind if he'd stop. He began to feel better.
"Take your time," he warned himself. "Don't get stuck with
a dog. These all look alike. How can you pick?"

There were only two men in Loch Lomond. One was
white-haired, well-preserved, pink-cheeked, old. He sat stiffly
upright as though he were either unused to or disdainful of
this mode of travel. The woman who had the seat facing him
looked plainly unhappy about him or something. She was a
nice-looking female, pink and white skin, a halo of blonde,
fluffy hair. When Corbett passed, she looked up. Her eyes
were blue Wedgwood china. He thought for an instant of stopping. She wasn't exactly the dish but she wasn't too bad, different, appealing and soft. Then she glanced down at his
ribbons and averted her face. "She's not having any," he
thought. "No soldiers today."

The other man in the car was a Signal Corps Captain. A
giggly, homely young girl with a shoulder-length, straw-colored
bob, had him in hand. In both hands. She was sharing his
seat and ruffling his hair. "You've got dandruff," she squealed.
"Such problems. Such problems."

The Captain's young face was crimson and desperate. He
threw Corbett a glance of appeal. Corbett saw the E.T.O.
ribbon with four tiny bronze stars. "Hell, no!" he decided.
"He's had battle experience. Let him get out of this one
alone."

Two bedroom doors at the end of the car were shut; a
drawing room open, revealing two men in a gin rummy game.

He went out of Loch Lomond into Glen Argyle. The scene

was the same: the staterooms exposing card games or children and mamas, the tawny-skinned, bauble-hung dolls in the chairs.

At the end of the Pullman, a door stood ajar. An X marked the spot.

The X was a pair of superlative legs. They were slender with just enough of an arc at the calves, smooth at the ankles, without evident bones. They looked brown, nude, knee-dimpled and hairless, which meant that the stockings were sheer. They began with small, high-heeled slippers of a raspberry-plum tinted fabric, vanished under a skirt hem of wheat-colored wool.

For a full minute, Don Corbett stood in the doorway, enjoying the legs, before the girl knew he was there.

She was reading a magazine, a large sheet affair, and when she flipped the page over, she chanced to look up.

Her face matched the legs. It was perfect and lovely. It was brown and it glowed with good health. Its shape was a heart; its features were small; chin round but firm, with a beautiful mouth. It was the first face he had seen on the train that was not merely pretty, but friendly and clever and warm.

Half of her hair stood in two burnished black wings, parted above a wide forehead and handsome dark eyes. The rest dropped in a snood at the nape of her neck. Her earrings were gold filigree shells so finely made that they seemed like carefully brushed hair. Her jacket—raspberry plum like her shoes—was wool, simply cut, perfectly fitted, pin pointing her breasts. An ascot of wheat-colored silk was tied under her chin. Her fingernails matched the shade of her lipstick precisely.

She tipped her chin with the poise of assurance of beauty, smiled, said: "Oh, hello," as if every day Air Force officers stood in her doorway and admired her limbs.

He entered before she invited and slouched just inside the door. "Hello," he said, dawdled a moment to decide on his line and began: "Well, how's civilian morale?"

She smiled again, this time a trifle unsurely. "Oh, it's fine, simply grand." She had an agreeable voice, without sectional accent. Her teeth flashed, brilliantly white, a credit to dental hygiene.

"No complaints? Fixed all right for steaks, Scotch and nylons?"

A pucker sprang between her eyebrows. "Oh, I'm doing all right, quite all right, as you see." She uncrossed her legs, slid slightly forward until her heels touched the floor. She pulled her skirt over her knee-caps.

He said: "I'm just back. I've been hearing about the hard time you folks have been having. If I can do anything—"

There was no doubting his irony now. A blush crept up her cheeks, under her tan. "Don't believe all you read." There was a trace of annoyance in her eyes. "First time I've heard that line. I'm not sure I like it."

His heart sank. He thought, miserably, itching with nervousness: "Bum start. You don't make a girl by getting her sore."

He felt her eyes, as much as you can physically feel a curious stare, probing the scars of the war on his face: the network of lines, the grooves in his cheeks, the wry twist of his mouth, moving down slowly past his chin to his chest. Her frown lingered, a small tepee above her nose. "Well, you've been places. And done things." He was aware of a smile behind her eyes, so faint that it was almost imperceptible and so detached that he sensed she was looking at him and smiling at something that only she knew. But because he had made the bad start and wasn't quite ready for a new conversational gambit, he merely said "Yes."

"That brown and green ribbon is Africa?"

"Africa. Europe."

"I see. What are the others?"

He minded her tone. It was business-like rather than personal. Yet he touched the blue on his right breast. "Presidential Unit Citation. The whole gang got that one."

"What for?"

"For Ploesti." His thumb sought his thumb. He pulled it away.

"And the others? The orange and blue?"

"Air Medal." He shifted from one foot to the other.

"What's it for?"

"Oh nothing." He shrugged. "For letting the jerks shoot at you."

Her eyebrows arched. "You're too modest. What's the blue, white and red up on top?"

He sighed. If you had to humor the dish, you had to. She wouldn't be satisfied till she had all the answers. "D.F.C., Distinguished Flying Cross." His face was frozen, his voice cold.

"Oh really!" Her dark eyes opened wider. "I'm thrilled. Then you're a real hero!"

"Skip it," he growled. His thumbs were rubbing each other. He frowned over her head at the white towel antimacassar on the seat.

"What did they give you that for?"

"Nothing." "I'll take off the fruit salad," he thought. "I should have known better than wear it." He glanced hopelessly around the tiny compartment, hunting for something that would give him an angle, a safer bypath for conversational wandering.

A short beaver jacket, as brown, as soft as her skin, hung on a wire hanger on the opposite wall. A pancake of wheat-colored straw with a raspberry bow swung by a wide ribbon from the hook. Her hat. By golly, he thought, I could talk about hats. Silly hats. Her magazines cluttered the dark green settee. *Harper's Bazaar, Vogue, Mademoiselle, The New Yorker* and *Time*. There was a flat tin of cigarettes—a name new to him: *Parliament;* a wide box, tied up with ribbons, probably candy; a small overnight case of airplane gray; a handsome red handbag. "Way out of my class," he decided. "A dish. Unquestionably. But not for Corbett."

Then, quite without warning, she asked: "Why don't you sit down?" However, she made no move to gather the magazines up and make room for him on the sofa. Instead she waved, her bracelets pleasantly tinkling, toward a square, green-brocade covered stool. "Sit down on the can." She laughed. "You don't mind sitting down on the can?"

He lifted the green brocade lid. "By God, it is!"

"It's indecent." She made a face. "That in your living room."

He put down the lid and sat on the stool. This line was better. Very much better. You never could tell about women. He hadn't guessed this girl had it in her, that touch of vulgarity that put you at ease. "Don't tell your public," he smiled. "They'll never guess." He hitched up the knees of his trousers. "Say, this place isn't bad. Nice room."

"Oh it's all right." The bangles jingled again. "I suppose I'm very lucky. It's the first time I've been on a train in I don't know how many years."

An old joke popped into his head. (It was odd how these bits and pieces that you had all but forgotten leaped out of your past when you got back home.) A gag that belonged to that far distant time called depression, about the two bankers who were forced to give up their cars and kept telling each other in the subway sardine tin how many years it had been since they'd been on the subway, until the little straphanger between them spoke up: "Gentlemen, you don't know how we've missed you." He started to tell her the joke, but she stopped him. "I know it," she said. "You don't know how we've missed you. That gag has whiskers. You'll have to do better."

"I won't try," he said. It pleased him that they knew the same jokes. That helped conversation. You talked in taglines.

"But it isn't funny." She bent forward earnestly. "You see, in New York you use cabs all the time. And whenever you go out to the country—Connecticut, Westchester, the Hamptons, you know—there's always someone with a car."

Her chatter had a fairy tale air, something out of his world, but after a fashion, amusing.

"This was the first time I'd taken a winter vacation. I've really been working so awfully hard. I didn't want to. Really,

I didn't. Somehow in war time, you don't think you should. But all my friends said: 'Nina, you must.' "

So she was called Nina. The name was pretty, just right for her.

Her agreeable voice rattled on: " 'Three weeks in Florida will make a new woman of you. You can afford it.' Of course, I had always abhorred the very thought. Florida seemed so—" She paused, hunting the word to describe it— "so *nouveau* . . . But it really has something."

He thought: "You bet it has. A good chunk of my pay."

"I drove down with some friends and they're stuck. That OPA just won't let them have gas. And you can't buy a ticket. Why, I even thought I'd have to go home by day coach. Just a fluke I got this. Poor darlings, they're simply frantic. Why, if they can't get any gas, they'll have to dispose of their cars."

He smiled, disarmingly amiable. "That just breaks my heart."

A flicker of exasperation crossed her face, but she tried to make him believe that she too thought it was not really tragic. With a slight laugh, she said: "We can't worry soldiers with our little troubles." You could see she was trying to be careful, not to upset him, not to injure his feelings but she didn't quite know where his sore spots might be. "Let's talk about you. Let's hear why they gave you that D.F.C."

He shook his head sharply.

"Won't talk?"

"Won't talk." He thrust his hands into his pockets.

She pouted. "I'm sorry. You see, you're the first. Oh, I don't mean I've never met soldiers before. Good heavens, no! What else is there these days to go out with? But they're all going over. Not coming back. It's a little bit early for heroes. This is the first time I've met one of you boys."

The "you boys" annoyed him and his mouth twisted. "Can't see how you missed. Miami's crummy with heroes."

"I stayed at Palm Beach."

He said: "Oh."

The monosyllable told her as much as a paragraph. She

hurried to say: "I'm not one of the indolent rich. Really I'm not. I'm a hard working girl. Why—" She smiled as if what she was saying was a joke on herself—"I work in a store."

"Macy's basement?" His voice deepened with sarcasm.

"Well, hardly. Fifth Avenue. Fifties. Believe it or not, I do styling."

His glance ran over her raspberry and wheat-colored outfit and filigree earrings. "I believe it."

She pretended her skirt needed smoothing. "I have to dress up to my job," she said primly. "I'd be a fine stylist if I looked like a frump. It's my job to guess what women will wear and make them wear it."

His answer showed he hadn't heard or cared what she said. He asked, very seriously: "May I touch your legs?"

She looked startled. Her blush rose again. Her back stiffened. He knew a second of panic, of dreading that she might well be the kind that turned Queen of Sheba. He knew that he had to explain. "It's been a long time since I've seen first-class American legs."

She studied his face for a moment and he saw her expression change, something like pity enter her eyes. She thrust her legs out.

His fingertips touched her kneecaps, ran in the lightest sort of caress, down her calves toward her ankles. He felt a faint tremor and wasn't quite sure whether it was in her legs or his fingers.

She laughed. "Make you happy?"

"You bet."

"Oh well," she jangled her bangles to cover the confusion that both of them felt. "The best isn't any too good for the boys."

He sat motionless for a couple of seconds. Then he said: "I wish you wouldn't say boys."

Again, her eyebrows arched and her face held that anxious uncertainty of wanting to say and to do the right thing and not knowing what. Then without answering him, she opened her box of *Parliaments*, took a cigarette out, fingered the

match book a moment to see whether he would offer to light it.
He didn't. Instead, he asked: "May I have one of yours? I
don't think I've ever smoked those."

Her blush mounted again. "Please do. Where are my manners?" She struck the match, held it for him. She lit her own
next. "How far are you traveling?"

"New York."

"Oh really! Is New York your home?"

"After a fashion."

"No kidding!"

He wondered why that should cause comment. He said:
"What's wrong with that?"

"Why, nothing. Nothing at all. I just found it startling and
I'm surprised that I did. Sergeant York spoiled me, I guess.
You can't be a hero unless you come from the sticks. The Ten-
nessee hills. The Iowa farm. The maple-shaded small town
in Ohio. You sort of forget that the city boys make heroes
too."

He mumbled lamely again: "I wish you wouldn't say boys."

He again was aware of the probe of her eyes, running deeper
this time, past his skin to his mind. Let's see what makes this
guy tick. Let's see what the war's done to a big city slicker.

"What part of New York do you come from?"

"Brooklyn," he said.

She said: "Oh!" He caught the inflection, saw the slight
crease over her nose. He said, inwardly smiling: "Brooklyn
Heights. Is that better?"

"Oh, much."

"Don't be such a snob. Pierrepont Street. Good enough?"

"Oh please," she protested. "I'm really not so . . ."

He said: "Take it easy. I understand." He drew on the
cigarette she had given him. It was mild, almost tasteless. Its
cardboard mouthpiece diluted the flavor still more. He wondered: "Is that what I picked? Ultra refined? Superspecial?
Smooth surface? No flavor?"

She asked: "Home on leave or for good?"

"Twenty-one days."

"And then what? Back to Europe?"

He shook his head. "To Miami. Air Force Redistribution Center. Know about that?"

She nodded, although it was plain from the blank look in her eyes that she didn't.

"That's where they give us the works. Rest us up, check us over, decide what they want us to do."

"You're not wounded?"

His lips thinned. "I'm not wounded," he said.

Her face cleared and then brightened. "Oh, I know. You're one of those combat fatigues."

He stamped out his cigarette, bending a moment more than he had to over the black ash receiver alongside the washstand. "That's what they call us."

She didn't seem to have any answer to that but merely leaned back, again probing his face. He looked over her head, at the wall, wondering with bitterness whether "combat fatigue" in her mind was the same as "psychotic." Her next words were a jolt. "You want to get back just as soon as you can?"

"Don't be a fool."

She smiled delicately. "Those bad gremlins get you?"

His sharp answer was almost an outcry. "For Christ's sake, no whimsey."

"Oh." She had reddened again. Her face looked as though she was sorry, sorry she'd bothered with him. She said, rather stiffly: "Excuse me," and looked out of the window. Her profile was lovely, clear as a cameo. To fill the awkward pause with politeness, she asked without turning: "I suppose you're going to paint the town red?"

"You bet."

That was better, although both of them still felt they were treading the quashy terrain of a morass. "If my dough holds out, I won't draw one sober breath."

She turned toward him again, once more smiling. "You'll see all your old friends?"

"I'd have to travel from Suez to Alaska."

She laughed. "That's why it is. I've been wondering why men were scarcer than nylons."

That was the good side, the kidding around side. That's what you wanted. Easy, light banter with a good-looking girl. That got you where you wanted to go. Not question and answer. Not third degree.

"I shouldn't imagine you'd have any trouble getting plenty of both."

She gave her stockings a deprecating glance. "You won't believe one word I say, but I assure you I get them for free. I mean for free."

"Just teasing the boys?"

She said, rather tartly: "Don't be a pig," and then switched off quickly. "I suppose you'll drop in at the various canteens."

"No ma'am. Seen all the soldiers I want for a while."

"They have lovely hostesses. I ought to know. I worked in one."

"I'll take the phone numbers. Meet them outside."

"Against the rules."

"Fish for the rules."

She lit one cigarette from the butt of the other. "Got to save matches." She inhaled. "For all your big talk, I'll bet there's one special girl."

He drew himself up, his jaw tightening. "There isn't."

She guessed what he meant. "But there was?"

He bent forward, his thin-lipped smile tipped in lye. "Let her have her fat, 4F babies in peace. Corbett's out on the town."

"Oh, Corbett's your name?"

"Donald Corbett."

"Lieutenant Corbett," she corrected. "Pilot?"

"Bombardier."

"Oh." And after a pause. "Mine's Nina Gilmore."

"Hello."

She put out her hand. They shook gravely. Then he said: "Now that we've been introduced, may I touch your legs?"

She laughed. She raised her legs, held them straight out.

A voice said from the door: "Hi Buddy! You doin' all right?"

They looked up together. The smile froze on her lips.

The horseplayer lounged in the doorway. His black eyes ranged boldly from Nina's legs to her wrists to her ear-lobes, veered off to her handbag and luggage. Then he winked. His wink was high praise. It said: "A dish!"

Corbett flushed. He muttered: "Saw you back in the lounge. You were making out."

Kalchis raised his thin shoulders. "I'm takin' my time." He rested his spine against the door frame. No one spoke. When the silence confirmed his unwelcome, he shrugged again: "Be seein' you, Buddy," and wheeled and went on.

Nina waited until enough time had passed for Kalchis to be well out of earshot. Then she made a snoot: "Your friend?"

"Oh, please! Do I look it?"

She frowned. "No, I can't say you do . . . You look like—" She hesitated.

It was important for him to know what he looked like to her, if she thought him attractive, desirable. He said: "Go on. Tell me the worst. What do I look like?"

"Well—" Her smile was encouraging. "You have nice, honest eyes. What color are they?"

"You tell me."

She pretended to squint. "Would you say hazel?"

"I'll say what you say."

"Let it go hazel. You could do with a haircut. I thought officers had to be neat."

"Just give me time. I've been busy this morning."

"Making a nylon survey?"

"Know a better business than that?"

"Perhaps I do." She glanced at her magazine pile.

"Am I taking too much of your valuable time?"

She pursed her lips. "I do have some homework to do."

He stood up, not quite sure of whether that was his cue to go out. This light persiflage was fine for an exit. That would be best to pick up later on. "If that's the case, I'll be stepping along. I've got business myself."

"Business?" Her eyebrows rose.

"See a man. Reconnaissance tells me my porter can sell me a pint."

Her shining hair rested against the seat towel. "You're simply amazing. You don't seem to have the least trouble finding whatever you want."

He didn't reply for a moment but stood swaying above her, looking down at the bow of her lips, the curve of her breasts. The impatience was rising again, prodding and driving. He forced it back savagely, thinking: "Not yet. This isn't the way. You're home now. You do this right."

He said: "If I get the pint, will you? can I?"

"Could be."

His spirits rose. He felt almost gay.

"See you later," he said.

"I'll be here. It's a long trip to New York."

"I'll be back."

He started down the aisle of Glen Argyle, stepping so lightly that he scarcely felt the jerk of the train. Then he suddenly stopped. A serpent of doubt curled through his mind. "Maybe she isn't. Maybe I ought to look further." He turned and went back up the aisle. Her door was shut.

He went out of Glen Argyle, crossed the platform and opened the door of Duquesne. He saw Benny Kalchis before the horseplayer saw him.

Kalchis was on his way back, weaving up the aisle, moving quickly and catlike, shifting his eyes from one side to the other. He wasn't looking at faces, but rather at laps.

Corbett's forehead knotted. What was there about that lean, shabby figure? It was stalking, that's what it was. Hunting for something. For someone. "Christ! What else am I doing? I'm doing the same."

A kid, a boy about five, reached out from one of the seats. The swath of his arm hooked Kalchis just under the knees. The man stumbled, gripped the back of a seat.

The kid's mother lunged for her child. From his stance near the door, Corbett saw the woman's black handbag slide from her seat onto the carpet. He heard her mumbling some words of apology, saw Kalchis swing low as if bowing or bracing himself, then straighten up, move on without answering the woman.

He slid past Corbett, holding his arms stiff at his sides, not even seeing him. He entered the washroom at the end of the car.

The black purse was gone from the aisle.

Corbett's scalp tingled. If it was what it looked like, it was slick sleight of hand. "No," he decided. "She picked it up . . . Mind your own business, Don Corbett." He went through Duquesne very swiftly, barely glancing at women. Halfway through Mount Royal, behind it, he gave up his quest, at last perfectly sure that the incomparable dish was behind a closed door in Glen Argyle. He turned back to go after his porter and pint.

CHAPTER FOUR

The gunner's mate's Joanie and a tow-headed boy, slightly older, were playing prisoner's base in the rocking aisle of Sixteen, gleefully shrieking when they bumped a valise or a passenger's arm. Their mamas took turns at trying to stop them, screaming: "Chuckie, come here" or "Joanie, stop that," but the kids went right on.

Most of the passengers seemed tolerant and even amused, as if a rodeo in the aisle was what you took with your ticket, along with the cinders, the smells and the noise of a train. A Sunday-at-home atmosphere pervaded the car, people lolling in upholstered chairs, reading the funnies, watching the kids, or half-falling asleep.

Chuckie whacked Corbett's thigh when he tried to weave past and turned up a sassy, freckle-nosed snoot. Corbett ruffled his hair and when he came to Joanie, yanked one of her pigtails. "Go git 'im," he growled in her ear. She giggled, flashed him a smile on the wing, and swooped after Chuckie.

The man in sunglasses and the motherly woman who had held the baby had moved into the seats he and Kalchis had left and were talking. She started guiltily, asked: "Is this your chair? I didn't mean to—" and began to get up.

He waved her back. "Don't disturb yourself, ma'am. I'm trying to locate the porter."

He walked to the end of the car, went out to the platform, saw no trace of the Negro, came back to the coach. "Might as well squat," he decided. "The guy'll turn up. No sense in walking all the way to New York." With a date on the books, he felt pretty good.

The Marine's place was filled with brown paper bags and an open lunch box, reeking of dill. Grandma, ignoring the mess, dozed over a Yiddish newspaper. The sailor's wife had propped her baby and Joanie's doll in the pudgy man's chair, had tied a blue blanket across like a guard rail. The apple-cheeked baby was wide-awake, drooling, his head waggling drunkenly with the bounce of the train. The doll was nearly as big as the infant. It snuggled against him, flipping wax lids.

There was just one available seat at that end of the coach, next to the sallow young woman in black. Her back was turned to it but when Corbett sat down, she shifted uneasily, aware of his presence, without seeing him.

He asked: "Do you mind?"

"I don't mind," and the apathy in her tone seemed to prove that she didn't. Nevertheless, she hitched around, craning her neck to see where her companion had gone.

He hurried to put her at ease. "I'm just parking here till the porter turns up."

"You can stay."

Her indifference was faked, he decided. Covertly, pretending not to, she was looking him over.

Her lashes, sweeping purple hollows under her eyes, were long and the slate-gray eyes large, yet with a curious glaze. Her face might have been handsome if it weren't so haggard, so gray in spite of its tan. With ten extra pounds on her bones, with lipstick and rouge and a wave in her hair, she had possibilities—of being a babe—not quite a dish. He wondered idly why she had let herself go. She looked like the type who was used to nice things. Her black dress seemed expensive, but was spotted and mussed. You could see where a sleeve seam had ripped at the armpit. The brown hands in her lap, mangling a handkerchief, wore a diamond band and a big topaz ring. Their nail polish was ragged and chipped.

The young woman's eyes had stopped at his ribbons, stayed there till she asked: "You were overseas?"

He nodded.

"In Europe?"

He detected a note of excitement. He nodded again.

The hand with the diamond band went up to her mouth to smother an "oh." After a moment's pause, she said dully: "My husband was there."

He was sure she was getting ready to ask if he'd met her G.I. and to forestall her, he said: "He and two million."

"Max was at Anzio."

"The Son of a Beach!"

She winced. He thought he knew why. "Watch yourself, Bud," he warned himself. "You're home. The dirty talk's out." "The men called it that," he began to explain "because it was—"

She shut her eyes. She said: "My husband was killed there." Her voice was as toneless as a robot announcing the time.

He plummeted down from his peak of elation.

He knew a moment of rage with himself for making the error of sitting beside her. Then he turned hot with shame for his callous wisecrack. His fingertips scratched the rough blue upholstery while he tried to think of the right words to say. All he could bring out was: "Too bad."

He told himself miserably that he should have known what

that black dress stood for. Africa, Italy, England were full of these women in black with those gravepits of eyes. Yet it gave him a genuine shock to come aware now that America must have many young women like this, girls, grown old overnight, putting on black, not for style but for sorrow.

The simple fact was that when a guy died over there you thought only of him, of the pity it was for him to be finished, of the pain and the fear he had felt, of the clothes and the pictures and trinkets left behind in the barracks that had to be gathered and packed and sent

To women like this.

Yet somebody had to be told, had to grieve. Someone whose name was stamped on the dog tags. Someone called next of kin . . . "Like my father," he thought, and he saw a gaunt, aging man in a musty, furnished room, opening a telegram. His body felt sticky with sweat.

The young woman was talking in a low, colorless voice, but the mind with which he was listening to her was so clouded with thoughts of its own that it took a while before he heard what she said. "—They write such nice letters. Tell such beautiful lies. How he died a hero." She seemed to be yanking her words out of a nightmare. "They mean somebody else. Not Max Weston."

That was a new one, belittling her husband, even in death. He welcomed his surge of resentment. It transferred to her a part of the anger he felt with himself.

"You see," her voice scratched, the way a worn phonograph needle does on an old record, "Max wasn't the type. Not the type for a hero."

This was the place for her to start crying and he was surprised that she didn't. The emotion-drained voice went on without changing timbre. "A sweet, gentle person. Live and let live . . . They made him a machine gunner! A killer! . . . Oh, how could they do things like that to people like Max?" Her eyes were fixed on his face, without expectation, as though she knew, already and hopelessly, that there wasn't an answer to what she was asking.

He ran a finger around the inside of his collar. "Look here, Mrs.—— What did you say your name was?"

"Elaine Weston."

"Well, Mrs. Weston, you must understand, you must make yourself see, that it's a job that has to be done. By guys like your husband. It's win or lose. We daren't lose." He looked at her features intently and thought: "If she's what I think, she should know."

She paid no attention to what he was trying to say. "Max never killed people." Her head moved very slowly, denying the thought, shaking it off. "He couldn't have changed. Not that much. Not that way." She paused, twisting her handkerchief. Each time she stopped you got a feeling of pain creeping up, catching her breath, that had to be borne and absorbed before she could go on. "He was in business, you see. Selling electrical things. Frigidaires. Oil burners. They said he had mechanical aptitude. That's why they made him a gunner."

He wished she would stop. He tried to make her. He said, trying to be gentle: "If you'd rather not talk."

She stiffened with offense. "Do you *mind* talking to me?"

He reddened, pulled at the knot of his tie. "I don't if it helps you."

"Helps?" Her mouth writhed. "Nothing helps. Do you think it helps me to see you coming back when he won't? Do you think it will help when the other husbands come home?"

Sweat poured through his shirt. He moved as if he meant to get up. "Enough is enough," he told himself. "She can't do this to me."

Elaine Weston put her hand on his sleeve. "You're running too." For the first time her voice had taken on color, the gall-green of bitterness. "You're like all the rest. A woman in grief is a leper. No one can stand someone else's trouble. Laugh and the world laughs with you. Cry and you cry—" She twisted her handkerchief savagely.

He set his back teeth. He thought: "Christ, I've got to do something for her!" Wretchedly, he tried to think of adequate words, words that would carry some comfort or common sense. A chaplain might speak about God's will and purpose, a divine plan and an ultimate good. Walk through the valley of the shadow of death. *Walk*. Not linger forever—

He was about to try those words on her but she cut him off. "What I can't understand is where Max got his courage. Where does a plain, simple man get courage for that?"

He cleared his throat, certain he had the answer this time. "You don't really have it," he said.

The slate eyes opened wider. "You mean"—Her voice cracked as though it was at last getting to be more than she could endure— "he was frightened, too."

He shifted his gaze, over her head, beyond, through the window, toward the sun-drenched Florida green. "We all are." His thumb started to rub.

This time, she had no reply, but merely sat, lips parted, staring at him, her eyes narrowing, finally focusing on the thumb moving steadily against its twin. After a moment she moaned: "Why did it happen to us?"

The small part of his mind that was listening to her heard only the "us." He was shocked to hear her cry out. "Why do you do that?"

"Do what?"

She touched his hands. "That. Rubbing your thumb . . . As if it was dirty."

His face flooded with heat. He jerked his hands apart, thrust them into his pockets. For a half minute he didn't reply. Then, when he was finally ready and able, he said: "Maybe it is."

"Oh! That's what it was like." Pain wrenched her features. She swung around to the window. Her handkerchief went to her eyes. He saw the shuddering throb of her back, heard the long slups of her tears. Yet now that she wept, he no longer felt sorry for her, but rather aggrieved.

She had slammed a door in his face, a door he had tried so long and so hard to pull open. She had pried; she had pushed; had forced him to open that door, and then slammed it shut.

Some day, he had known, the obscenity of killing and dodging your death would have to be put into words. You'd have to tell someone; share, divide the horror in parts, to have less to carry alone. Yet the first person to whom he had tried to tell what it was, what it did to a man, had cut him off with her tears, had turned her back, left him high and dry at the instant of climax.

He sat completely still for several minutes, admonishing himself with a terrible urgency not to let his thumbs rub, trying to decide whether to stay or to go. Even that choice had to be weighed with exactness. At this moment, he felt his whole future lay in that simple decision.

Joanie bumped his elbow and jogged it into his lap. She paused, with the brief butterfly lighting of children, panted "h'lo," laughed up to his face, flitted on.

The contact jogged more than his elbow. It reminded him that he sat in a blue and chrome seat on a train. He glanced around hurriedly to see whether any of the people in the car were watching him and the young woman in black. No. The high seat backs gave you privacy. They fenced you in.

Across the aisle, a man and his wife were exploring a lunch-box. She gave him a chicken wing and he growled: "No drumstick? You know I like dark meat best."

The pair back of them were asleep.

The coach was one world. These two seats were another. He thought: "I have to get away from here fast. I can't bear her near me."

He got up without speaking to her and went through the car to its rear platform, lighted a cigarette, smoked it down, lit a second from the stub of the first. After he finished the second, he went into the washroom, pushed the button marked PORTER, crouched on the slippery black leather settee, waiting, smoking one cigarette after another.

Chuckie, all sweaty and dirty, came in with his father, made faces at him, wriggled and squawked while his face and hands got a scrubbing. A stoutish, mulatto-tanned man in the forties came in, sat down beside him, lit a cigar and remarked that the way they were running they'd be at least an hour late reaching Jacksonville but maybe they'd make time tonight. It didn't disturb him that Corbett made no reply. He went on to announce that train schedules were cockeyed, just cockeyed, why his brother-in-law had been nearly twelve hours late getting in from Florida two weeks ago, held up by these troop trains all the way in, and God, you took your life in your hands when they tried to make time because the equipment was just shot to hell and had Corbett noticed that this train had roaches? Never happened before and he ought to know because he went down every year. The railroads were certainly getting away with plain murder, making dough hand over fist, but did they give a damn for the public? They did not. No, sir. Why, last week when he went to the Miami station to ask for a sleeper, the ticket man all but laughed in his face. Some nerve, some crust! Why isn't his money as good as the next one's? He told the man off. He told him all right. He said: "You better take care of us or we'd be damned if we come back next year." We'll go some place else. Mexico, maybe. They say Mexico is running wide open, no war down there at all. Miami's gone straight to hell. They treat you like cattle. Thirty dollars a day for a room and what food! Say, did Corbett eat on this train? That's an experience. Fast service, all right. The bum's rush. They all but spilled that slop they call coffee right down your throat. And ask for a small piece of butter! By God, where was all the food? Who was getting it, anyway? Probably the Russians. Europe, not us. We worry about the whole world. That's us all over. Give it away. No butter, no cream, no good steaks, no liquor. Oh, the liquor he knew because that was his business. The black market was getting all that, and believe me, you can't blame them at all. Those crooks in Washington. They had fixed that all right. Those OPA ceilings. You got your hands on a few cases of Scotch. Could you make a few dollars on them? You certainly couldn't. They told you what you should charge. Try to make a few dollars and the first thing you knew some inspector—a Gestapo—that's what it was, a Gestapo—

Corbett got up, dropped his cigarette into the hopper, went out and entered the diner. The steward was totalling breakfast checks at one end and the waiters beginning to spread clean cloths on the tables. He passed through to the lounge.

A pall of smoke hung over the car. It had begun to look frowsy with twists of empty cigarette wrappers, swirls of cigar cellophane, gray puddles of ash on the carpet. The people were talking, by twos, or trying to read while they smoked.

One seat was vacant, the one Kalchis had had, next to the redheaded grande dame with the Peke. Corbett sat down, lit a cigarette, let the smoke slowly out. The woman made a moue of annoyance, picked up her dog, turned it around on her lap, so that its head faced in the other direction. She said: "Pitty Sing doesn't like smoke in her face. Do you mind?" She herself was smoking, in a long holder, carefully held high.

He said: "I don't mind" but he did. It was only a pinprick, but the kind you could scratch until it became a big, ugly sore.

He got to his feet, stood teetering a moment, trying to decide whether he ought to stalk out. To where? To wait on a platform or back in the latrine until the diner was ready or the porter showed up?

He moved across the aisle to the desk underneath the big mirror. It was spread with discarded Sunday newspapers. War headlines stared at him. Impatiently, he shuffled the sheets all together and sat on the pile. The blonde in the silver fox jacket, down near the door, looked his way, flicked her lashes and smiled. The man in the chair nearest the desk pushed an ash stand over, glanced at him fleetingly through rimless bifocals, turned a page of his book. It was a pocket-size thriller, Corbett saw. The man was only pretending to read it. The Marine Corporal sat next to him, looking redder and hotter than he had before. He was down to the final inch of his butt. He leaned forward, mashed it out on the metal bowl of the ash stand and hoisted himself clumsily out of his chair. He nodded at Corbett, beckoned, with a tilt of his head, from him to the chair, smiled at the man with bifocals, and went out of the car.

Corbett slid off the desk and took the Marine Corporal's place. A woman leaned over the arm of his seat and said: "How nice! I wondered if I'd have the pleasure of talking to you." She was the old girl with the flowers on her hat, lilies of the valley they were, heaped on a crown of black straw. Under the hat brim, gray hair straggled down rouge-pinked, flabby cheeks. Her bosom was motherly. Between shoulder and armpit on her black dress, she wore a spread eagle of glittering stones, red, white and blue, stabbed by a capital V. She spoke in a thin, high, affected voice. "I saw you go through. Oh, some time ago. Twice. Wasn't it twice? I always notice the boys."

He shook off some ash on the carpet. The man with the bifocals moved back the ash stand. He had a good face, Corbett thought, gentle but adult. The blue eyes behind his lenses looked kindly and bright. His sparse hair was entirely gray, plastered down on the tanned top of his skull. He smiled at Corbett and asked: "Going through to New York?"

Before Corbett could answer, the woman with the V and the eagle plucked at his sleeve. "Going home, aren't you?"

He nodded uncomfortably, looked straight ahead.

"Your dear mother will be so happy to see you."

"My mother's been dead a good many years."

"Oh!" Her mouth corners drooped. "One misses one's dear mother so. Her prayers and her love. So many of my boys"—Porcelain jackets gleamed in her smile—"I'm chairman of our canteen, you know. They're all my own boys. I haven't a son of my own, you see. Just one precious daughter. You must meet my little girl. She's on this train, too. So many of my boys tell me I'm just like their own mother."

Corbett crossed his legs and uncrossed them again. Nowhere on a train were you safe from a pest. Except with the dish. He thought: "Shall I go back there now?" but decided "No. You can't be a nuisance, show you're too anxious." That wasn't the reason. He knew that he had to get the bad taste of the black widow out of his mouth, rinse it in alcohol, before he saw Nina Gilmore again.

The old girl with the V squeezed his arm. "Now, don't run away. Don't be nervous. I understand. You've been through so much. Talk if you want to. I know you're just dying to talk, but you feel if you do it'll be quite too shocking to us. Some of my friends just can't bear to hear the boys tell what they've been through."

Mosquitoes buzzed like that voice, in your African tent, shrill and insistent and threatening. The mistake was to notice. If you shut yourself up, made an armor of surliness—

On his other side, the man with bifocals asked: "Enjoying the trip?" and closed his book on one finger.

Corbett tried to sound curt. He said "Yes and No," glanced across the aisle.

In the end seat of the opposite row, a well-padded man, mahogany-tanned all the way up to a receded hair-line, was sounding off loudly, with gestures, to a carbon copy in the chair next to his. "So I said, 'Okay, if that's the only way to get rooms for my family, I'll *buy* the hotel.' You think I was kidding? You know what I did? I called up my partner, long distance. I called up New York. Person to person. He's in and out all the time. You never know when you can get him. I put in the call four o'clock. Know when I got him? Eleven at night. That's service for you! He said: 'Okay, go as high as two hundred thousand. No more!' Well, you know what happened? In the morning, I came down to talk turkey to them, I found the place sold. Two hundred fifty. All cash!"

The man next to him whistled. He said: "You see. Money like dirt." He flicked off his cigar ash. "Money like water. I say you're lucky. That stuff's no good. That's inflation. That's what it is. Just inflation. Remember what happened in twenty-six, twenty-seven?" He clucked. "Lost their shirts. They'll lose them again. Who knows if you'd bought that this month, next month the Army would take it away?"

"But they pay for it, boy. They pay plenty, believe me.

I figured I'd turn the deal over fast. Pick up five or ten thousand . . ."

The man with the bifocals coughed loudly, as though he hoped to drown out the voices. He gave Corbett a sidelong, searching look. "The fortunes of war," he said, framing his mouth with his hand. "I mean dollars and cents."

He closed his book, tucked it into his coat pocket, turned around all the way. "Don't, I beg you," he said soberly, "judge all of America by what you see and hear on this train." He was speaking softly, but in a clear, even voice that carried no further than Corbett. "Not all of this country has been on the joy-ride. Don't let what you hear, what you see, make you bitter. Some people—most people, I like to think—have known or have tried to know what was happening."

He waited for Corbett to comment but when Corbett didn't, he coughed again, looked down at his shoes, said: "It's funny, I find myself apologizing for what I'm a part of myself. Perhaps that's why I am."

He paused again until Corbett had lighted a fresh cigarette, had inhaled once or twice. Then he said: "You'll forgive me if I seem a bit, well, emotional. I'm usually not. But seeing you and that lad. Two heroes. That boy was wounded in action, you know. Malaria, too. Won't discuss it, of course."

"You don't," Corbett muttered.

The man seemed encouraged by the fact that he'd made a remark. He hitched up in his chair, as if sitting straighter could bring him closer to Corbett. "Naturally not. It's impossible to get things across to people who have never experienced them. You can't know how pain feels until you've felt pain. Am I right? You see, I know a little. I was in the other. The first. . . . I'm a doctor. My name is Peck."

Corbett said: "Corbett," and thought how oddly you traded names on a train. You talked about anything under the sun, the most intimate or the most casual things, till you got to a point where you couldn't go on without names.

Dr. Peck said: "Glad to know you, Lieutenant," and then "Going home?"

"Three weeks' leave."

"And after that?"

"Back to Miami."

"Lucky boy. To tell you the truth"—Dr. Peck's smile was diffident—"while I was down in Miami, when I saw all those boys . . ."

"I wish people wouldn't say boys."

The man blinked. "I stand corrected. Rightly so, sir. We sent them in boys. We get them back men. When I saw all those Air Force *men*, back from the front, I wanted so much to converse with them. But I couldn't. For the first time in my life I felt tongue-tied, inadequate. Awed. Simply awed. When I looked at their ribbons—that's the D.F.C., is it not?"

Corbett nodded. He gripped his cigarette firmly between thumb and finger.

"I thought so." The man bobbed his head, self-approving, before he went on: "It was the sort of experience a patient of mine once had in a somewhat—oh, quite different—situation. You'll get the point, I believe, when I tell you the story. My patient was a newspaperman."

Corbett's chin came up, his head cocked. He turned at last completely away from the woman with the V and the lilies.

"He was reporting, covering, they call it, I think, a sensational murder trial in New York. The Snyder-Gray case. A corset salesman and a stupid blonde housewife. You remember, perhaps?"

Of course he remembered. That case was a legend. American *crime passional*. He said: "I do."

"I trust you'll forgive the analogy. From the sublime to the ridiculous, almost." Dr. Peck cleared his throat. "But homicide *is* one of the facts of our national life. Well, this was a sordid affair. They bludgeoned her husband to death for insurance, with some household implement." He scratched the short hair at his temple. "I can't quite remember."

"Sash weight," Corbett said.

Dr. Peck chortled. "So you do remember! What an impression individual murder makes on our public! Why, just a few months ago some young chap in New York killed his wife. It seemed to me every person I met was discussing that. Forgot the war. One killing, one killer, is something we grasp. Down on our level." He hitched up the knees of his trousers. "Let me get to my point. My patient was a first-rate reporter, and so his colleagues chose him to ride with the condemned murderess up to the death house. Only one newspaperman could go on that journey. They selected him. When he got out of the car at Sing Sing, they crowded around him, and asked: 'Well, what did she say?' 'She didn't say anything.' 'What did you ask her?' 'I didn't ask anything.' 'You didn't ask *anything?*'" He lifted his eyebrows to mirror the astonishment of the men he was quoting. "'You rode with that woman and didn't ask her one single question!' 'I couldn't,' my patient said. 'How could I? You just don't ask questions of people in hell.'"

His eyes were on Corbett, to see whether he'd gotten the point. "It hit me that way, that same way. I desperately wanted to talk to those boys—those men—with the ribbons. To ask all sorts of questions. I couldn't. I couldn't intrude. Do you know what I mean? Can you ask them about war? Say: 'Excuse me, sir, did you enjoy that mess over there?' And to talk about anything else seemed a cruel impertinence."

Corbett dropped his cigarette into the bowl. He knew that this man had deliberately chosen this roundabout way of revealing how deeply he felt, using loquacity, self-interruptions, to keep hero-worship from sounding too maudlin. Yet, he was, in a way, another way, glad Peck had taken the detour of the old murder case. It was one of the things that made you feel you were really back home, like the gunner's mate at the depot remembering the Good Humor man. "I think," he said finally, "they'd have been rather glad if you talked to them. About practically anything American. Baseball. Politicians. Or even murder. They like to feel they haven't lost touch."

"I wonder." Dr. Peck's face was grave and paternal as he shook his head. "They seemed so terribly absorbed, so quiet, preoccupied, as if they all had enormous problems to think through." He paused. "Like yourself."

Corbett blushed. He fumbled in his pocket for his cigarettes and lighter, muttering as he pulled them out. "Haven't we all?"

Dr. Peck shook his head vehemently. "It's part of our present catastrophe that the world is divided in two. One part's getting all of the bad—the suffering, the sacrifice. The other is getting the spoils—the easy money, excitement. We here at home, even those of us who have some sort of conscience—" his shoulders hunched—"have given, have felt, just nothing at all. I mean, compared to the things we've demanded of you. Take me, for example. I practice medicine. White Plains. Know where that is? Westchester County, New York. My practice has doubled because some of my colleagues have gone off to the war. I take night calls, for the first time in ten years. I drive out in blizzards. My arthritis doubles me up. I flatter myself I'm doing my part in the war."

"Well, then—" Corbett began.

Dr. Peck brushed his interruption aside with a wide wave of his hand. "Well, nothing! I go home to a steam heated house, sleep between clean linen sheets on the best innerspring in the County. When I wake up, my good wife has excellent coffee, all hot and waiting. I read my bank statement. For the first time in my life I can, if I wish, worry about surtaxes. My patients are paying their bills. They've got enough money. And when the ache in my bones gets too bad, I travel to Florida and bask in the sun. Now, those young fellows whose patients I'm treating work seventy-two hours at a stretch in the jungles, live on atabrine, slosh in mud. No, son." His head wagged again. "I'm not kidding myself. There's a gulf, a chasm between us. It's going to get wider. I can't see how we'll ever cross over—"

"Please," Corbett begged. You could stand this gush only so long. Then it began to stick in your throat.

Dr. Peck looked at him sharply: "Do I bore you, sir?"

He colored: "I have to see—"

The girl with straw-colored hair and the Signal Corps Captain staggered into the car, stumbled against him. The girl said: "H'lo" instead of "Excuse me." She was a tall, gangly kid, badly dressed and made-up.

The woman with the V cried: "Patsy, darling!" and gave the Captain a critical stare. Beside her a man with furry eyebrows broke off his own conversation, shifted his cigar from one side of his mouth to the other, mumbled: "Well, Pat!"

"I told Captain Metzger he had to meet you and dad." The girl swayed in front of her mother. She clung to the Captain's arm.

The Captain seemed flustered. He looked young, Corbett thought, to have double bars, probably one of those kids who'd been smart enough to take R.O.T.C. and hang on to commissions.

"Captain, meet my father, Senator Hastings. You have heard of *him*. And my mother. She's been killing herself with canteens and things."

Corbett turned half-around. That face had seemed familiar. Something out of picture magazines or the newspaper morgues, one of those public figures you always have known without personal encounter. In the flesh, the abundant flesh, Senator Hastings was far less impressive than in his pictures; slack jowls, nose pinched, purple-veined, eyebrows twin mustaches over the nose.

His name meant nothing at all to the Captain. He took the introduction completely dead-pan.

The Senator boomed: "Glad to know you, sir. My little girl been behaving herself?"

Corbett got up, moved quietly back to the desk.

Mrs. Hastings beamed at him fatuously. "That's a dear boy. Pat, the Lieutenant's sweet. He gave you his chair."

"Sit down, Pat," the Senator ordered. "Sit down and behave."

Pat Hastings let go the Captain's arm, slid into the seat between her mother and Peck and eyed Corbett.

The Captain took a step back, preparing to leave. "Oh

don't go," the girl cried. "Don't you dare run away." She opened her handbag, took out a compact, slapped a puff on her nose.

The young Captain sighed, spread his legs for a stance.

"Mother, he's just the most wonderful hero. Been in all the big battles."

Mrs. Hastings exposed her teeth and bent forward. "You poor boy. You must have had a terrible time."

"They rolled me over a barrel," the Captain said calmly.

"I envy you, sir," the Senator began. "If I were younger, I'd like nothing better than to march shoulder to shoulder with—"

His daughter broke in. "You can't worm a thing out of him, dad. I've tried till I'm tired. Just worn out." She unscrewed her lipstick.

The Captain glanced uneasily toward Corbett. The bombardier smiled.

Mrs. Hastings tapped the Captain's wrist. "How lucky, how wonderful you're back safe and sound. Your darling mother will be so glad to see you."

He shook his head. "I won't see my parents this trip. They're out in Ohio. I'm spending this leave with my wife and baby."

Pat Hastings held the lipstick away from her gaping mouth. "Why, you never told me!"

The Captain's smile broadened. "You didn't give me a chance." He raised the hem of his tunic and reached for his wallet. "Ruth sent me pictures. If you'd like to see them."

The girl held up her compact mirror, slashed her red pencil against her lips.

Dr. Peck said: "Let me see. I'm an expert on babies."

The Captain moved down to in front of the Doctor and gripped the edge of the desk, boxing Corbett into the corner. He passed the pictures to Peck, grinning self-consciously, as if he weren't quite sure whether he ought to be proud or embarrassed. "I've never seen the kid. Just his pictures."

They were in a small folder, a half dozen framed snapshots.

Dr. Peck leafed the pictures, nodded approvingly, passed them to Corbett. It was the wartime Madonna, a thin, bobbed-haired girl, smiling gallantly, and a fat and expressionless infant. Every married man in the Air Force pulled out a folder like this the minute you met him.

Dr. Peck said: "Remarkable infant. A boy or a girl?"

"Boy." The Captain seemed especially proud of that fact.

"Something to fight for," Dr. Peck said. "To save from more wars like this. . . . How old is the child?"

"Sixteen months."

"Fine. Excellent. She's taking good care of your kid."

"Isn't she though!" A worried frown started between the young captain's eyes. "It seems funny to be coming home to a kid. Hard to get used to that. Me and Ruth . . . well, you know how it is, batting around, furnished rooms, dancing joints, movies . . . Now, spending a leave sitting home with a kid."

He took the pictures from Corbett and looked at them as if he hadn't seen them before. "Imagine telling that kid: 'This big lug is your daddy!' I hope I don't scare him. Ruth says he says 'Daddy.' " He put the folder back in his wallet. "It's a big jump," he said. "Being a family man. Ruth, she's had time to get used to the business, but to me—well—"

Corbett said: "Please. I'd like to get through."

Dr. Peck looked up quickly, first at Corbett, "Leaving us?" then toward the diner. "They're not ready yet?"

"Got to see my porter about something."

"I see. Fine to have met you. I enjoyed our talk. Going all the way through?"

Corbett nodded.

"Then I'll see you again."

The Captain flattened himself on the wall. He said: "See you again," as if sharing his pictures with Corbett had made them old friends.

A waiter opened the door from the diner, precariously balancing an enormous tray, swathed in linen, heavy and bulbous with crockery and silver. Corbett side-stepped to let him go past.

He saw Senator Hastings's eyebrows leap up. "We were told there's no seat service on here."

"Special pah'ty." The Negro's face was impassive. "Drawing Room A." He lurched through the car.

"There's a prisoner of war in Drawing Room A." That was the voice of the man who had almost bought a Miami hotel. "They have him in handcuffs. I saw him. He killed a guard at the camp."

Corbett heard a quick gasp. The blonde in the fox said: "My God!"

Pat Hastings's lipstick dropped from her hand. As it fell, it made a sharp ping on the base of the ash stand. It rolled before Corbett's shoes down the aisle.

"Well, I'll be goddamned," the Senator said. "He gets better service than us."

CHAPTER FIVE

Coach Sixteen smelled of fried chicken and pickles. Half of its passengers were eating their lunches out of shoe boxes and bags. The sailor's baby lay on his mother's lap, contentedly guzzling a bottle. Joanie had moved up the aisle to Chuckie's family's seats and was nibbling a chicken bone. It all looked like a family picnic.

Corbett swung through Sixteen, out and into Fifteen. There, an infant was yowling and the car looked more cluttered than the one he had left. He threaded his way through the valise-narrowed aisle to the platform. A trainman was tightening a door catch.

Corbett asked: "Where can I find my porter?"

The man shrugged. "Prob'ly catching a doze. Need him for anything special?"

"You bet."

"Trouble?"

"No trouble."

"We're coming to Wildwood. Ten minute stop. He'll turn up by then."

Corbett went back to his coach and into its washroom. The young Marine was on the black leather sofa, his feet propped on a chair. He let his slow, pleasant smile ripple over his face. "What's a matter? You got a weak stomach?"

"I'm feeling all right," Corbett said.

"Aw no." The youngster shook his head. "Can't kid me. I took it longer'n you. They make you sick." He jerked his thumb toward the lounge.

"You bet." Corbett pressed the porter's bell button.

The Marine yawned. "Oh, they mean well. They don't know the score. That's all it is." His nose puckered and his grin turned mischievous. " 'But Corp'ral, the boys do pray in the foxholes, don't they?' " He had the tone and the airs of the old girl with the V and the lilies down pat. "Sure, ma'am, sure. You betcha my life. They say 'Jesus Christ' alla time."

Corbett took out his limp cigarette package, held it to the Corporal. The Marine hesitated politely, counting the smokes "Go on," Corbett said. "I know where there's more. I know a girl with a carton."

The Marine helped himself, mumbled "Thanks." He lifted his shoes from the chair, dusted it off with his hand. " 'Do tell us about your wonderful experiences. Wheah were you wounded, you deah, deah boy?' " He snickered like the kid he obviously was.

Corbett snapped his lighter open. The Marine drew in, held the cigarette up with his pinkie stiff. " 'Oh deah, I don't think I can beah to heah your experiences.' Force yourself ma'am. Just force yourself." He guffawed. "You came in too late. You missed the best part. The way I fixed *him!*"

"Fixed who?"

"Her husband. 'The Senatuh.' " He put his cigarette down on the lip of the ash stand. "You meet her old man?" The grin smeared his face. "He's a card. Know what he asks me? 'What do the boys in the foxholes think of John Lewis?' "

Corbett stared at him coldly. "Well, what?"

The Marine squinted. "One guess."

"They don't think."

"You said it, Bud. They got somethin' else on their mind. I told him better than that. I told him I worked in the mines. My old man works in the mines. We think John L. is damn good for the miners." He chuckled. "My old man will laugh himself crazy. First time a Tamaqua Polack told a Senator off."

"They give you a pain in the ass," Corbett muttered. He stretched his long legs from the chair to the edge of the leather settee.

The Marine sat up, visibly wincing as he straightened his spine. "Who *told* you?"

"Told me what?"

The youngster touched the purple strip on his tunic. "How I got that." His smile twisted a little, wry with remembrance of something unpleasant. "I'm the Marine that got goosed by the Japs." He picked the cigarette up, winked through the nimbus of smoke. " 'But Corp'ral, why can't you tell us where you were hit? You're just bein' modest, deah boy.' . . . That's no lie, sister, believe me, it ain't . . . We're in the jungle, see. They're throwin' the works. I'm sweatin', see. I'm thinkin' the next one is gonna get me. An' then, Jesus Christ, I feel a pain in my spine, like a knife. I think: they got me, they got my spine, I'll be crippled for life. I pass out cold." He guffawed again and measured a foot span with his big, shaking paws. "That big. Like a needle. Right through my pants. Goddamdest thing you ever saw in your life."

"It's funny as hell," Corbett said. He didn't smile.

The Corporal's quizzical stare wondered why the Lieutenant stayed glum. He raised his shoulders. "I'm goddamn lucky, that's all I can say. Ain't many lucky as me." He slouched back again.

After half a minute or so, Corbett asked: "How much leave did you get?"

"Thirty days. I stop off in Quantico first. Thirty days after that."

"Lucky bastard. I got twenty-one."

The washroom curtain swung open. A young man came in, glanced quickly at Corbett and the Marine, went into the toilet.

The Marine looked at Corbett. He said quietly: "Over eighteen."

The young man bustled out, stepped to the basin, avoiding the servicemen's stares. He pressed the hot water tap, got a sputter and trickle. He pressed the cold. The water ran in a thin, brownish stream. He clucked impatiently. "I wanted to wash up before lunch." In the mirror above the washstand, he could see the two uniformed men watching him. Color rose under his tan. "Well," he began, forcing a heartiness, "I hope they've got something simple to eat in that diner. My ulcer's been acting up . . ."

He paused as the long curtains flapped. His relief was plain when a man in civilian clothes came in. It was Kalchis. The horseplayer stood in the doorway and leered down at Corbett. "The dish give you the brush?" he inquired.

Corbett didn't reply. Instead, he looked swiftly, almost involuntarily, at the horseplayer's coat pockets.

The young man side-stepped at the basin. "I'm just about done," he said amiably to Kalchis. "Take this if you want. How late are we running?"

Kalchis shrugged.

"Golly, I hope we get in on time. I've got a lunch date in New York tomorrow."

"Oh yeah." The horseplayer was examining the young man's attire. "Kiss it good-by. You'll be lucky you get in for supper."

"Don't say that. It'll cost me a job. A good job." He caught himself, glanced over his shoulder at Corbett.

Corbett looked at the Marine. He asked: "Going in the diner?"

The Marine moved back on the leather, nursing the tip of his spine. "I'm saving my dough for Tamaqua."

Corbett got to his feet. "See you," he said.

Kalchis, soaping his hands, called over his shoulder. "Wait for me, soldier."

Corbett pushed the curtain aside and went out.

All the twos in the diner were taken. At one of the twos at the far end of the car Corbett saw the bright raven wings of Nina Gilmore's coiffure and the brown heart of her face. The second seat at her table was filled with padded civilian shoulders, a mahogany neck and sleek haircut. He brushed by the waiters, hoping without hope that the man might be persuaded to sit somewhere else.

The steward stopped him halfway down the car, waved him, with a peremptory frown, toward a table for four that already had two. A man and a woman had the seats beside the broad window. Their faces seemed remotely familiar, possibly passengers he'd noticed before on his first scouting trip through the Pullmans.

The man was New England antique: straight-backed, distinguished, white-haired—the clean, silver-white you get from a few drops of blue in the rinse—with a thin, Puritan nose, a rectangular jaw, scrubbed, rosy cheeks, tight, magenta lips, eyes ice-bright and cold. The scrawny, shaved back of neck above a stiff collar looked like a plucked rooster's.

The woman seemed young enough for his daughter but she obviously wasn't. They were much too polite to each other to be closely related. She was pretty, as a Persian kitten is pretty. Her light hair, fluffing out, her round, china-blue eyes, gave her an appealing air of fragile femininity. Her cheeks were pink, without obvious rouge. She didn't wear earrings. Her tweed suit bespoke quality. Ladylike, that was the word, the womanly woman, with the suggestion of clinging, of brave little woman facing the world, that brought out the Sir Walter Raleigh in man.

When Corbett noticed her eyes, he remembered. The first time she had turned those Wedgwood eyes up to him, he had almost stopped in Loch Lomond. It had seemed to him then as if she was imploring him to save her from something or someone; likely as not the old fox. Well, old thin-lips had turned out to be more wolf than fox. The glare he gave Corbett when the officer pulled out a chair and sat down was possessive, defensive, as though he had to preserve genteel ladies from the lecherous contacts of soldiers.

More to gild the good name of the Air Force than because it was actually called for, Corbett asked: "Do you mind? All the small tables seem to be taken."

The woman purred: "It's quite all right." The "quite" had the British inflection, good breeding. Her demeanor was pleasant. Then, dismissing him with her nod, she looked down at the menu. "Of course, I shall have melon. I can't ever seem to get quite enough of your American melon. But that isn't a meal. Oh dear, there's really so little to choose, if one doesn't want fish, ham, omelet or salad." She glanced up at the old man with a helpless deference that was charming. "If you would suggest—"

He folded his menu, picked up the pencil that lay on the cloth alongside his order blank, said: "I shall have lamb chops."

The Wedgwood eyes scurried over the card. "But it's not on the menu."

"They'll manage to get it for *me*."

Corbett smiled to himself as he watched the liver-spotted thin hand, scrawling its order. The old geezer's terrific, he thought, he expects them to stop the Palm Queen and run out to the butcher.

The woman said brightly: "Then I'll have chops too." She folded her menu, tucked it under the water carafe. The man pushed his aside with his elbow.

Corbett wondered mildly why neither of them had had the good manners to pass the card over to him.

The waiter, in a grease-spattered coat, set down three glasses, half-filled with ice, sloshed in the water and with one swoop of his big, dusky paw, gave Corbett a menu and picked up the pad on which the old man had written. He scowled, pointed down at the paper.

"Can't you read?" the old man asked coldly.

The waiter wrinkled his forehead. "It looks lak lamb chops."

"It is."

"Ain't no chops on the menoo."

"That makes no difference." The old man's fingertips pressed together.

The waiter shifted from one foot to the other. "Cain't get no lamb chops on heah."

Corbett touched his sleeve. "Can I order a drink?"

"On'y beer."

"Give me beer." He wrote out his order, gripping the pencil against the jounce of the train: Tomato juice, ham and hashed brown potatoes, ice cream and coffee and beer.

The waiter snatched up the paper and waited again until he was able to catch the eye of his steward. The steward came over. His forehead and under his nose were beaded with sweat. "What's wrong over here?" His suspicious glance was at Corbett.

Old thin-lips spoke up: "Your waiter refused to fill my order."

The woman's color was high. She was making the fluttery hand motions of unease.

The steward slanted a suspicious glance at his waiter, snatched the slip from his hand. He said brusquely: "He can't fill orders for what's not on the menu." He crossed out the spidery handwriting. "Please order something we have." He flung the sheet back on the table.

"There is nothing else."

"Please, mister, if there's nothing you want, I've got people waiting for seats—" The steward gestured toward both of the entrances.

Kalchis slid into the chair alongside the old man, nodded at Corbett and picked up a menu.

A purplish tinge was spreading from the old man's lips through his face. The woman fidgeted, bleated: "Oh, Mr. Voorhees, let's order anything. Just to get done."

"What's your name, man?"

"Listen." The steward rested the heel of his hand on the table. He sounded as tired as he looked. "Right now this road needs me and my waiters and chef a good deal more than it needs you. Why don't you stay home if you don't like the service?"

Corbett thought the old man would have a stroke. He turned blue, clutched the rim of the table. The woman reached over and patted the back of his hand. "There, there," she said, soothingly, "you mustn't let these things upset you."

The waiter picked up the slip on which Kalchis had written his order and scooted. The woman reached for the menu. "Please, Mr. Voorhees, do let me order your luncheon. I'm sure I can find some things you can eat. See here." She wrinkled her forehead, prettily anxious. "I think that some bouillon. Clear bouillon. Sliced chicken on toast. White meat of chicken. And tea. A melon dessert. Now, how does that sound? There! And I'll have the same. Shall I write it?"

The old face was softening. It looked almost grateful. "My dear Mrs. Forsythe, please let me."

She sat back, dabbing her lip with her handkerchief, half-smiling, glancing at Corbett, expecting some sign of approval. He toyed with his silver, pretending to be so absorbed in aligning his knife, fork and spoon that he had neither listened nor seen.

"There," she said briskly. "That's taken care of. Now do let us forget the whole horrid business."

"I should very much like to." The cheeks looked almost normal. "But I hardly think you know what this means."

The waiter set a glass of tomato juice before Corbett, without plate or ice-bowl. He crowded the glass with a plate of gravy-drowned ham and charred fried potatoes, a metal bread tray with two soggy rolls, a chip of half-melted butter, a brown bottle of beer and a glass. He snatched up the order and slithered away.

Corbett heard Kalchis say: "You know what that looks like? Like a dog's vomit," but he didn't look up or reply. The horseplayer was right. The food looked disgusting. Corbett drained his tomato juice, broke a roll, smeared on the butter, poured out his beer.

The woman was talking to the old man, gently, patiently, almost caressingly. "Really, Mr. Voorhees, you must not let yourself become so upset. "It's horrid, I know. One must put up with these things in a war."

The ham and potatoes blocked Corbett's windpipe. He sputtered. The old man glared, drew his thin shoulders indignantly up, expecting apology. When there was none, he snorted, said stiffly: "I had been told of these things. I had been told they were happening. It's the first time they have happened to me. Why, do you know—" He picked up his water glass, grimaced at the chunk of slimy, soot-flecked ice, set it down. "I've not been on a train in at least twenty years."

"Mister, you too," Corbett thought. "You don't know how we've missed you."

"Each year I've gone down to Palm Beach, we have driven. They forced me to leave my car there this time. No gasoline. I know what they're up to. They're determined to take our comforts away, one by one. To humble us, make us subservient to their every whim, get us ready for . . ."

The woman broke in: "It's so hard for a man of your years to travel by train."

There was a bridling, perhaps at her mention of age. "You might have thought, when they deprived me of the use of my car, they'd provide something else. Suitable transport. They told me I ought to consider myself most fortunate to get one lower berth."

She bent forward, her blue eyes bulging slightly, "Oh, but you are! Why I have an upper. Just fancy, an upper."

The old man looked down at his fingertips thoughtfully. "I'd offer to change—"

Her hand went over the tablecloth quickly to touch the back of his hand. "I'd never accept it. You just must not think, because I find it so hard to get used to your sleeping cars— this intimate contact with all sorts of strangers—" She darted a look across the table at Kalchis.

His bold pupils stared back.

Her shoulders hunched forward. "One never knows who—" Her voice trailed off.

The waiter set down the horseplayer's lunch. The old man looked up, half-timid, half-defiant, tapped on his water glass. "Bring me fresh water. No ice." You got the sense from his tone that it was one final stand, one last test of the virility of his petty authority. "Yours, too, Mrs. Forsythe?"

She said "No, thank you" and sipped at her goblet. "I have learned to enjoy your American ice water. I used to think it was a barbarous custom. But one comes to accept—"

Corbett pushed back his plate. "Lady," he thought, "if you come from the same place as your accent, you've got a crust being snooty about one single thing over here."

The waiter set down two cups of bouillon, removing the scabrous tin lids. The soup splashed over the rims of the cups into saucers. He put down two chicken sandwiches, charred on the outside, depressed in the centers, whisked off Corbett's plate, slid down a brick of strawberry and vanilla ice cream and orange ice. Corbett hacked with his spoon.

The old man said, over his soup cup: "But you are going back?"

She smiled at him ruefully over a spoonful of soup, tasted it, reached for the pepper and salt. "But of course. I must."

The switch-off was startling. When you eavesdropped on trains, you had to guess the beginnings, the backgrounds, the ends of whatever you heard.

Mrs. Forsythe was sipping soup daintly, talking between

spoonfuls. "Rodney's sister wrote me the letter . . . Oh he wouldn't himself . . . He never could bring himself to compel me. He's always been so considerate of me . . . That's why I left when I did. The Prices, my friends—they have a *most* charming house at the Gables—aren't leaving till well into April. They *begged* me to stay . . . But I had to go back. See the consul. Talk over the chances of passage . . . She, Rodney's sister, I mean, thinks the danger is over. She thinks Rodney misses me so very much."

"You miss him as much?"

She waited until she had reached the bottom of her cup. Then, after a nervous clearing of throat, she replied: "But of course. Except that it's hard to be sure how much you miss someone whom you haven't seen in four years."

"Four years!" The old man's white store teeth crunched his toast.

"He sent me here in that dreadful spring. 1940. My nerves! He was certain I could never have stood the air raids."

"And quite right."

She lowered her eyes to her plate. It looked like an act. Frail little woman was a powerful line. Better men than the Puritan iceberg had melted before it. Yet the tone of her voice sounded as though she meant what she said: "I know I must go back. But I can't. It's hard to find the words to express it. I don't really mean I'm afraid to go back." She set down her knife and fork. "Perhaps that is what I mean. It's all so confusing." She brushed back the fringe of her hair. "You see, there's more than an ocean between us. There's what they've been through all these years. Why, they—I really think they'll actually hate me when they come to know how very different it's all been for me. I have loved it here. My friends—" She traced a circle on the cloth with her fore-finger. "Why, they've been like a family . . . better than family. Took such good care, as if I was something they had in trust, that had to be returned in perfect condition." She laughed delicately. "I feel closer to them than to my own people." Her shoulders hunched again, in that gesture that was near to a shudder. "Why, even Rod. It's hard to remember just what he looks like."

"I can tell you, lady," Corbett said to himself. "He's thin as a slat and gray, his hair and his skin, because he hasn't been sleeping too well all these years. He has a catarrh. It's been cold as a barn where he works and he lives. He looks shabby and tired, much older than you. Not much of him left but his guts."

The waiter set down a chipped metal coffee pot for Corbett, for the others two thin slices of melon, a steaming silvered pitcher, two cups, dangling strings of tea bags; he scooped up Kalchis's plate, banged down his coffee and pie.

Kalchis gave his unpleasant chortle. "Hey, why the rush!"

At the sound of the horseplayer's voice Voorhees jerked around. So absorbed had he been in what the woman was saying and he was replying, that he had forgotten that some one was seated in the chair next to his. He drew himself up. His mouth made a purse of disdain. He glared at the Greek. The horseplayer's eyes met the ice-blue and a long curious look passed between them. The Greek's eyes were cool, almost contemptuous. The old man's were malignant with hate.

The woman must have sensed it too for her voice quavered a little. "Shall I pour your tea now?"

Voorhees turned slowly back: "If you please." He glanced at Kalchis again.

"You see," she began tentatively, trying to pick up the thread of her problem while she stirred cream into her tea, "I do want to go back if they need me, but I almost wish— Sometimes I think, if I had something here . . . In four years, you begin to belong . . ."

Voorhees was less than half listening. He was plainly uncomfortable next to the Greek. He drank a few sips of his tea, set his cup down. "As soon as you're ready—" He opened his coat, took a plump, tan leather wallet from an inside pocket. The waiter, balancing a tray of dishes, caught the gesture of cash, slid to a precarious stop at the table. Corbett asked for his bill, took out two single dollars.

The old man opened his billfold, fingered the thick stack of greenbacks, laid a ten-dollar bill on the check. He put down the wallet, let it lie on the table while he waited for change.

Kalchis was eating his pie, was drinking his coffee. His eyes slanted sideways, fell on the wallet and stayed.

The train was slowing and Corbett looked through the window. The sign on the sun-bleached depot said: WILDWOOD. He decided to pass up his change and hunt for the pint and the porter during the stop.

He opened the pint in the men's room. It was rye; it was raw; it had cost five dollars. He offered a drink to the Marine from Tamaqua, but when the Corporal said: "Why not? Any time you get something for free from the Army," and stretched his arm for the bottle, Corbett yanked a flat paper cup from the wall container and poured out a drink. It was ticklish work, with the sway of the train and his own unsteady hand.

The Marine sniggered. "Gettin' perticklar. Acts like a civilian awready?"

"Damned if I'd trust a Marine with my bottle." He handed the paper cup over, three quarters full. "Make it last. I'm saving the stuff for a party."

"What kind of a party with only one pint?"

"She's a lady. She'll take what she gets and be happy."

"Lady? What in hell is a lady? What good is a lady?"

"Any time the Air Force needs advice from the Marines."

"Okay, okay." The Marine held the paper cup up. "In your eye."

"Short war," Corbett said. He drank from the bottle.

The Marine emptied his cup at one gulp, crumpled it, tossed it into the ash stand bowl. He said: "We got better from the mules in the mines." He ducked his head into his collar, pretending to be dodging a blow. When Corbett merely sat down without menacing gestures, he asked: "How was the lunch?"

"One guess."

"But what did they do to it, hey?"

Corbett laughed. "I know that gag." Whatever it was, the company or liquor, he had begun to feel good.

"I'm smart," the Marine said. "When I blow my pay I want somethin' for it. See my old buddies?"

Corbett shook his head. "Saw plenty. Heard plenty without them."

The kid nodded sagaciously. "They're somethin'. Believe me, they're somethin'." He eased himself back on the settee. "Makes you feel lousy," he said.

Corbett pulled down a fresh paper cup for the youngster and filled it.

The leatherneck shook his head. "Empty stomach. I better not."

"Aren't you going to eat?" He drained the cup.

"They'll be sellin' sandwiches somewheres along . . . I'll have one of your butts."

There was just one in the pack. He let the Corporal have it. The youngster drew in, let the smoke dribble from the end of his mouth. "Lieutenant." The rye had a funny effect on the kid. It was sobering him up. His broad, pleasant face seemed almost solemn. "I'm glad, I'm goddamn glad I'm just a dumb Polack. My people are different. They know the score. You want to know somethin'?" He put his big hand on the officer's knee. "My mama, she saved my life at Guadal." It dawned on him then this was a First Looie and he drew his hand quickly back. "You don't mind me gettin' familiar?"

"Hell, no. The latrine's no place to be pulling rank."

The Corporal smiled absently. "I ain't never told nobody this, but it's God's honest truth." He jutted his chin so that it creased like a bulldog's. "You know when we hit the Beach at Guadal, I was so goddamn scared, I couldn't shoot. I was paralyzed. Stiff." He held his arms tight at his side, acting it out. "We come in right through the water. And then they open up." He gestured widely with the cigarette. "I see all around me. Jesus Christ! What I see! My buddies. My pals. Good guys I know."

"You don't have to tell me." Corbett felt his right thumb where it lay on the bottle, stirring to life.

"I'm just like a stone." The Marine went on as if Corbett had not said a word. "I can't shoot. By Jesus, I can't even move. Then, all of a sudden, I hear my mama. I hear my old lady just as plain as I'm talkin' to you. She's talkin' to me. She's sayin': 'Come on, Stan, what you been doin'? You been doin' somethin' you shouldn't. Tell mama what's wrong.' Just the way when I was a kid and I done somethin' wrong. I holler out: 'Mama, I'm scared. I can't shoot. I'm so scared I can't shoot.' An' I hear her sayin' to me plain, like we're in the kitchen back in Tamaqua: 'They can't do that to you. Stan, they can't do it to you.'"

The youngster's eyes widened, his face took on surprise as if he couldn't believe that he was actually relating this miracle and that an Air Force officer was listening to him, seriously, intently, believing his words.

"Go on," Corbett said.

The kid's nod said thanks for permission to speak. "I could feel her alongside of me, holdin' onto my arm, steadyin' me. 'Go on, Stan. Give 'em hell.'" He sucked in, expanding his chest. "'Okay, mama, okay,' I hollered. 'They can't do this to me.'" He blew out his breath. "My old lady, she saved my life. I tell you she saved my life." He glanced at Corbett again, expecting approval or censure, puffed the cigarette a few times, then lowered his head and grinned sheepishly. "First time I told anybody. Why I picked you—"

"Want a drink?"

The kid shook his head. "Funny about trains. You clam or you spill. You spill all you know." He stayed silent a moment and then he pounded the hard leather seat with his fist. "Tell them fat asses a story like that! They think you're nuts. They been to the movies. They know all about it. Can't tell 'em anything."

Corbett squinted into the paper cup in his hand, tilted it into his mouth, let a few drops roll down his tongue. He asked: "Going back to the mines?"

"You betcha."

Corbett scowled. "That's the better world they tell you you're making?"

The Marine returned his scowl. "What's wrong with the mines? It takes a man to work in the mines." He put his cigarette out. "What you work at yourself before you went in?"

"Newspaperman." Strange sensation to say that here and now, to drag a word and a world out of shadows.

"No kiddin'?"

"No kidding. Night copy desk. U.P."

The Marine wrinkled his forehead, stared queerly at Corbett. "All yours," he said. "I did awready. While you was eatin'."

Corbett laughed. "Dope, *United Press*. U.P. stands for United Press."

"I'll be damned! Know what I thought?"

"I know." He laughed with the kid. "You should hear the switchboard operators when they're in a hurry. 'Good morning, U.P. . . . Good afternoon, U.P.'"

The Marine threw back his head and guffawed. In a moment, they both were rocking and roaring with laughter. When he slowed down for breath, Corbett knew the old gag wasn't half as funny as that. It was obvious. Infantile. Every halfwit in the world had tossed it around. Yet he roared. The rye and the words had touched the right spot. He laughed till tears streamed from his eyes, rolled down his cheeks.

The man with the sunglasses thrust back the green curtain and bustled into the toilet. As if a signal had switched, they stopped laughing. Corbett reached for his handkerchief, mopped his face and his eyes.

By the time the man came out again, they were quiet, sedate. The man pressed on the tap to wash his hands, beaming at them while he shook on the soap. He was small and squat, so round-shouldered he looked like a hunchback. The dark glasses gave his pudgy face a weird hollowness. "You are enjoying your journey?" He spoke with an accent. Teutonic.

The Marine scowled and tried to sit straighter.

"It is good to see soldiers laugh." He yanked a rough paper towel from the holder and painstakingly blotted his fingers. When he had finished his drying, he sat down beside the Marine.

Corbett covered his bottle with the tail of his jacket.

The Marine's face was hostile. The man continued to beam. "Do I stop your goot time?"

Corbett stretched his legs, preparing to rise. He mumbled politely: "No, not at all."

"I am so surprised, so pleased to see soldiers laughing. War is a grim business. No?"

The Marine muttered: "You bet!"

"But you do a great deed. You safe humanity." His head bowed. "I congratulate you."

The Marine looked at Corbett and thrust his lips out.

"You are home from the war?"

Corbett answered him gruffly. "Temporarily."

"Aha, you go back! Perhaps to bomb Hitler?"

Through Corbett's mind flashed the placard at the end of each car, the bald, printed warning about enemy spies and saboteurs. "I go where they send me," he said curtly.

The man nodded, conceding that that was correct. "If you go over Berlin, drop one bomb for me. For Doctor Kurt Frankel. With his best regards." He paused, stroking his thigh with a circular motion that wasn't unlike the way Corbett rubbed his own thumb. "Berlin was my home," he said gravely. "I lif there fifty years. I was a lawyer. Doctor Jurisprudence. I sat in the Reichstag ten years."

The Marine's chin came up. You could guess what went through his head. A big shot. A guy whom you ought to respect. Corbett smiled to himself. "One of their great brains," he thought. "One of the birds who let Hitler in."

Dr. Frankel was studying his ribbons. "You haf been over Berlin?"

Corbett nodded. He touched his left thumb with his right.

Frankel bent all the way over, clapped his hand on the Lieutenant's shoulder. "You have done a goot job?"

"I hope so."

The man sighed. "It was a beautiful city. I lofed every street, every building and tree." He paused until his voice and his face had grown stern. "I hope you have left not one single stone in its place."

Corbett's chin sank. He made no attempt to quiet his hands.

The German hadn't noticed his hands. "Only your heaviest bombing, please," he went on grimly. "Hitler made them a promise. No harm will come to their soil. Let them know. Let them learn. They will learn only through pain." He raised his plump palm. "Oh I know, I know well, one does not kill an idea with a bomb. But it is sometimes a conwincing argument. No?" He saw the Marine squirming and abruptly altered his tone. "Forgiff me if I lecture," he tried to smile placatingly. "It is my business. In America, I am now a lecturer."

The Marine stared at his face. "Are you a Jew?"

Dr. Frankel's jaw firmed. He said with a trace of hauteur: "Has only a Jew the right to hate Hitler? Has a Christian no brains and no conscience? You look like the Aryan. Why do you fight?"

"My people are Polish." The Marine gave a short laugh. "That's a pay-off. Me hatin' the Nazis, down in the jungle, killin' the Nips."

Dr. Frankel shrugged. "You fight an idea. Not races. We fight against Fascism, not people." He wagged a fat finger. "Listen, I tell you. All over this country, I travel. Each place I say the same thing. Make no mistake, you are not fighting Germans. Not Japanese. You fight an idea. That idea is effrywhere. In Europe. In Asia. In America too. Look." He slid forward until he was practically on the end of the seat. His face glistened. "Last night, I make a speech in Miami. This beautiful city is crowded with people. One hundred come to my lecture. They tell me that is goot in the season. People come down for their pleasures, to forget the war and their troubles. Goot, I say, if I talk to one hundred—if I talk only to ten and they understand, it is goot. I say: 'You must fight this evil thing. You must fight it all ofer the world. You must fight it right here, in your home. Your own Ku Klux Klan—" He broke off, his face working so that he could not continue.

The Marine looked down at his fingers, rootched on the seat in discomfort.

"So." Dr. Frankel's twitching had finally subsided. "They come up to me after this lecture. They are very polite. They say: 'Doctor Frankel, we found your lecture interesting, in-formatif.' I thank them. They say: 'Doctor Frankel, you make one mistake. One big mistake. We are sorry you men-tion the Klan. The Klan are our neighbors. Our friends. Look, we will tell you just how it is. Sometimes we haf trouble with Communist Unions, with some of these . . .'" He lowered his voice and his crimsoned face. "Forgif me, I find some words too hard to say—'nigger-lofers down from the North. Our friends in the Klan take care of these people for us.'" His shoulders hunched, his mouth screwed itself into a tight, bitter knot. "'We know our own problems better than you. You refugees come here and try to tell us how to run our own country.'"

The Marine muttered under his breath. "Ain't it the truth?" He pulled himself up, stretched and yawned. "Might's well go in and catch me some sleep. So long. Be seein' you, Doc." He winked at Corbett, lurched out.

Dr. Frankel's chin quivered. He looked toward the frosted glass pane. "Forgif me," he murmured. "I forget myself some-time. I forget how easily children are bored."

Corbett felt that he ought to defend the Marine. He thought: "Christ, this guy has a nerve. Children, hey? That kid's been in the jungle. That kid's been rotting in hell, catch-ing malaria, while this fat ass with the accent is here making speeches. Safe. Making dough. Ran out on his people. Ducked out. Saved his hide. Let someone else do the job on his Adolf . . . Come here and criticize." Yet he sat still, not saying a word, because there was nothing to say, since the German was perfectly right.

He felt the old nervous impatience rising again, tingling through all his body, demanding release. He knew that he had to stop talking and listening. He knew that he had to get high.

Deliberately, so that the German could see what he was doing, he held out his bottle, made an elaborate job of finding a pocket, thrusting it in. He said: "See you later," and swaggered out of the washroom, back through the diner and lounge car and Pullmans to Bedroom C in Glen Argyle.

CHAPTER SIX

Nina Gilmore wasn't alone. There was a man in her bedroom, a civilian, the one who had almost bought a Miami hotel. He sat on the sofa beside her as if he belonged there. He smoked a cigar. It had a half inch of ash.

The room swam with gray smoke.

Nina broke off what she was saying to the man on the seat and tipped her chin up to Corbett. "Oh hello! So you didn't forget me." She reached to the ash tray beside the washstand, rested her cigarette on the rim of the tray. She smiled, self-consciously Corbett thought, and glanced at the man next to her. He was staring at Corbett with a curious frown, more approving than critical, on his long bronze brow. Corbett sensed they'd been discussing him.

"Lieutenant Corbett, Mr. Stengel," Nina said.

Mr. Stengel stood up and stretched out his hand. Corbett took it and shook it. Mr. Stengel remained standing before his half of the sofa, his eyes darting from Corbett to Nina. His were very sharp eyes. They took in Nina's heightening of color and the officer's unease. He smiled affably. "Glad you stopped by, Lieutenant. I was beginning to think I was boring our friend." He smirked. "Talking business," he added. He looked at the ribbon-slashed breast of the officer's coat, and then laid a plump hand on Nina's shoulder. "Got a gin rummy game, waiting for me back in there."

"Don't let me chase you," Corbett mumbled politely.

"Not at all. Not at all. Must make my expenses . . . Nina, take you to dinner?"

She slanted a questioning glance up to Corbett. "Could be," she said.

"Well, see you later. I'll stop by at seven and check . . . Glad to meet you, Lieutenant. Be good to yourself. Hope to see you again."

When he had gone, Nina got up and sat down on her legs. She tucked her skirt carefully around her knees, sniffed once or twice, like a puppy, at the heavy drift of cigar smoke that Stengel had left. "I thought you'd forgotten all about me," she began tentatively.

Corbett swayed in the doorway, looking down on the red and gold Buddha. "I knew you'd be busy—"

A triangle of annoyance leaped between her pencil-line eyebrows. "Oh, Larry Stengel's just—"

"One of the boys."

"—a guy." Miss Gilmore finished her own sentences. "A nice guy. Salt of the earth. Business. But strictly. You'll never guess what."

He saw her glance at his ribbons. He said quickly: "Won't try."

"Larry's in textiles. He's richer than God."

"I know," he said slowly. "A quarter million for a Miami hotel. To get rooms for his family."

Her eyebrows leaped up. "You get around." She laughed, not quite sure of why he had said it. "He needs a hotel. Six dozen children."

His expression was properly skeptical and her smile eased. "Don't stand there like that. Come in and sit down." She waved toward the green brocade square. It was littered with magazines.

He ignored her direction. He sat down beside her. The frown remained over her eyes although she didn't say "No" but merely tucked the skirt hem more tightly over her knee caps.

He said: "That's no fair." He fingered her skirt tentatively.

"It is too. I'm ticklish." She removed his hand. He let it rest on the sofa.

"That's funny. So'm I."

That was better, much better. Her forehead smoothed out. "I saw you in the diner," he said.

"Larry paid for my lunch."

"Big hearted, too."

"I waited for you. He passed by, saw me sitting alone."

"If I'd thought—"

"Oh, don't apologize." Her lips thinned. "I saw you, too. With your pal."

He bristled. "That's no pal of mine."

"Seeing's believing." She took what remained of her butt from the ash tray and puffed. "Where've you been all this time?"

"Shooting pool with the gang."

She liked his reply and picked up his bantering tone as though he had tossed her a cue. "Sissy! I thought the Army shot craps."

"Oh, not on trains. Dear, dear, no. It's too unrefined . . . If I'd thought, if I'd dreamed you needed lunch money."

She murmured: "I managed."

"Girls like you get along."

The triangle came back to her forehead. He was irked with himself, more than she was with him. "Cut it out, Christ, cut it out," he admonished himself. "Stop picking sores." "Sorry," he said after a small pause. "I got detained. Had some business to do."

"With your pal?"

He reddened. "I'll wash your mouth out with soap. Can I help it if that guy has the seat next to mine?"

"In the coach?"

He nodded. He sensed disappointment, wrong side of the tracks. "Lucky to get even that."

"Is it terrible there? Awfully crowded?"

"Come and see. You're the type who goes slumming."

Her eyebrows hitched up. "Say, soldier, only my friends can talk that way to me."

"Do you have them?" He bit his lip. The sarcasm wasn't called for. Yet his skin was so thin it couldn't pass by the least bit of needling.

"You'd be surprised at my friends." There was a lilt of coquetry. It relieved the tension.

"Mr. Stengel?"

"Mr. Stengel. Mr. Smith. Mr. Jones. Mr. Brown. The cream of the crop."

"My, my, how you get around."

He leaned back on the sofa, resting his head on the towel antimacassar. He planted his legs on the stool.

"Make yourself comfortable," she said with the least hint of asperity. "Nothing's too good for the Air Force."

"You said it, baby. You said it."

She put out her cigarette, blew the last wisp of smoke from her mouth. "A fine situation. Boy meets girl. Boy starts picking and squabbling."

"That's *your* disposition."

"Mine? Why, sir, how dare you? Me thinking I'm being especially nice."

"Oh, sure. Hiding those beautiful legs."

Her eyes dropped to her skirt.

"Come, come," he wheedled. "Don't sit on those tootsies. Bad for the posture."

She laughed. With a show of demureness, she thrust her legs out, sliding down on the sofa until her heels touched the stool. "There! Happy now?"

"An improvement. You listen to reason. That's something. What do you think I came in here for anyway?"

"To call me names."

"Guess again."

"Read a book?"

"Come, come, sweetie-pie, don't play dumb."

"Not conversation?"

"Not conversation."

"Oh dear, and I've such a wonderful line." She laughed. "Oh, now I remember. You promised to bring me a drink."

"So I did, so I did." He lifted the hem of his tunic, pulled the half-emptied pint from his pocket. "You're one hell of a girl. Drove it clean out of my mind. Why!" He scowled fiercely. "You made me sit. I might have sat on that bottle and zingo!"

"Tsk, tsk, it's all my fault. Everything's me . . . There must be more where that came from."

"You try to get it."

"But you got it. Wonderful man. Send him on a mission—"

He was uncapping the bottle. He stopped. He said sharply: "Bite your tongue."

She looked puzzled. "Why, what on earth? What have I said now?"

He got up for the glass. "Straight or with water?"

"Straight, if you please."

"Good girl." He filled the glass one quarter full. It made a substantial hooker. "A glass for your company? A paper cup?"

She shook her head. "I don't think so. You'll have to drink from the bottle. Don't you know there's a war?"

He said: "If you pull that, I'll slit your throat. So help me, I will."

"Excuse, please." She frowned over the rim of her glass, took her legs off the seat.

He clinked the top of the bottle against her glass. "Short war," he said.

She answered "Short war" and drank. Her face puckered.

She shuddered as raw alcohol seared her gullet, yet she was
game and finished the dose while he took a long swig at the
bottle.

"Have a chaser?"

"I'd better."

"Brutal? Not what you're used to?"

She shrugged. "Hardships of war."

He got up and filled her glass from the carafe. She said:
"While you're up, there are pecans in that box. We might as
well make this a party."

He brought back the box and she opened it, offered it.

"Who told you I'm nuts about salted nuts?"

"Intuition."

"A genius!"

"You catch on fast."

He asked: "Have another?" He held up the bottle.

"Not yet, do you mind?"

"Speak fast. A pint goes."

"I noticed you got in some work on the bottle before you
came here."

"My hospitable nature. There was a Marine in the washroom."

"Thought you boys didn't speak to each other. The Air
Force talks only to God."

"That's Cabots. You mix up your jingles. And remember,
I warned you this morning. Don't say 'you boys.'"

She ran her hand over her forehead. "That rotgut is potent."

"Glad to hear it." He sat down beside her. She edged toward the window, just enough to make him aware she still was
distrustful. "I scare her," he thought. "She's beginning to
worry. A drunken serviceman in her room." He took a handful of pecans from her box, munched them slowly, to give her
a chance to relax. Meanwhile he studied her legs. Through
the thin nylon film, he could see the minute pencil lines of the
veins on her shins, the hair follicle dots. "Your shaving's been
sloppy. You missed four hairs."

She thrust her lower lip out. "Magnificent eyesight."

"Need it in my business." His fingertips touched a spot over her instep. "Down there. See!"

She bent over with him. "So it is, so it is. Sorry. I've been so busy this morning." He was aware of her perfume, rich, heady, fragrant.

She sat up again. "Pass me my cigarette box, will you please." She took a cigarette out, looked around for her match book.

He said: "Let me light it," took out his lighter, flipped the hood up. The flame waggled in front of her face.

She asked, watching his hand: "Were you always like that?"

"Like what?"

"Jittery. Nervous."

"If I were, could I get in the Air Force?"

He could see her eyes somber behind the flickering flame of his lighter. He snapped the hood down.

She appeared not to have noticed his upsurge of anger. "Aren't you smoking? Light yours from my butt."

He took one from her box. His face came close to hers. Over the length of their cigarettes, he inhaled with his smoke, her rich perfume. He asked: "What's the scent?"

"Chanel Number Five."

He said "Oh!" though the name had no meaning for him. "What flower is that?"

"Flower? Lord knows. I've never asked. City slicker."

"Aren't you the girl who drives to the country? Westchester, Connecticut and the Hamptons."

"You remember. You seem to remember every word that I say."

"Of course, I remember. I listen. I always have listened. A habit of listening. Old training." He had begun stammering but now he found himself speaking fast as though there were a long speech in his larynx that had to be hurried before some one called time. "I've been away so long, in so many places, that just hearing American talk is like listening to music. Like music you haven't heard for a very long time. Like those records you had and played over and over and then put away. When you take them out and play them again—"

She broke in: "They sound lousy."

He frowned over her head at the window pane and the sliding landscape. "Sometimes they do. But just hearing the old familiar refrain—there's something about it. Why look—" His eyes drew away from the window. He inched nearer to her. "All this morning, I've been prowling this train, like—like a lost soul, just listening to people."

"Enjoy what you heard?"

He sat back and looked at her skeptically. "What makes you ask that?"

She blew out a gray whorl of smoke. "I just wondered."

He was silent a moment and then said, very slowly: "I can't figure you out. Sometimes I think you're on my side, and sometimes I think you're on theirs."

She said, smiling gravely. "I'm trying my best to cross over to yours. You don't give me a chance."

That wasn't good either. They were treading the morass again.

She sensed it too and she made a fresh start. "Words seem to have different meanings to you and to me. I say something that doesn't mean anything special and you're up like a kite. You dish it out, you dish it plenty, but you can't take a thing. And I'm trying so hard—"

The way she said that, with her crimson lips bunched, made him anxious to kiss her. But he merely said: "I'll try to be good. Honest, I will," and "Let's have a drink."

"Just a drop."

He tilted the bottle up toward the light. "Drop's all you'll get. Mix it this time?"

"I'd better. If you won't think I'm just being snooty, that rye is—" She crinkled her nose. "It tastes of the barnyard."

As he poured, he pretended to bow with a waiter's stiff dignity. "The management deeply regrets, modom. We are serving our best. If modom prefers something else, perhaps modom would try some place else."

She giggled. "That isn't a joke. Let out a yip about service or liquor or food and they tell you to go some place else. And don't you know there's—"

In duet they chanted: "Bite your tongue," and then laughed together.

She *was* cute; she *was* fun. He thought: "If I can just stay off the edge. If I can only be human, this'll turn out all right." He began again: "There was an old rooster at my table in the diner—"

She smiled archly: "Bedtime story?"

"I hadn't thought of that—yet."

"Oh no." Her eyebrows flicked up. She made a pattern of dots with her fingertips on the glass. Then peremptorily: "Tell me about your old rooster. Is it funny?"

"Not very. Enlightening. To me. He was raising a fuss about not having lamb chops for lunch. Just a spoiled baby. Going to tattle to teacher if he couldn't get them."

"You came back from the war to listen to that!"

"Hell, sister, I didn't mind. It was a pleasure to hear the steward give him come-uppance."

"Come-uppance, tuppance. Does it matter as long as you're healthy?"

Pouring rye into her, he considered, might pay off in the end. He held the bottle up to her glass. "Short war."

"That's better than 'Mud in your eye.' "

He drained the bottle, hurled it into the soiled towel rack near the floor. He said: "Or a kick in the pants."

"You brought that home too?"

"Brought back what?"

"Short war."

He laughed. "Thought you meant kick in the pants."

"You boys—" she began.

He waved his forefinger.

"You *men*—" she corrected "have brought back a new language. 'Mae West's'. . ."

His glance swept the arc of her bosom. She colored, murmured: "You know I don't wear them." And added, continuing the sentence before, "and 'Roger.'"

"And 'fruit salad,'" he said, touching his ribbons.

"Not really! That's darling!" She paused. She was thinking of something. In concentration, she produced a slight squint. When she spoke again, her voice and her manner had completely changed. She was business-like, crisp. "We could call them *Fruit Salad Prints*. It's so much more gay than *War Hero Prints*."

He said: "Excuse, please. If modom's in conference—" He shifted his haunches as if he meant to get up.

She caught his hand, pulled him down, said abstractedly: "Sit down, don't be silly." Then her brows knit. "No, not *Fruit Salad*. That isn't chic. It hasn't—Oh, it sort of plays down what it stands for." Her fingertips touched his ribbons, played a light tattoo over his heart.

"Hey, cut that out," he said quickly.

"I've got it." Her face brightened. "*Valor Fabrics*. Perfect. Right on the button."

Whatever it was that was right on the button meant nothing to him at that moment. She noticed the baffled look on his face and she laughed. "Oh, you don't know. I forgot you don't know. It was Larry's idea. And *sensational*. I was telling him about you. About your ribbons and stuff—You don't mind, I hope—and it popped. 'By God, Nina,' he said. 'Know what I'll do? I'll get out a line of War Hero Prints. It's a natural, baby. A million bucks in it.' Fabrics. Dress materials, you know. Larry thinks, and he's right, that they'll sweep the country." She raised her chin, smiling as though she expected him to applaud, blandly unaware that he was stifling a swift surge of nausea, forcing his face into an impassive mask. His breath came hard. He muttered: "The fortunes of war. Dollars and cents."

She couldn't possibly miss the double-edged irony in his tone. She took a moment to decide what she wanted to say and then said it decisively: "Look, one of the things you seem to have forgotten is that life goes on in this country you've left.

People wear clothes. People make them and sell them. People have money to buy. And what's wrong with that?"

"Oh nothing! Nothing at all."

"Then stop acting as if," she said tartly. "People like Larry Stengel aren't heels—any more than I am—unless you think that I am"—She gave him a side glance and when he made no movement or sound, she went on. "Larry has a kid in the Navy—somewhere in the Pacific. That doesn't mean he's got to stop earning a living or living."

He growled: "Cut it out. Let's drop it."

She waited a few seconds before she said: "I'll be glad to." She touched the back of his hand. "I'm sorry. That's the schizophrenic in me. Split personality. Business woman. Two words. Two people." She settled back on the sofa. "Let's see, what started all this? Oh yes, we were talking about words. The new language that's come out of the war. 'Mae Wests' and 'Roger' and 'fruit salad.' What else is there, soldier?"

"Well, there's 'eager' for keen. There's 'ronchie' for sloppy and careless. There's 'rugged' for tough."

"I know one: 'sweating it out.'"

He squirmed. He felt his nerves tightening again. "I don't like this game. Let's play something else."

She gave him a quick glance. "Why don't you smoke?"

"I hate to bum yours. I've run out."

"Don't give it a thought. I've got plenty."

"I'll get some when we stop. Where do we stop?"

"Jacksonville."

"When?"

She shrugged. "Eventually. Running late. Do you care?"

"Me? I should say not. I could ride this way—well, for twenty-one days."

"Oh, thank you. You *can* say nice things when you try."

When she smiled that way, with the come-on in her eyes, you forgot all the nonsense—the Valor Fabrics nonsense. Then she was the dish. The desirable, essential dish. His hand reached toward the doorknob. He swung the door a few inches shutwards. Not looking at her, he said with studied casualness: "We may be disturbing the people outside. Do you mind if I close it?"

"Oh, I wouldn't. It would get fearfully stuffy in here, with all this tobacco." Her tone was as deliberately nonchalant as his own.

He pushed the door back to its catch, took his hand off the knob, as if it had burned.

She smiled, with a bland air of triumph.

"You're smooth, baby," he thought. "You know your on-ions." He drew on his cigarette, watching her silly hat bob and dance on its hook on the opposite wall, trying to think of what to say next.

She spoke first. "You make me think of a joke I heard long ago, about an American girl, traveling in Russia. She was sharing a compartment with one of the comrades, and reading her book and minding her business . . ."

He interrupted: "Enough of this bourgeois romancing. Take off your clothes."

"It saves so much time when you know the same jokes."

"And you know all the answers."

She lowered her eyes to the empty glass in her hand. "I'm sorry, my friend, I got you so bothered."

He sneered: "A mind reader, too."

"I don't have to be especially literate, soldier. You're aw-fully obvious. There's only one thing on your mind." She was twisting a braid loop on her jacket. "Look, soldier, I've no objection to kidding around to pass an hour on a train . . ."

"Teasing. Give the boys a good time."

She said somewhat wearily. "You said 'boys' that time," and then paused to prepare a fresh start. "You needn't go bitter on me. I'm just not the girl who likes wrestling with strangers after two drinks. I travel this way to be able to pick my own company You looked like a gentleman. I invited you in. If I've made a mistake, why then—"

His face, he knew by its heat, must be crimson. He stamped out the cigarette she had given him, so savagely that the black ash receiver fell out of its clamp, spilling ashes and butts on the carpet. "May I ask," he said, his tone frigid with frustration, "what do you usually do with a Sunday? Pose for Holy Pictures, perhaps?"

She stared at him in amazement and then threw her head back and howled.

While she sputtered with laughter, he crouched to pick up the butts. She said: "That's enough. I'll get the porter to clean up the rest. I should make you do K.P. for penance, but I won't. That line saved your neck. . . . Now, sit down. And be a good *boy*. I meant *boy*. You act like a kid."

He sat down at the far end of the sofa. He studied the carpet. It was the ugliest carpet he had ever seen, a grotesque interweaving of tan and black, with small flecks of bright blue, the sort of floor covering they had in the cheaper commercial hotels. He heard the empty wire hangers beneath her coat whine with the sway of the train.

She had lifted her legs from the stool and again drawn them up. The gay, easy, rye-stimulated give and take was all gone, evaporated with the speed of the liquor itself.

Minutes sped by like the landscape, while they sat apart, silent, he studying the carpet, she the green swamps. Finally, he sat straight, turned in her direction. He summoned his most formal air. "Madam, may I ask how you like our Florida scenery?"

She turned half around. He could see relief in her eyes at his change of manner. "Is that your best? I find it—well, repetitious."

"And warm for March, don't you think?"

"Outside or in?"

He bared his teeth in a wide smile. "Quite cool inside. Chilly, in fact. The air conditioning does seem to be working."

"And when it works it works for Mr. Birdseye. It's so chilly here now, it freezes you solid."

"Look, I know where to get more of that rye."

She shook her head. "Don't waste your money. Where'd the last bottle get us."

"Would you care to go for a walk, to warm up?"

She glanced at her wrist watch. "Florida's long but it can't last forever. We ought to be pulling into Jacksonville before long. We can hop off there for a stretch."

"If you'd like to go slumming—meet the people—see how the other half travels."

"No, thank you. I might meet some more like your chum."

"He isn't my chum."

"He acted that way."

"Look, has that guy been pestering you?"

"Not me. He couldn't. My grandma warned me against people like him. 'Don't talk to strangers on trains.' That's what she said. She must have meant you, too, Lieutenant Corbett."

He answered, "Oh yeah," automatically. He was threading his fingers and she knew by the scowl on his face that he was thinking of something he hadn't told her. When he suddenly asked: "Say, have you heard anyone on this train mention losing a purse?" the detour bewildered her. Then she caught on: "Why, has he? Did he? Do you think—"

He shrugged: "I've been reading too much Dick Tracy."

"Dick Tracy?"

"The all-American detective. The funnies."

"No kidding! You read the comics?"

"And why not?" The sharp edge turned up again.

"Oh, my dear, not men like you! Men with all those ribbons!"

"Listen, sister, some of the best guys I know, some of the best guys on earth read the comics."

"Superman?"

"He's my boy. And Mandrake the Magician. The Batman."

"You slay me."

"Okay, then, you're slain."

"That's America for you! Our heroes read comic books. No serious reading, discussions?"

"Certainly, certainly."

"For instance what?"

"Topic A."

"And what, pray, is Topic A?"

He was irked by her tone, Queen of Sheba, all right. "Topic A, my dear friend, is dat ole debbil sex. Girls, women, females. Too bad we can't all spend the war on your high intellectual plane . . . Let's see what you're reading, my beauty."

He reached to the stool and picked up the top magazine. He studied the cover a moment, flipped over the pages. He stopped. He read a few lines to himself, then read them aloud: *"Women today have never been so busy nor so active. No wonder underthings have assumed a new importance."* He stole a glance at her face. A blush brightened the tan. "Tin drawers? That what they're selling?"

She muttered: "Shut up."

He leafed one page, and another. Again he read: *"I've decided that this is a year of decisions and what decisions! The future of mankind on this globe, for instance. We're standing on that breath-taking peak of history. 1944. How can I comport myself best as a tiny but very proud atom of that history? . . . I'll try to look as well as I feel . . . I'll clothe myself in color and softness."*

She said angrily: "Look here, soldier, that's my trade. I make my living from that."

"That's the old Einstein gag," he said placidly. He was enjoying himself now, chortling over each page. He read: *"The girl who landed a pilot. Her complexion was always so charmingly fresh, so wonderfully real looking."*

"Stop it," she cried and attempted to snatch the magazine from his hand.

"Oh no, you don't, sister." He hugged it to his chest. "This is funny as hell. You ought to send this across to the gang. They'd give up a whole stack of Mandrake for just one of these." He waited until she was back in her corner and then again turned a page. *"A ruffle is a secret weapon, dangerously flicking beneath a hem,"* and another . . . *"Memorable moments, snatched perhaps between trains, a lifetime lived in miniature, comfortingly confident in her smart appearance, she secretly thanked her stepin and bra* . . . Sister." He leaned back on the sofa. "What world is this?"

"But you don't understand," she said hotly. "These things are important to women. You know perfectly well that you boys—"

"Don't say boys."

She ran past his red light. ". . . expect us to be glamorous."

He put his thumb in the page. He snapped: "Don't be a fool."

She gnawed her lip. But she came back in a moment more sharply than he. "You're the fool. Just playing wise guy. The boys in the foxholes dream about American girls. Pin up their pictures. You *know* they do. Why look, you yourself—there's no shortage of girls on this train. Why did you come here to me?"

"That's easy. Because you're a dish."

"I'm a dish. Oh, I'm a dish. Thank you so much. You're so generous with compliments. I'll tell you why. You picked me out because I had all of that glamour you boys have been dreaming about. Because I make it my business to look well and dress well and even smell nice."

"You're not kidding," he murmured.

She took that for encouragement. "It's no less than our duty, our patriotic duty, to keep things going the way they were before, the way you expect them to be. I suppose you'd like it better if you came home, saw us dowdy and shapeless."

He began: "Those English girls. They manage to—" but she cut him off.

"They'd give their right arms for a lipstick, a good pair of stockings."

"Listen, sister, you don't know those girls."

"I know women. Just because we've been luckier than they are—"

He said wearily: "Look, sister, why are we quarreling again?"

"Just because you've implied that I'm Mrs. Hitler because I believe war or no war, it's the duty of women to look as

glamorous as possible. I'm trying to tell you that it isn't trea-
son to try to look smart."

He growled: "Don't be a dope."

Pouting, she reached over him for her box, took a cigarette
out, lit it herself, without offering him one, and turned toward
the window again. He stared at her snood for a moment. She
was smoking furiously, puffing the smoke out in front, clouding the window pane.

He turned back to the book, flipped a handful of pages. A
line struck his eye. He couldn't believe it. He bent closer.
He read aloud: *"Tell them in time of war, patriotism is not
enough."*

Nina's head moved. "You're going dramatic. You sound
like the Fourth of July."

He said: "I should slap you for that."

She turned. "What gives you the right—?"

He lowered his voice. "What gives *you* the right to sneer
at a very great lady?"

"Who said that?"

"Edith Cavell."

"And you just *happened* to remember it now?"

"I didn't just happen. It's here in your book."

She bent down to look over his shoulder. It was there: a
caption over an old movie still, heading an advertisement.

He said, in a voice deep with disgust: "They're selling rayon
with Edith Cavell . . . Your pals are terrific. They don't
miss a trick."

"Oh, shut up," she said. "You make me tired."

He closed the magazine, tossed it on the brocade-covered
toilet.

"Lady," he said, "for my dough, this country stinks and all
the Chanel Number Five in the world can't clean it up."

She said frigidly: "You just don't understand. You won't
understand."

He sat still, his face in his hands, reviewing the design in
the carpet again. This was dead end. No place to go down
this street. A mistake from the start. Can't judge the goods

by its package. Lovely face; pretty clothes. No heart and
no brains. The wrong kind of brains . . . There's a chasm
between us. Who'd said that? Some one in the lounge car . . .
that garrulous doctor . . . Hard to cross over . . . Get together . . . You don't know how hard, Bud, you don't know
the half . . . She said it, too . . . "I'm trying to cross over
to your side. You make it hard" . . . Take a few steps yourself, Donald Corbett. . . .

He looked almost timidly at Nina Gilmore, and then past
her out of the window. The Palm Queen was slowing. Mean
houses groveled, next to each other. A cluster of small Negro
girls in bright Sunday dresses stood alongside the track, holding hands. In a yard, he could see kids in toy commando hats,
digging a foxhole under a palm.

He asked: "If it is Jacksonville, do you want to go out?"

She gave him a keen, probing glance before she nodded yes.
She reached for her handbag, took out a huge tortoise shell
compact. "You won't mind if I put on some glamour?"

He began to growl.

"I like you," she said. "You're so gentle and sweet."

The train rasped to a stop before she finished her lips.

He let her go first, out to the rear platform of Glen Argyle.
Its door was still shut. On the other side of the accordion
snubbers, the Duquesne porter was opening his door. An im-
pulse moved Corbett. He whispered a question into the
porter's ear.

The Negro blinked. "How you know that lady done lost it?"

"Oh, I just thought I saw a pocketbook kicking around in
the aisle when I went through this morning."

The black face stayed suspicious. "Ah found it. Out by this
do'."

"Good."

"Routine. Jus' routine. Passengers is always losin' they
things."

"Who's losing what?" Nina asked.

"Watch your step," Corbett said. "Come on through here.
I'll help you down."

CHAPTER SEVEN

When they walked side by side up the Jacksonville platform, he saw with surprise how little she was. The top of her burnished black hair reached just under the wings on his sleeve. Yet Nina walked as if she thought she was tall and walking tall made her taller, with an air of carrying a spotlight on her own beauty and the knowledge that even in this grimy, hot train shed she would be noticed.

Corbett shortened his stride to match the quick tap of her heels, proud to be walking with her. It felt good; it felt normal, strolling along in American sunshine, with a smartly dressed, beautiful American girl, touching her elbow to guide her in traffic, conscious that other men stared and might envy. He felt twinges of shame for the way he'd been acting before; the irritability, flip-flops of mood, flares of temper, the behavior as if she were a floozie or half-wit or heel. He looked down on the white line of her scalp between the hillocks of hair and he thought: "I'll have to apologize. Explain it later. She's more than I rate. Didn't need to put up with my guff. Well, why did she?"

This was the right way to begin: a stroll in the sunshine.

March was like June, mild, lazy warmth, and Jacksonville was deep South. Plump Negresses in slacks, well filled out, red bandana turbans and gold hoop earrings meandered alongside the Palm Queen, dragging hoses to fill washroom tanks. An elderly Negro, overalls black as his face, slouched along with his oil can, flipping the journal box lids.

The train shed was littered with papers, empty milk cartons, cigarette wrappers and butts. Outside the diner, garbage was piled in malodorous open crates. The woman with the crest of green feathers was walking her Peke.

Disheveled passengers piled out of the cars and stopped to exclaim over the streamliner on the parallel track, a gorgeous concoction of silver and purple, beginning to move. Its carefully shut windows were lined with faces. Some of its passengers waved; the Palm Queen people waved back.

When the streamliner pulled out, they saw the long train, sprawled on a track further over, a string of dusty, old-fashioned coaches. Those windows were open and each window sill was crowded with the khaki blouses and young, heat-pink faces of soldiers. The servicemen stared across the stretch of track and platform and the vacationists stared back at them. Some of them pointed.

Corbett touched Nina's elbow. "Don't gawk at the suckers. Let's do my shopping." Outside Sixteen, coatless coach passengers were mobbing a small rolling stand. "Nina, what shall I buy you? Orange drink? Milk? Candy? Sandwich?"

"Thank you, nothing. Just get your butts."

Using his elbows, he cut through the crowd. A harassed colored boy was trying to quote prices, serve trade and make change, all at once. Dr. Frankel had stacked up a half dozen sandwiches, cartons of milk. "I buy for the ladies." He felt the need to explain his big purchase to Corbett. "That Mrs. Taylor, that sailor's wife, would you believe it, she has no lunch. Nothing at all. So busy feeding her babies. That young Mrs. Weston. I make her eat."

Corbett's long arm stretched over the German's shoulders to get to the cigarette tray. The assortment was scanty, the brands unfamiliar. He selected two packs at random, tossed the man a half dollar, waited for change. Behind him, a husky voice said: "Get one for me, will you, soldier." It was the frizzy-haired hag with the coral earrings. He pretended he hadn't heard her. She lifted her voice. "Where you been hiding? I missed you, Lieutenant." He knifed through the crowd in another direction without waiting for change. On the fringe of the crowd, he saw Kalchis. The horseplayer said: "Hi! What they selling?" but he didn't answer.

Nina was petting the Peke and the elegant dog-walker was apparently relating her life story to her. She seemed aggrieved when Corbett took Nina's arm. "Let's get on. It's too warm out here."

"You've got your nerve," Nina said as they walked toward Glen Argyle. "That cute little pooch is a Frenchman Made the trip in the Clipper. With mama. They're refugees. From the Riviera . . . It's a wonderful air-traveler. Not sick a minute."

"Get on," he said gruffly. "I can't trust you in public."

When they came to her bedroom again, dust motes were dancing in a sun stream. The room was a mess, with the cigarette ends on the carpet and the literature strewn on the sofa. Nina stooped, picked up a few butts, raised the green brocade lid, dropped them into the bowl. She shuffled the magazines all together, set them down on the floor in a corner.

When she had finished housecleaning, she noticed that Corbett still stood in the doorway. "Staying or going?" she asked.

"That's up to you."

"Oh, sit down. You've got your full growth."

He sat down on his usual end of the sofa, broke a cigarette package open and offered it.

"I'll smoke my own, do you mind?"

He held his lighter for her, then lit his own, drew in and spat. "Hay and manure!"

"Take one of mine."

He shook his head. "The filter's confusing. I light the wrong end."

"Suit yourself." She settled back in the seat, tucking her skirt decorously over her knees. Her face was pleasant, bland but determined. "Look," she said. "Let's don't fight any more. I'm sick of sparring."

He said: "Suits me fine." The train jerked and jolted, beginning to move. He waited until its racket had ground down to the rumble of riding. Then he asked: "What do we do? Tell each other jokes?"

"I seem to know all your gags." She slid forward. "Let's talk about you."

"Ixnay." He put his hand up.

"Meanie!" She made a snoot. "Why not?"

"Tell me about your thrilling adventures?" He tried to produce Mrs. Hastings' manner and tone and did it badly. " 'Why did they give you those lovely ribbons? Oh, you're a hero . . . Do tell us stories.' No soap. I'm no talking dog."

She frowned: "I don't get it."

"Just a notion I got on this train. Soldier, speak for the people. Do tricks. Give them some war to keep them amused."

She flushed. "I'm sorry. You seem to have met the wrong customers."

He clasped his hands over crossed legs. His cigarette's smoke flowed lazily off his knee-caps. "They're not all of one kind. Obnoxious in different ways." His mouth twisted. "In twenty-four hours on this beautiful continent, I've been treated like a sucker and bum and shining white knight. Nobody's caught on to the fact that I'm only a guy. A guy that knows jokes, reads books and papers, takes showers with soap."

She picked up the line: "A human being, in short. Under that brown masquerade suit—"

"There beats a pure heart of gold."

"I doubt the *pure*."

"Ooops, sister," he said. "There we go again."

She said: "I'm sorry," once more, and her brow wrinkled. "You're much more complex than I thought."

"Problem child?"

"You bet."

He unclasped his hands to wag a forefinger at her.

She watched his face through a veil of gray smoke. Then she said quietly and with kindness. "Look, Don, I don't intend to pump you about what you've been through. If you don't want to spill, that's up to you. Your business, strictly. All I'm trying to do is to get to know you as a person. You barged into my life. We've been scratching and biting—I think it's high time we got decently acquainted."

"Tell me, Lieutenant, who is your family? How much cash do you have in the bank?" His short laugh was bitter. "Let's have your references, before our Miss Gilmore wastes more of her time."

She raised her hand to protest. "This seems to be where I came in. Or you did." Her voice and expression were weary.

He ran past the warning. "Or would you prefer the psycho-analytic approach? Let's discuss your childhood, Lieutenant. Did your mother resent your birth? Did you ever play doctor with little girls? Did you dream about murdering your father? No, professor, my mother was damn glad to have me. She wished she had more. Ours was good stock. Average American. Scotch-Irish way back. A few drops of German. On my mother's side. I had a pretty good childhood. Got along fine with the kids on the block. With both boys and girls. Had a dog and turtles and rabbits. I did my homework. No trouble with teachers. My old man had a nice business. Burlap importer. Now retired. We always lived on the Heights. Brooklyn Heights. In a house with a yard. Saturday afternoons my old man took me to ball games. Ebbet's Field. We both like the Dodgers. Does that make us crazy? Went to Columbia College. Marks not too bad. My mother died the year I graduated. Cancer. By the time she passed on, my old man and I were pretty relieved, for her sake, believe me. We gave up the house when she died, took furnished rooms. Together. I got a job on the *Eagle* in Brooklyn. Leg-man. Moved over the bridge to U.P.—*United Press*. Copy desk. I liked my job. Voted for Roosevelt, Fiorello La Guardia. Went to the movies, the concerts and shows. Knew lots of people. Nice people. Interesting people—so called . . . Sorry, but Corbett isn't a case." He pressed out the three-quarter inch of his cigarette in the ash tray, then took out another, opened his lighter. Over the flame, he stole a glance at her eyes. They were thoughtful, the least bit puzzled. "Your witness, counsel. You may cross-examine."

She spoke softly. "The girl?"

He colored. "Who said there was one?"

"You did. Remember? 'Let her have her fat 4F babies in peace.' "

He stalled for a moment before he shrugged and replied: "Just a phony. Flash in the pan. 'But, Don, dear'—" He tried female impersonation again. " 'You can't rahlly expect me to just sit under the apple tree and chew my nails while you're playing soldier.' "

She gave the back of his hand a small pat and a smile that said what a louse she thought the other girl was. "You enlisted?" she asked.

So she wouldn't take no. Right back to the war. Yet this time he let himself answer since he felt almost at ease, as if by identifying himself, recalling his personal past, reliving the unhurried span of his youth, he again was a person, not a soldier on leave, a cog, compressed in the tight vise of time.

"Day after Pearl Harbor. I'd had a low number. Or was it a high one that kept you down on the list? Just stalling along. Hoping I wouldn't have to . . . I was visiting friends. Up in Stamford. We had a date to go somewhere together. You'll never guess what it was. Memorial meeting for Heywood Broun. Remember him?"

Her brow creased. "The columnist?"

He nodded. "We were sitting around my friend's house, enjoying the Philharmonic. And then we got the flash. Pearl Harbor attacked. We were in. We were fighting the Japs . . . About time, we said. About time, my friends kept saying to me . . . and I to them. I know I felt relieved, the same way I did when my mother finally died of that cancer. The long sickness is over."

The cigarette was burning unnoticed between his fingers, dribbling its ash on the carpet. Nina gave it a glance, began to reach for the ash tray, stopped herself. This was what he most needed: to unload his burden, in his own way, without interruption.

He wasn't looking at her but rather over her head into the sunshine. A sense of distance seemed to fill his whole face.

"All of a sudden, I thought of a kid I'd known in grade school. A private school, over in Brooklyn. A Japanese kid, Sandikichi Misigouchi. One of the swellest damn kids I ever knew. His father was in the silk business. The kid had come here when he was a baby. He talked Brooklynese. The goddamnedest thing you ever heard in your life, that Brooklyn accent coming out of that Japanese face. When he was fourteen he went back to Japan, but he wrote to me and I wrote to him, all through high school. I wrote him about how the Dodgers were doing. I sent him Babe Herman's picture for Christmas. All I could think of was: 'My God, I'll have to fight Sandi!' Mind you, not him fighting me, but me fighting him. I wasn't sore at the Japs. To me all the Japs were just Sandi Misigouchi. Oh, in a sort of a way I was sore at the Nazis. That Master Race crap made me vomit. But hell, if we minded our business, kept our own noses clean . . ."

She murmured: "So you were one of those too?" and unobtrusively took the ash tray from its clamp, held it under his hand.

"Weren't you? We were the Pacifist kids. Veterans of Future Wars. The Yanks aren't coming. They rooked us once but never again to die for the British Empire . . . Well, my friends finally shut off the radio and said: 'It's time to go over to Libby's.'"

She repeated: "Libby's" and added a question mark.

"Libby Holman's house. That's where they were having the Memorial for Broun."

"Oh really." She wriggled a little in the pleased way people do when a celebrity is mentioned as an intimate.

"There was quite a crowd when we got there, down in a room in the basement, the game room it was, a big room with a bar. Actors and writers and agents and editors and politicians, all kinds of people who'd been friends of his or friends of his friends or who just wanted to see Libby's house. They were drinking highballs and trying to make small talk but couldn't. Every few minutes someone would come in with the latest word from Hawaii. And then we'd shut up and just drink. It was funny, but nobody so much as mentioned Broun all the while we waited for his meeting to start. Well, after a while, somebody said the meeting was supposed to go on the air from some local station and a couple of people read speeches into a mike and Libby Holman got up and sang *'Give Me Something To Remember You By'* and I thought of a Christmas card Sandi had sent me and I said to myself: 'I'll have to kill Sandi. I'll have to go out and kill Sandi. Why, he'd have to kill me, if I got in his way.' They'll put him in intelligence, I thought. With that Brooklyn accent, he'll be pretty damn useful to his lousy country. 'Lousy country.' You see, I was working myself up a hate. A hate I'd never been aware of before."

"You weren't original. Plenty of people knew one good Jap or German."

He looked up, quickly as if he meant to contradict that. But, instead, he went on, in the same high-pitched, mildly excited tone. "My mother had German blood. I'd assumed her people were good. I knew the first thing I'd have to do was get Sandi out of my system. I made myself remember the German kids who'd been sent to Norway after the last war, fed and fattened and loved by those decent Norwegians, who came back to lead the Nazi invasion. Knew every fjord in the country. Knew how to destroy those good people. 'Sandi's your enemy, now,' I kept telling myself. 'The past is wiped out. If I have to kill Sandi, I have to.' I couldn't wait to get out of that house and back to my place and next to a radio. I sat by that radio all night. Didn't shut it off once. In the morning, I took a shower, drank black coffee and went over the Bridge to see if the Air Force would have me. If I had to be in, I wanted to be where—"

Nina ended his sentence "—it would hurt most."

He squirmed but he said: "Exactly." He sat back, winding his long legs, resting his head on the towel. He stroked his thigh nervously and then gripped his hands. The bright afternoon sun lay on his face, sharpening the gullies beside his mouth, etching the web of fine wrinkles around his eyes. He looked terribly tired, almost old.

She spoke up, with a forced cheeriness that made you aware that her mind wasn't with what she was saying: "It's amazing how easy it is to talk on a train. Words just flow. It's as if there weren't much time. You have to get everything said— said fast—before you get to your station."

He bent over his tightly locked hands. "That's it. There isn't much time. That's one of those things . . . You know it when they disappear . . . Good guys. Just go out and never come back."

The way he said that made her afraid he was withdrawing again to his private world of unspeakables. To bring him back quickly, keep him on the plane of question and answer, she asked: "But why did you go into the Air Force? A newspaper man—after all. There was Public Relations."

His snort was eloquent. "Look, I wanted to do—"

"I know. What would hurt most." She saw his hands clench and unclose and waited for an easing of strain, before she said: "You've done things to be proud of. Don't forget that."

"Proud?" His lip thrust out.

"Those ribbons. You didn't get them for—"

His mouth writhed. "Valor Fabrics."

"Oh, please! Please!" Color mounted under her sun tan. "You worry a word the way a dog does a bone . . . Let it go. Let one thing pass. Just once."

He lifted his eyebrows but kept silent.

"Your father will be proud when he sees your ribbons."

"My father?" There was an indignant note in his voice as if so long and so far had he traveled without them, he almost resented the right of his family to know what had happened to him.

She made a new try. "At least," she said, lightening her tone. "You can write a book."

"It's been done. By better men."

"There's always room for one more."

He said nothing to that, and she began to think he again had lost interest in talking to her. "You're confused. Is that it?"

There was no answer from him for a while but finally, he said: "Do you mind if I pull down the shade? The sun's awfully strong."

"I'll do it." She yanked the shade down.

Diffidently, he began: "You won't think . . ."

"I won't yell rape, if that's what you mean." She smiled at him with a forthrightness that struck a new note in their contact, and she slid down the seat until the flare of her skirt brushed against him. The atmosphere in the room had perceptibly changed. The distrust had gone. Dusky and quiet, the little compartment had almost the hush of a hospital room —an operating room, he decided. Through the expectant silence he could hear the whine of the hangers, the monotonous drone of the wheels on the track.

She stroked his sleeve. "Don, tell me about the Air Force."

"What's to tell?"

"We got to where you went down and enlisted."

"Oh yes. I tried out for pilot. Washed up. Poor depth perception. You have to have that. By Jesus, you have to have that." She saw his jaw tighten. "I applied for bombardier school and I made it."

"Don't you need some mechanical aptitude?"

The last words struck an echo but he didn't try to recall who had said them before.

"Oh sure, sure you do. I drove a car in Manhattan traffic. That's enough and to spare. I didn't do badly at science and math at Columbia." He pushed back his hair with the flat of his hand. "Like most kids that grew up in our times, I wanted wings. That's all the adventure that's left. I used to cover LaGuardia Field—the airport—for the *Eagle*. Watch the Clippers come in from Europe, Bermuda. I remember one day, the Bermuda plane was getting ready for takeoff. They were cleaning her up. I saw them bring out a carpet sweeper. It gave me a jolt. You don't sweep a plane with a Bissells, I thought. You should use a moonbeam."

She squeezed his arm. "I love it when you talk like that. The small things you've seen and remembered."

"My newspaper training."

"Big jump."

"The slot to the Plexiglas nose."

"That's a name for your book."

"Cut it," he said, and then with a trace of his former irritability: "I can't see why you keep harping on that. There's nothing special about newspapermen. You find all kinds of guys in the crew of a B-24. Why, look here, in our group we had one rancher, one clerk in a hat store, a college sophomore, a garage mechanic; one ran a greenhouse, raised flowers—"

"Which was the pilot?"

He didn't reply, but she knew that he'd heard her question because one of his thumbs drew up to the other. He pulled it back, pushed his hands into his pockets, before he repeated: "You find all kinds of guys in the crew of a B-24." Then he drew out his pack, lit a cigarette. His hand, she could see, was shaking again. She let him inhale and exhale and then she asked: "Weren't you old for the Air Force?"

"More or less. Twenty-seven when I went in. Twenty-nine now. Only First Looie." He tsk'd. "Shame on you, Corbett. No push. No ambition. We've got Colonels at twenty-two."

She laughed, glad of the remotely comic relief.

"Don't laugh," he barked. "It's a hell of a joke." His smoke made a veil for his face. All she could see was the gleam of his eyes. "Nina, know how those kids get to be Colonels so quick? Not genius. Or pull. Mortality rate. Vacancies come fast in the E.T.O." His hands had emerged from his pockets.

She touched one of them to let him know she understood what he meant and said soberly: "Those kids make me wonder. What on earth can be the future of a kid who's a Colonel at twenty-two?"

He waved his cigarette hand. "Oh, he'll be the guy who wipes off your windshield, puts air in your tires, fills up your tank."

"I don't mean that." She shook her head. "I mean, he'll be

so terribly let down, after all that authority, being a big shot."

"If he lives . . ." His thumbs moved toward each other but before they came together his hands had gripped, knuckles white. She could see only his profile, his lips straight and shut, the crease in his cheeks that made him look old and spent, the sharp angle of jaw. "He hasn't much time to do postwar planning."

She waited again and then asked, trying to keep her tone casual: "Yet I suppose to some of the kids it's glorious adventure. A grand shooting gallery."

A tremor rippled along the hard line of his jaw. "I can't speak for them. A soldier isn't one guy. He's ten million. All different. I can just speak for me. For Donald Corbett. One person. *It isn't*." He halted. When he spoke again his speech had lost some of its sharpness, was almost bemused. "Why, it's queer to think, to talk of myself as a person."

"I noticed that." There was a pleased smile behind her eyes, so faint that if he perceived it, it could scarcely offend him. "You're quite a different man when you talk, open up."

He went on as though the last few sentences hadn't been spoken. "I only knew one who thought it was glorious adventure. A kid. Fighter pilot. He used to talk about how exciting it was to watch a convoy blown up on the road, the munitions trucks bang-bang-bang. Fireworks. Fourth of July. He thought it was a hell of a sport to chase Messerschmidts, see them go up in flames, fall out of the sky. . . . I watched him bail out. Without his chute. His plane was on fire . . ." He stopped. After a long pause, he said: "You don't want me to talk about that."

"But I do. I want to know what it's like."

"Oh, you do?" The caustic was back in his voice. "Stories to tell at Westchester house parties. I met a bombardier on the train and he told me—"

"Stop it." She had her hand on his arm. She could feel it trembling beneath the coat sleeve, could see the pulse in his throat pumping furiously. A hysteria was sweeping him. "You'd like to know what Ploesti was like? Well, it was hell.

Hell with trimmings. Flak so thick you could walk on it. Smoke, flames hiding the damn target, hiding our planes and theirs. You had to get through—"

Her grip tightened. "But you got through."

He laughed. She thought she had never heard anything more ghastly and terrible than that acrid laugh. "I ride with an angel. Up on my shoulder."

He groped in his pocket for cigarettes. Before he could get his lighter out, she struck a match, held it for him. "Give me one of yours. I'll try your poison." He held out the pack. The room filled up with their smoke, with the mumble and grind of the train.

Nina stared at the blank green window shade and then jerked it up. The gold of the sunset swept in. They both blinked. She said: "If you care, we're going through Georgia. See the beards on the trees."

He looked over the polished, dark, sun-gilded wings of her hair, without interest, yet relieved by the distraction of merely seeing, not talking or listening or thinking, at swamp waters as brown as the bosoms of mammies, at jungles of cypress and oak, festooned with the eerie gray draperies of moss, at forests of straight-standing pine, at piles of cut yellow timber.

They whizzed through a hamlet and on shacks near the depot he caught a sign: JESSUP'S PRESSING CLUB . . . and another: ROBERT C. COLEMAN: CIGARETTES, CIGARS, ICE-CREAM AND SNOWBALLS—eating and smoking and tidying your clothes.

He looked down at his wrist-watch. "It's nearly six. Are you hungry? Shall I see if the diner is open?"

She shook her head. "I'm not hungry."

He thought he detected a petulant note. "Look, Nina, I'll be damned if I'll cut out my guts to humor a female."

Her eyebrows went up as if she was hurt by his vehemence. "You've got me all wrong," she said. "I thought I was helping you by making you talk yourself out. I noticed before—this morning, earlier this afternoon, that whenever we mentioned the war—your experience, even your pilot . . ."

He said: "Shall I tell you about him?"

"If it will make you feel better to tell."

"Like hell it will . . . You asked for it. You can have it . . . The guy that raised flowers, that kid who raised roses, he was the pilot. A 20 mm shot off his head, blew it clean off his neck."

She blanched under her tan, raised both hands to stave off the horror. Through the bars of red fingernails he could see her eyes, enormous and glassy. Yet he kept on, watching the misery in her face, with a grim satisfaction that was almost sadistic. "Ever see one of those? A neck without a head? It's obscene. It's filthy, I tell you."

She put her cold hand flat on his mouth. She whimpered: "No wonder you're sick."

He slumped back in the seat. She let her hand stay on his mouth. The triangle of uncertainty settled over her nose. It was still there when she finally got up, walked across the room, snapped on the side-lights at the basin and the ends of the sofa. She swung the door shut. "*I'm* doing it this time," she said pointedly. She sat down in her corner, selected a cigarette. While she lit it, she turned a grave face to him. "Look, Don, I'm not kidding, you're sick. Very sick. Much more than you think. I noticed it first when you came in here this morning. You had the darndest trick of rubbing your thumbs, as if they were dirty."

He shot a glance at his hands.

"You were jittery and jumpy," she went on. "But this whole afternoon, since we left Jacksonville, you've been almost normal. You've talked in paragraphs, not single words, half sentences. You've let your thumbs be. You were getting things out of your system."

He jeered: "Doctor Gilmore!"

She shook her head, the way a dog shakes off water. "This morning you talked about combat fatigue. Almost as if you were ashamed that you had it. You were scared green all the time? Is that it?"

His chin came up. He said tartly: "Who isn't? You're a liar

or a dope if you say you're not. We're not Superman. We're people. Remember we're people."

"And all the while they were pinning those medals on you, you felt like a hypocrite, faker?"

"I did not."

"What then?" She sounded chagrined. Her diagnosis had missed.

"I thought only of time. I counted. Twenty-one, twenty-two, twenty-three . . . How many more missions."

"How many?"

There was a pause, almost breathless, before he replied: "Thirty-five."

"I see." She looked away, out of the window again. The sun was a red hemisphere, burning through pine and cypress, smearing the swamp pools with scarlet. When the last arc was gone, its glow stayed in the sky, tinting a cloud, a pink fleece on clear cobalt that changed, while you watched, into ebon-tipped crimson and merged with the darkening sky.

While the night grew, Corbett's angry voice rasped in her ears, tore at her skull. "So you think I'm queer, teched in the head. Flak-happy, we call it—there's a new one for your book —Well, I've been treated like everything else on this train. Listen, my sweet, a soldier's a guy who's doing a dirty job for his country. He has no choice. We're in and he's in, and it's kill or be killed. He's not going to die. If he can help it. He wants to live . . . to come back to the girls. He knows what it means when you lose to Tojo or Hitler. So he's not going to lose. He isn't thinking in broad ideologies. He leaves that to the statesmen. Not because he hasn't the brains, I assure you. Not because he doesn't give one goddamn. Oh no, darling, but because all he hears, all he reads—Darlan and Giraud and Badoglio—gives him the cramps. No, baby, we'll take Flattop and Pruneface. We'll take Mandrake The Magician. Give us our phantasy straight. Where black's black and white's white. This guy is bad; that guy is good. Get what I mean? Labels plain and clear and unmixed . . . Christ, if you once let your-self think about the reaming we're going to get when it's over, you'd slit your own throat . . . They tell me the Russians don't get combat fatigue. Don't even know what it means, because they know what they're fighting for. Mebbe so, mebbe so . . . They tell me the guys in the Pacific don't get it as we do. Because they know what it's for. The Japs shot up Pearl Harbor. They hate the Japs. It's plain A.B.C. I wish to God we knew too, but we don't . . . and that's that."

Her hand ran the length of his sleeve from shoulder to wrist. "That's better," she said soothingly. "It's all out of your system."

He shook her hand off. "There, there, little soldier. Don't cry. Mama fix."

"Don, listen to me." Her smooth face and her voice were still determinedly kind. "We've come a long way since this morning. Then I was legs. Only legs. And after that I was merely a female to make. But now I'm your friend who knows all about you and wants sincerely to help—"

"Like hell you do."

She shook her head reproachfully. "I'm trying my best. I really am. This is my war as much as it's yours."

"Don't make me laugh." His eyes ranged deliberately from her raspberry-plum colored shoes to her filigree earrings. His lip curled. "You're the girl who thinks we're fighting this war for your glamour."

She flushed all the way to her eyes. She cried hotly. "Stop that. Don't say that. We feel this war. We all feel this war."

He patted her hand, as patronizingly as she had done his, before. He said: "Listen, there's a girl in my coach—younger than you—with two little kids. Her husband's a sailor. One of those guys on the raft. He's been shipped out again. She's on her way home to mama. No husband. No home. Only worry. And there's a widow in there. About your age . . . Her guy died on the Anzio beachhead . . . *You* feel the war? You've got nothing to feel. It doesn't touch you. Doesn't get in your way. Why, you haven't so much as—"

She cut in. "What would you expect me, people like me, to do? Feel something that isn't there? Torture ourselves? Go hungry and ragged when we don't have to? We're lucky. Is that our fault? If we'd had to, we would have. If we'd had one little bombing, it would have been different!"

His jaw dropped. He stared at her blankly. "Do you know what you're saying?"

"I certainly do." There was an air of triumph about her, as though she knew she had said something final and clever. "I know what happened to England. When the Germans started bombing their cities, they began to wake up, to get in the war."

"Baby, I've seen English cities. You haven't." He was talking to her with a spurious gentleness, the way you address a not very bright child. "That man Broun once wrote a piece, during Finland, during that time we all were so hopped up over that Russian war on the Finns, about class-conscious bombs. It seems they could duck around a city, pick out the capitalists, leave the workers alone. He was being sarcastic, in case you haven't caught on. You're thinking about something like that, aren't you? A nice, considerate bombing, that would miss Central Park and the kids, the Empire State and the Chrysler. Just knock down a couple of shacks on Long Island . . . Baby, I drop my eggs on rail yards and bridges. I don't have the time to send them a post-card and tell them to move out the kids who live near the tracks . . . I've seen kids that have been through the bombings. Kids, without arms, without legs. Can't run. Can't play. Sit out their childhoods, waiting until they're full grown and can get wooden legs . . . I've made a few kids like that, myself."

He was rubbing his thumbs, rubbing them hard, as though this time he meant to rip flesh from the bones.

For a long while, she just sat and stared until she could stand it no longer: "Stop that!" she cried. "I can't bear what you're doing." She covered her eyes. Through her muffling sleeve, once more she begged: "Oh, please stop."

"You wanted it, baby. A story to tell the 4Fs and their floozies at bars. 'I met a war hero on the Florida train. He told me what it was like to bomb cities.'"

She had started to cry. She was shaking all over with big wrenching sobs.

His insides were churning so terribly that he saw only a blur of raspberry and gold. It took minutes before he became aware of how bitterly she was weeping and at first he was startled, then baffled and then he felt sorry for her and remorseful that he had hurt someone he'd wanted. He inched slowly toward her until he could smell the Chanel Number Five. His arms went around her small, quivering body.

She snuggled against him, her head on the blue of the Unit Citation.

He kissed her lips. She lay passive, not responding or rejecting. He bent down again. His hand moved over her shoulder and around the cup of her breast. His fingertips sank into softness. His whole body tingled, every nerve pushing, demanding. He turned her to him and crushed her mouth with his own.

She wriggled convulsively in his arms as though she had just awakened. Her eyes opened wide. Her hands pushed, thumped his chest.

He caught her wrists, gripped them tightly.

She struggled, cried: "Stop. Don't you dare."

He let go her hands.

She rubbed her wrists on the rough wool of her skirt. She was frightened. He saw it in her eyes, in every line of her features, in her trembling and it left him perplexed and dismayed.

She moved toward the bell button, keeping her eyes on his face.

He got to his feet. "You won't have to call help."

The closing door snapped at his heels.

CHAPTER EIGHT

D<small>r.</small> Peck fell in with Corbett on the platform of the Savannah train shed, his arthritic limp not quite in step with the airman's long stride. "Have a good afternoon?" he inquired sociably.

Corbett threw down his half-smoked cigarette. On the black pavement it glowed like a coal. Dr. Peck glanced at him curiously and then side-stepped behind him and stamped out the ember. "I missed you," he said. "We had quite a session in the lounge. Senator Hastings. An old goat named Voorhees. Brass Castings. Rauchmeyer, the publisher . . . Know he was with us?"

Corbett didn't and he shook his head "no." Another time, another place, the chance of a contact with the head of the Rauchmeyer newspaper chain might have meant something. Now it was merely intrusion. Like the talkative presence of the stocky, spectacled man shuffling beside him.

"Big shots on this train." The doctor panted a little with the effort of keeping step. "Ordinarily they give me the pip. But when they let their hair down, I got a great kick out of listening to them. Learned how America's thinking—or isn't." He caught Corbett's arm at the elbow. "Not so fast, if you please. This is no way to get to New York." He chortled. "They've certainly fought a tough war from those Florida cabanas. Their hindsight is staggering."

Corbett yanked his arm free, pulled out his flaccid cigarette package, removed the last smoke, crushed the wrapping and hurled it away.

The doctor kept still, watching his face while he took the first puffs. Then he asked: "Have you had your dinner?"

Corbett growled: "No."

"Then, why not? Make a dash for the diner." Dr. Peck stopped under a bulb, pulled out a round platinum watch, snapped its case open, held it up to the light. "I'm probably the last man in the country who uses a turnip." He whistled. "Ten minutes to eight. We're more than an hour and a quarter off schedule. Might make up some time overnight." He put the watch back in his vest pocket. "They may still be serving. Why don't you try?"

Corbett muttered: "No, thanks," said he'd rather keep walking.

The doctor glanced at him quizzically. "See here—" He seemed embarrassed. "I've already eaten but I'd be glad to go in with you. Have you as my guest."

"I've got money. I just am not hungry." It sounded ungracious, he knew, but even the best of them couldn't get over the notion that a serviceman always expected a handout.

Dr. Peck cleared his throat as though he had read Corbett's thoughts. "But you'll be hungry. There's a long night ahead. Do I see a cart, up there by the coaches? They sell some food, I believe. Sandwiches. Milk. Fruit. How about it?"

"I'm not hungry," he repeated. He moved toward the train.

Dr. Peck edged around to the inside before Corbett could start up the steps. "Oh, don't go in yet. It's a balmy spring night. Feels like May. Get all you can of this air. I hear they have snow in New York." Without deliberate rudeness Corbett couldn't push him aside to get on. "Savannah's beautiful. Ever been there? Old South. Gracious, friendly. Of course you never can judge a place from its train yards. If it weren't so dark, I'd show you a hell-hole. Right by these tracks. Frogtown, one of the places where their colored folks live. Sometimes, I've thought it would be a Godsend if someone had blasted our slums off the map the way they did London's."

Corbett's teeth clamped on his cigarette. He coughed when the smoke filled his throat.

"You haven't caught cold?"

This was his chance. He growled: "Maybe. I'd better go on."

Dr. Peck held his arm. "I wouldn't. Get all the fresh air you can." He paused, catching his breath. "My, do you realize before we wake up, they'll be turning on steam?" He stepped briskly aside to avoid bumping into a crouching figure. A man was bent double alongside the wheels. "What's that for, do you know?"

Corbett shrugged. Dr. Peck tapped the man on the shoulder. A brown, tired face turned up.

"Cap, what do they call what you're doing?"

"Checkin' juhnal boxes."

"Is that so?" The doctor laughed. "I know just as much as I did."

The man grunted: "Grease on the axles. Cain't run 'thout grease."

"True enough," The doctor moved on. "Have you ever thought"—His manner was reflective—"how much we're at the mercy of human capacity. All these lives on this train—If one man's too tired or too careless . . ." He stopped, glanced at Corbett's grim profile and took a fresh tack. "Say, I sat with an odd little fellow at dinner. One of those queer characters you don't often meet. Picks horses, makes a profession of following the races. You'd have found him amusing." He saw Corbett's jaw tighten and hurried to add, "I don't want you to think that I personally spend much time at the track." He paused for a moment before he started again. "Well, my strange dinner partner paid much more attention to my watch than to me. Asked me the time several times. Asked to get a look at the case. Probably figuring what it would hock for, if I were careless enough to leave it in his reach." He paused once more, to see whether this line would draw better conversational results and when it didn't, he walked a few steps beside Corbett and then, clearing his throat first, he asked quietly: "Are we getting you down?" He slanted a long, searching look up through the murk of the train shed, hunting a flicker of assent or dissent, and then he went on: "It's unfortunate, it's much too bad that you're getting your first eyeful and earful—and bellyful, too—of the folks back home on this sort of train. This isn't all of America, believe me, it isn't."

"I know," Corbett grunted. "That's what you said this morning."

"Did I? Well, let me say it again and again." He paused, breathing in, to get wind for emphasis. "I'm terribly anxious for you to believe what I say. For all of the boys—the men— like you to believe that we aren't your enemy."

"My enemy?"

A faint smile crossed Dr. Peck's face, echoed in his voice. "Well, you're certainly acting that way. Lieutenant, it's been our war, too. We've felt it and we *have* tried to do . . ."

"So I've been told," said Corbett.

Dr. Peck stopped, cocked his head sharply, but continued to talk as if Corbett hadn't spoken. ". . . whatever was asked of us, whatever we could. And wished it were more. I think—I think, perhaps, because thinking anything else would be too bitter a dose—that most of America is worth fighting for. Oh, the flashy stuff you see on luxury trains or in the night clubs, why, bless you, that isn't America. That's the froth. Some might say the scum. Are they synonymous? Why, I can take you from house to house, people I know, substantial people, who haven't set foot in a night club in all their lives and don't care if they don't. I'd like to show you the people with sons in the service, working hard, going about with lead in their hearts, tight bands of strain on their heads, working like . . ."

"Making Valor Fabrics. War Hero Prints."

The ceiling light caught the glint of Dr. Peck's glasses as his face tilted up. "Come again. I don't understand."

"Dollars and cents. The fortunes of war."

"Oh! You throw my own words back in my teeth . . . Well, granted they are making money, but there isn't as much left to spend as you think after taxes and War Bonds. Don't let yourself fall hook and line for those stories you hear about fabulous pay in the war plants. A hundred a week. Twenty-four fifty's more like it. At dull, tedious jobs. I get around. I meet all sorts of people. I know those who're so anxious to send their blood off to war that they cheat, go from blood bank to blood bank, offering their blood, to give more than five pints a year. I know those who stand out in the cold all night long, standing watch on the docks for the Coast Guard. Why, up in my County there's a group of men, middle-aged, hard-working men, who come in after work to man our hospital ambulances, do the dirty night work, orderlies' work, porters' work, without asking thanks . . ."

"And go home at night to their families and friends, sleep in good beds between clean sheets on the best innerspring in the County."

Dr. Peck sighed deeply and said: "You pick things up fast, don't you, lad? It seems to me I said that to you, not too many hours ago. Well, when you're right, you're right, and I've sense enough not to argue. The chasm is there. The gulf between us and you. Between men who are free, free to come and to go as they please, and men who take orders. Between men who live horror and men who read horror in press dispatches." He halted a moment and started again. "You're probably too young to remember, but after the war, the one before this, my war, there was a very fine play that tried to get across something of what it was like. *What Price Glory*. I seem to remember that one character cried out: 'Goddamn every son of a bitch who wasn't there.'" His shuffling feet dragged along the pavement, beside the quick, angry tap of the bombardier's heels. Finally, he said very softly: "Don't hate us. I beg you don't hate us because we've been lucky."

They were passing Glen Argyle. Dr. Peck stopped. "I'm in this Pullman. Want to get on?"

Corbett wheeled. "No, thanks."

The doctor turned with one foot up on the stool. "Why, I saw you get on here at Jacksonville. I assumed you were in this car."

"I'm in the coaches. Sixteen."

"I see. Sit up all night." He squinted down through the sphere of his bifocals. "I can't say I like it. A Nazi prisoner of war is sleeping tonight in a drawing room bed while our own heroes sit up in the coach." He hoisted himself from the stool to the train step. "Come down and visit with me. I'm in lower twelve. I retire rather early. Let's have a visit before."

Corbett walked down alongside the train until he came to Sixteen. The food cart was deserted. The passengers, believing the timetable claim of a ten-minute stop, had already gone on. The porter swung from the open doorway, looked up the track. Red signals stood set in the yards.

"They're movin' sojers." The porter offered conversation. "They goin' some place." He wagged his gray head portentously. "Palm Queen gotta wait for the sojers."

"Got some more of that rot-gut? Sell me a pint."

The Negro stopped watching the signals, leaned back on the wall of the platform, took note of Corbett's strained, furrowed face, shook his head. "Cain't sell no likka on Sundays in Geawgia."

Corbett snorted. "What's that got to do with *your* business?"

"They's a law. Cain't sell on Sundays."

"You sold me a pint this afternoon."

"That there musta been way down in Flahda." The porter scratched his grizzled head. "They got diff'ent laws. Ev' state, it got diff'ent laws."

"Do you get me that pint?" Corbett tried to sound tough.

"Cain't do it, sojer."

"Listen, you get me that rye or I'll slit your black throat."

The man's eyeballs grew whiter and larger. He looked scared and he sounded that way. "You meet me in the washroom aftuh the conductuh's been by." He stamped on a knob in the floor of the platform to fold up the steps, pushed the door to, tightening the hasp. "We'll git goin' now. Ah gotta git in. See if mah people is raidy fo' pilluhs."

Corbett stayed on the platform. He broke open the last of his Jacksonville packages, lit a cigarette, slouched back on the wall. He stared through murky glass of the door, at shadowy yards, at twinkling lights and black building shapes.

Two slim girls in slacks opened the coach door and came out

to the platform. From habit, more than desire, he glanced at them. One seemed very young—eighteen or so—had a long, golden brown bob, a small, kiss-or-pout pointed mouth, a fuzzy pink sweater, tight over breasts no bigger than peaches. The other seemed slightly older and attractive in a quite different way—short, curly auburn hair, light, freckled skin, turned-up nose, a businesslike blouse. Both of them wore wedding bands. The girl with the sweater had a very small diamond.

They glanced at Corbett but didn't address him until the red-headed girl had taken a packet of Luckies out of her handbag and had said: "Got a match, Sue?" and both had scoured handbags and pockets for matchbooks. Then they both looked at him and the redhead asked: "Lieutenant, may we have a light?"

He crossed the platform, snapped open his lighter and held it.

The girl in the sweater drawled: "Is tha-ut a win' proof?"

He nodded.

"Wheauh do you git it?"

"PX."

"Mah husband cain't git 'em down at his caiump."

He shrugged, said: "Too bad," and went back to his corner. The girls made no effort to keep him.

"Mae, what time we s'posed to git into Richmun'?" The younger girl's drawl was nasal, high-pitched.

"Lord only knows. You getting off there?"

"Ah take a bus to mah home. We're s'posed to get in aroun' fo' in the mawnin'. Ah'm kinda scared." She wriggled a little, as if hugging herself for protection. "Ah ain't nevuh been out so late."

"Oh don't you worry. Don't you be scared. Nobody bothers you if you don't bother with them."

"Ah heard some maiun say we're runnin' a hour and a half late. That makes it what tium?"

"Half past five. Six o'clock . . . Who knows? You got all night. If you go in right now you could catch a night's sleep."

"Oh. Ah don' figguh on sleepin' to-naht. But ah don' ve'y

much caiuh. Ah slep' las' night. Ah declaiuh las' night's sleep
Ah haid with mah husban' was the soundes' night's sleep Ah
had since he went in the Ahmy. You think that was because
Ah was sleepin' with him?"

The other girl hooted, glanced shyly at Corbett. "Of course,
dummy. You just finding out it ain't no good sleeping alone?"

She had a raw look, a sex-hungry look, and Corbett idly
wondered whether she'd be worth trying for. Hell, no law said
it had to be Nina. This girl had a ring. And so what? If she
was willing. Probably be much obliged.

He looked again, more intently this time. The girl seemed
aware of his notice. She turned deliberately, stared through
the door on her side.

The kid in the sweater sucked her cigarette gingerly. "We
only haid jus' this week-aind. Thuhty-six ouahs. Ef he come
up, he'd jus' have the tahm to say 'hello' an' 'good-by.' His
mothuh said ef Ah wanted to go to be with 'im she'd stay with
the baby. Ah hope she don't give her no trouble. She's a awful
good baby. You know how it is, ef they're baiud, they blame
it on you, you not raisin' them raht."

"How old is your kid?" he heard the redhead inquire.

"Jus' fahv months."

"Mine's a year and a half."

Well that was that. Or was it? Oh sure, to hell with it. To
hell with them all. He banged a door shut in his mind.

"I left him with my mother," the red-head went on. "I been
living with her since Michael was shipped. She takes care of
the kid when I'm working. Gees, I hope the job is still there.
I'll need that job now, believe me, I will."

"This yo' vacation?"

"Nope. Just walked out. Say, when I heard Mike's voice on
long distance, I all but fainted away. When I heard him say:
'Honey, I'm down here in Miami, I'm in the hospital here. It
would help me a lot to get better if you could come down,' say,
I would have come down if I had to crawl. I just called up my
boss and told him 'You better get somebody else for my place.

I don't know when I'll be back.' Sat on my suitcase all night, going down."

"We'uh lucky, we got us them seats." The Southern girl mashed out her butt on the wall. "Ah ha'ut to waste yo' good cigarette, Mae, but Ah jus' cain't learn how to smoke . . . What kin' of job do you do?"

"Stenography."

"Does it pay good?"

"Not too bad. I figured I'd try to put a few bucks in the bank. When he comes back—getting started again—till he finds a job, I figured I might just as well have some put away."

The Southern girl frowned. "His muthuh's been helpin' me out with the money. Ah ain't nevuh wukked. He don' want me to wuk."

The redhead laughed, not pleasantly. "Sue, we do a whole lot of things we never did before. You'll find out. I figured if my husband was staying there long, I'd find an apartment and bring down the kid. Say, I walked my shoes off. Up one street and down the other. Not a chance. Not a thing. They look at my clothes and they say: "What does your husban' do?' 'He's in the service.' That's all you need tell them. They slam the door in your face."

The Southern girl hissed: "Jews!" and flashed Corbett a glance. His wavy brown hair, his bold nose, looked faintly suspicious. The other raised a fingertip to her lips.

The drawl rose belligerently. "Ah won't shush. Ef he is, Ah mean him to hear me. Ef he ain't, he'll know what Ah mean."

Her words went through Corbett's ears without touching his brain. Numbness had begun to crawl through him, in which the one thing alive was his craving for liquor.

Mae brushed her red hair back from her forehead. "Oh, it ain't only them. Believe me, it ain't. Baptists do that; good Methodists. All kinds of people. Before my husband was shipped, I traveled all over with him. I lived in every jerk town in the country. Believe me, I lived in more dumps. In the South. In the West. The minute they hear you're a serviceman's wife, wherever you go, they rent you the worst dump in town and charge you like it was the Ritz."

"They took ouah husban's away an' that's what they give us."

"They tell us stay home. What's the matter with us, running around just like gypsies, chasing after our men?"

"Jus' stay home an' let some she-wolf come get 'im!" The Southern girl sniffed. "Ah tol' mah husban' ef Ah heard 'bout him runnin' aroun' with some chippie, Ah'd jus' staht datin' the first maiun that asks me."

"Oh, you will. You will anyway. Sitting home is no fun. God, there's seven nights in a week. You got to go out or you start in climbing the walls."

For a moment or two, neither one spoke. Then the drawl asked: "How long is youah husban' gonna be theah?"

The red-head raised her shoulders. "God only knows. The doctors won't say. They took off his leg."

"They took off his laig!" Sue's voice rose, shrill with horror. "Ah think Ah'd die ef that happened to mine."

"Oh, you don't die. You don't die that easy. You just sit down and start figuring out how you're going to get by. I'm damn glad I saved all that money."

That was enough. That was an ear and a gut-full. Corbett went into the car.

The gunner's mate's wife elbowed him in the passage and he flattened himself on the corridor wall to let her go past. She nodded at him, paused with the green curtain in her hand as if she welcomed the chance to trade a few words. "I'm moving my kids in here for the night. If they don't sleep, at least they won't disturb the whole car." Her face was smudged and there were black half-moons under her eyes. She was wearing the red coat like a cape. Joanie held on to the hem of the coat and the baby blinked sleepily over her shoulder. The kid had his thumb in his mouth and his flushed face was blotched with the rings tears make on dirt.

She pushed open the door beyond the green curtain. The washroom was a sty. It reeked of smoke and stale tobacco.

Wet, crumpled brown paper towels littered the floor. The plumbing was bad. You could see the rivulet of a leak, creeping under the closed door from the john.

What pigs women were! Corbett thought, and the thought gave him pleasure. By the illogic of hate, he could attach it to Nina. The ladies' room is a pigsty. Nina Gilmore's a lady. Nina Gilmore's a pig.

The sailor's wife sniffed. "Disgusting! But it's six of one and half a dozen of the other. At least they can stretch out on the sofa in here. The love seat. Excuse me!" In spite of her weariness, she managed to smile.

Joanie tugged Corbett's pants leg. "Was you on my train all the time? I didn't see you on my train."

Her mother caressed the kid's hair. "Joanie thinks everything's hers. She thinks the whole world is hers. Well, I can't kick. She's not been too bad ... Say good night to the officer, Joanie."

The child smiled at him, as if he was papa or uncle. "Where you going to sleep?"

He gestured toward the coach. "In there. On the rack."

The kid's eyes opened wide. "Ooh, you'll fall off and get hurt." She put her hand into his. It was a soft, sticky nothing inside his big palm. "Sleep here with me." She sidled up to his leg, cuddled her head on his thigh.

"Joanie Taylor, behave yourself," her mother warned.

He smiled. "That kid's a honey."

"Her father thinks so. She's crazy about men. Makes a play for them all. She misses her daddy, I guess."

The train lurched, at last starting. Corbett steadied the child to keep her from falling. He gave her small bottom an affectionate pat. "Goodnight, Joanie. Sleep tight."

"Good night, Lieutenant," the young woman said. "See you tomorrow." She lowered the curtain.

The Palm Queen was running, rumbling and grinding and clashing over the ties to the North. Corbett felt slightly better and he said to himself, jeering at his own thoughts: "The touch of a little child's hand—"

The coach gave him a sense of home-coming. There were remembered faces; the familiar pattern of luggage and orange bags up on the rack. Most of the seats were already tipped back for the night in a comic position, neither sitting nor lying. The fat, middle-aged couple in one and two lay back with abdomens distended. Grandma in three had a soiled, crumpled handkerchief over her face. The two women in black slumped in their chairs, fur coats over knees, eyes shut against the bright light in the ceiling. The horse-player's seat and his own were vacant. He dawdled before it, trying to decide about staying.

The Marine, sipping milk through a straw in a carton, greeted him eagerly. Dr. Frankel, sunglasses at last taken off, put down the book he was reading and motioned to Corbett to sit down in the chair next to him. He shook his head, went back through the car. Chuckie, Joan's pal, put his hand through the arm of the seat where he was bedded down with his papa and lunged for Corbett's near leg. The frizzy haired female with the earrings gave him a leer, contemptuous this time. She had a sailor, a leather-skinned, middle-aged gob, who should have known better but actually looked pleased with his present companion.

He went on to the men's room. Kalchis was in there alone, asleep on the leather settee. His mouth was open. You could see the yellow fangs of his teeth, hear, over the grind of the train, his harsh snore.

Corbett went out to the platform, stood just back of the door, and watched for the porter. He thought: "If that dinge don't keep his promise, I'll slit his black throat." He kept repeating the threat in his mind until it became a part of the noise of the wheels on the track.

Georgia rolled past, dark cutouts of treetops against a black sky, the blink of the light from a cabin, the flash of a lantern from freights on a siding, the wavering, thin beams of a moving car's headlights.

He saw it merely with eyes, his mind fixed on one object, drawing down to a point as fine, as imperative, as the hair

lines of the bombsight, upon getting liquor and drinking himself into stupor. When, finally, through the glass, he saw the
porter fluffing a pillow, he went in and tweaked the man's
sleeve. "Well?"

The Negro stared at him blankly. "You ask me fo' a pil-
luh?"

"You know goddam well what I want."

"Mah closet's locked up. Cain't fin' the key." The man pretended to be completely taken up with the cushion, smoothing
its seams, pulling its corners meticulously square. "Cain't he'p
you ri' now. Ver' busy. You go back to that lounge cah.
Mebbe somebody got somethin' there."

                    *   *   *   *   *

There were two bottles of Scotch in the lounge: two of the
best—pinch bottle—and two pot-bellied quarts of Bourbon.
Corbett saw them through the glass half of the door, swishing
their amber elixirs to the sway of the train, in thickets of
brown White Rock, green gingerale bottles and tumblers of ice,
on a big tray on the writing desk at the end of the car. He
stopped, awestruck by the wealth, and it took him a moment
to grasp the fact that the big mirror doubled the number of
bottles, made them twice as alluring.

It was a country club party. The best people were there.
Yet something was wrong with the picture. With that liquor
supply, it should have been gay, but it wasn't. The party was
grim. Not a getting together, but rather a getting off, in a
huddle.

The mirror reflected the huddle, the heads of three men:
on the far end, the Senator's furry eyebrow, the purple-veined
nose, the cigar; on the near, the chiseled granite of a man in
gray with a trim gray mustache, and between the two, his silvery hair towering above them, the New England antique. The
two on the ends held highball glasses. The old man between
was telling a story, excited about it, you could see by the
twitch of his head, the gleam of his eyes.

Facing them in the unyielding armchairs sat the Senator's

wife in her spring garden hat and the kittenish Englishwoman. The Senator's wife was doing the talking. The Senator's straw-haired young daughter finished that row, sprawled back in her seat, swinging one leg, crossed high over the other, showing her knee-caps. She was drumming the arm of her chair, nervous with boredom.

Way down on the end, near the door, on the liquor side of the car, sat the blonde in the silver fox jacket with a man in a peacock blue sport suit. They were three seats away—three empty seats—from the huddle of men. The blonde was chattering, gesturing with an arm adorned by a diamond bracelet.

The Hastings girl, recrossing her legs, veered toward the door, saw Corbett and brightened. She smiled at him. He smiled at her and opened the door.

With the abruptness of pulling up brakes, the old man stopped talking. He drew himself up, glanced at his two companions as if he hoped one of them would get up and throw the intruder out. Corbett slouched in the doorway, feeling the chill of unwelcome. He thought of retreating. The sight of the bottles detained him.

Then Pat Hastings patted the empty chair next to hers and he went all the way in and sat down.

The situation, he was aware, called for craft and guile. He said: "Good evening. How are you this evening?"

Pat Hastings said: "Oh hello," and eyed his ribbons. The two other women gave him a nod.

He forced a propitiating grin. "You've all found the perfect way of passing the time." He glanced down at the tray with the bottles. "Most beautiful sight I've seen in two years."

Pat Hastings followed his glance down the car and then looked at her father. Corbett held his breath. The Senator gave a diminutive nod.

The girl touched his arm: "Lieutenant, can I give you a drink?"

He let his breath out. He nodded his "yes," fearful his voice would betray too much eagerness.

"Bourbon or Scotch?"

"Scotch, if you please."

She swayed to the front of the car, crooked a finger for him. "You pour it yourself. Too hard to tend bar on a train." He took up the pinch bottle tenderly. The jerk of the train nudged his arm and the hooker was stiffer than was conventionally decent. The girl whispered: "Hey! That stuff's scarce." She slipped her hand through his elbow. "I'm only kidding. Go right ahead. More where that came from."

Behind him he heard her mother: "Pat's a born hostess. Perfect with servicemen. Knows just how to treat them."

Pat Hastings ogled him. "Do I?"

God, she was homely, he thought, scrawny and pimply. But what the hell, she had a kind heart.

She raised his drink to her lips. "Let me taste. Just a sip. Daddy won't let me drink in public."

Her lipstick smudged the glass. He turned it around to get the clean side.

She pouted. "That wasn't nice." The come-on in her eyes was unmistakable and he wondered: "Where do these babies learn all these tricks?" A Senator's precious daughter and the Picadilly Commandos. Well, if you had to take her to get Haig and Haig, it still was a bargain. He finished his Scotch, extended his hand for the bottle. She tapped his wrist. "Not yet, piggy. We're rationing the stuff. Come back and sit down."

He sat on the end of the women's row and the girl's fingertips played with his sleeve, marching up toward his shoulder. "I just adore fliers," she cooed. She pawed his arm, squeezed the muscle.

"Lieutenant!" Her mama leaned forward. "Do tell us about your adventures abroad."

He thought: "Here it comes. Sing for your Scotch. Adventures abroad! The Rover Boys at Ploesti." Yet the double of good Haig and Haig had eased him up and so he merely pretended he hadn't heard.

"Lieutenant!" You couldn't play deaf to the Senator's gong. "You were in Europe?"

"Yes, sir."

"In the Air Force, I gather." The man uttered a commonplace as though it were Holy Writ. "Did you by any chance run across a young pilot named Hotchkiss?"

He shook his head. Christ, didn't the fool know how many airmen there were?

"Too bad. Too bad. You must look him up. Fine chap. He worked in my office."

"He wrote daddy's speeches," Pat Hastings whispered. She had worked her way around to the wings on his breast. "Daddy's not been the same since he left."

"Splendid lad, splendid." The Senator bit off the wet, ragged end of his cigar, spat toward the ash stand and missed. "When he left, I said to him: 'You're a fortunate boy. Yours is a great, an incomparable privilege. To fight for your country. By God, I envy you, sir. If I were younger'—Pat, remind me to write him a letter."

He was suddenly aware of a dimness, a chill in the car. His stomach was jumping. Again, there was decision to make: to get up and go, to give up the chance to get stewed or stay here and take this emetic with Scotch.

He heard Pat Hastings ask: "Another drink?" and he nodded, thinking "Just this one. No more at this price."

"Sit still, I'll pour it this time."

When Pat Hastings got up, the silver-fox blonde looked at him speculatively and said to the man next to her, raising her voice: "Of course, I may go back to Powers or I may go to the Coast. A gentleman I met down in Miami said any time I want, he'll get me a contract in pictures." She simpered at Corbett, certain she was making an impression on him.

The man in the sport suit breathed heavily. "You've got what it takes, baby. Got what it takes. Plenty glamour."

"You really think so?" she tossed her head. The roots of her hair, Corbett saw, were dark brown, like her oversized lashes. "I'm glad to hear you say that. My husband, my former husband, I mean, I keep forgetting that the decree's been made final—thought I ought to sit home and darn socks or something."

"Not you, baby. You've got too much life in you. Live while you're living, that's what I say."

"Of course"—Again the appraising glance across the aisle— "I don't believe a *girl* should do *nothing*. Not in these times. If Mr. Powers makes me an offer—"

Pat Hastings came back with a highball. "I mixed it this time. Put soda in. So you won't get done so quick . . . Now, undo. Relax. Oh, for Pete's sake, what makes you so glum? Don't tell me you're thinking about *your* wife and kiddies. Like Captain Metzger . . . That was a drip! He's gone to bed. Dreaming about what he'll say to the baby! I had to pick *that!*"

Corbett sipped the cold highball. She'd put in enough, but he regretted the ice and the soda.

"Take it easy." The girl was a chiropractor. Her fingers were working his arm. "You can't have any more till I decide you're a very nice boy. I've been nice to you but you haven't been one bit nice to me. Why, you haven't asked me one single thing about did I have a good time in Miami, and what I do with my—"

He sighed. He asked docilely: "Did you have a good time in Miami?"

"Oh, super! Why, there was the darlingest Lieutenant Commander. And a Major. An adorable Major. He danced like a dream. Of course, they were old. At least thirty-five. But I thought it was simply my duty to go out with them. Keep up their morale."

It was a mistake to let that get started. He said desperately: "Sh . . . Shut up for a while. I want to hear what your papa's saying."

She pouted again. "Silly, that isn't my daddy. That's Mr. Rauchmeyer, the newspaper publisher. He's just an old sourpuss. You wouldn't want to listen to him."

Now that she put it that way, he did, yet without curiosity, merely to have a pretext to get rid of the clack of her voice.

Rauchmeyer had said very little, just: "Go on, Mr. Voorhees," and clipped his words off so that they seemed even less than they were.

Old Mr. Voorhees went on in his senile treble: "Well, Ray Parsons called me—he's our executive vice-president—he felt he wanted me to have the last word. They're meeting on Wednesday. They wanted me there. You can see what it means for us to give in. It would be the end. Voorhees Brass Castings will no longer be run by its Board of Directors, its voting stockholders. It will be run by a Communist Union."

A stingy smile raised Rauchmeyer's toothbrush mustache. "Or by the Army," he said.

Purple spread over old Voorhees' face. "But they can't do that! Not in *my* country." He looked at the Senator, his eyes filled with desperate dread.

Pat Hastings pawed Corbett's shoulder. "You don't want to listen to that," she persisted. He put his hand over hers. "Be a good girl," he said. "And keep quiet."

"We've seen it coming," Rauchmeyer said. "Every step of the way. I knew the moment we entered this war, liberty was dead on this continent."

"That's it," old Voorhees quavered. "They're taking our country away from us. Why, only this day on this train, I had an experience I shall never forget . . ."

Corbett saw the blue-eyed Englishwoman turn away from the Senator's wife, flush, bite her lips.

"You told us about that," Rauchmeyer said coldly. "I'm interested in the other. The Labor Board matter. If we can help you at all, why we will. We owe it to our readers to present all the facts."

Senator Hastings sipped at his highball. "You didn't give me a break—not much of a break—when I made my address on the servicemen's pay." He glanced at Corbett over the top of his glass.

"We did our best. You know our policy. Raids on the Treasury, more loads on the taxpayer's back. This futile adventure is costing enough . . . And it's nothing, it's nothing at all to what will come after. When we're flooded with goods from Russian slave labor. When our own men come back, infected with Bolshevism"— He turned, looked at Corbett and scowled—"Clamoring for jobs that just don't exist."

"Filled up with refugees," the Senator quickly put in. "That's what I've told them time and again on the floor. (You'll find my remarks in the *Record*.) Why, this country's just running with foreigners, taking the jobs that belong to our boys. Why, we're sending tractors to Europe—to Europe, mind you—while our farmers can't get what they need. We'll have trouble enough, just mark my words."

"Oh, I know." Old Voorhees trembled as he talked. "I spoke with some friends in Palm Beach. Very wise men, men of foresight and vision. They're getting ready. They're training for after."

Hastings looked at Corbett again. There was a hint of discomfiture in his face. He pressed Voorhees's arm, whispered in his ear. The old man glanced quickly up, toward the soldier, and, then, with tremulous appeal, toward Senator Hastings. It was perfectly plain that all three of the men were wishing that Corbett would finish his drink and get the hell out.

He looked into his glass. There wasn't much more than melted ice. But the malice of stubbornness made him pretend he had a long way to go in the highball. He leaned back in the chair, stretched his legs. Pat Hastings said, "That's better. Now, you listen to me."

But he couldn't because her old man had started an oration, and the Senator's voice was used to large halls. He was staring at Corbett; the speech was plainly directed at him. "Some star-gazers are telling you about the world they're going to make. Well, I'm a practical man. I'm one of those old-fashioned, practical men. I believe in letting nature take its own course until our boys come home. I know what they want. They've written to me. They've told me what they want. They want to find Uncle Sam in his swallow tail coat, his tall hat, just the same as he was . . . Leave him be. That's what I say. Leave him be."

Pat whispered: "For Pete's sake, if somebody doesn't stop dad, he'll go on all night."

"I want prosperity. I want lasting prosperity. Not meddling and monkeying. I believe in taking care of the sick and distressed in my own home before taking care of any other country on the face of the earth. And I want peace, above all things I want peace. My heart is with all the suffering and sorrowing mothers of the world. My heart goes out to them because a mother is the noblest thing God ever created." He bowed his head in his wife's direction.

It sounded like double-talk. Through the alcohol fuzz, it even seemed mildly amusing, pleasantly soporific. Corbett yawned. The girl next to him grimaced. "Is that all I get for giving you Scotch?"

He roused himself, decided the time had come to be generous. He stroked her hand. "You're a sweet kid," and after a moment: "Think you could manage a refill?"

"Oh daddy'd—"

"He wouldn't mind. You know he wouldn't. I'm a vote, a potential vote. Take care of the sick and distressed."

"Are you sick?"

"Not so you'd notice it, darling . . . Come, come, be a good kid."

She ruffled his hair before she took his glass and went up to the tray with the bottles. "Just one little one, daddy," he heard her say. "Just one more. Oh, be nice!" and then the door of the car swung back with a bang.

Kalchis stood framed in the doorway, bracing himself by his lean, wiry hands, blinking eyes bloodshot from sleep. "Sa-a-ay, it looks like a pa-a-rty."

Every face in the car turned toward him. There was outrage and shock and, growing slowly, unmistakable fear, as though all their vague dreads and their hates were made immediate and personal in this one shabby stranger.

Kalchis seemed not to have noticed. He entered the car,

teetered a moment, getting his balance, deciding which seat to take. He sat down next to Corbett.

Pat Hastings gave Corbett his glass without speaking. She slid into her chair, tucked her short skirt over her kneecaps.

Kalchis touched Corbett's sleeve. "I see you rate. Crashed the party. What does a guy have to do to get one of those?"

Voorhees clutched the arms of his chair and pulled himself out. "I shall retire," he said primly. "Mrs. Forsythe, don't you think you had better?" His eyes were on Kalchis.

The horseplayer lolled back in his chair. "Don't let me chase you," he drawled amiably.

The Englishwoman stood. "But, of course. If you think our berths are made up." She blushed as she said it.

Corbett saw the blonde in the fox glance at her boldly and snicker.

Voorhees crooked his arm. Mrs. Forsythe held it tightly while they swayed in the aisle for good nights. "We'll continue our talk tomorrow, I hope," Voorhees said. "Shall I see you gentlemen at breakfast?"

"Not me." The Senator tamped his cigar on the ash stand. "I get off early. Washington. Back to work. Margie and Pat stay on to New York." He arched his spine. "Girls, what do you say we turn in? I've had a tough day." He picked up his pinch bottle and bourbon, put one under each arm. "Pat, leave that soldier alone. You've got him drunk."

The girl bent over Corbett. "I'm in twenty-four." She fenced her mouth with her hand. "Loch Lomond. Mother and dad have a bedroom way down on the end."

"I might—and I might not," he said.

When they had gone, Rauchmeyer, rising reluctantly with them, the lady in fox turned to her companion. "What some women will do!" She said crisply, "Did you see what that was? That dame with the baby blue eyes. To look at her, you'd think she didn't know which end was up. She picked up that old guy, right on this train." The rouged bow of her lips slipped sideways with contempt. "I hear she has a husband in England. They come over here—" She waved her wrist.

The wall bracket sent its light down, drove out a shower of sparks from her bracelet.

The horseplayer leaned back in his chair, knees crossed and hands folded, smiling benignly at her and the diamonds.

Corbett set his glass down on the floor and went out of the car.

CHAPTER NINE

The diner had put out all except one pallid night light. It was a weird, rattling cave, filled with long shadows of black men, swaying and stretching and bowing. The waiters were making their beds: three straight leather chairs in a row, wooden-legged canvas cots without pillows or blankets. The tables had vanished, turned into boards, stacked in a corner.

Corbett found the dismantled diner disturbing. With the taking apart of the car, the train had lost something, something of staunchness, solidity, permanent might. The Palm Queen seemed fragile, a shell, shaken by speed, hurtling through darkness.

He crossed the couplings, opened the door of Sixteen. The sight was so eerie that he caught his breath. Its window shades were all drawn, its bulbs were extinguished. At each end, blue night lights drained down on motionless heads on white pillows. It looked like a car of the dead.

Chuckie stirred in his father's arms and whimpered as Corbett tripped on a valise in the aisle. When he came to his place, he perceived there had been a few changes in the chairs nearest his. Joanie was back. He could make out her pig-tails in a crumple of light-colored blanket in the seat where Elaine Weston had been. The young woman had moved in next to Frankel.

She sat up, a taut silhouette, and watched Corbett climb into his place.

He fumbled around for the knob that would let down his chairback. It dropped with a thump. He heard sleepy murmurs of protest behind him. He took off his jacket, folded it on his lap, lay back, closed his eyes. For a moment or two, he listened to snores, wheezes, hackings, clearings of throats, shifttings of haunches. Then, utterly worn by the bone-break of travel, the exhaustion of overstrained nerves, the let-down of Scotch, he fell asleep.

A screech of iron on steel and a violent jolt woke him up. He sat rigid and tense, certain that something had happened. Then he let up the shade. A signal tower beacon glistened on a network of tracks, on black gnomes swinging lanterns. He pressed his face to the pane. On a curve up ahead, he could see the red signals. He settled back in his seat.

Light streamed through the unshaded window. It fell on the face next to his, a hollow skull that resembled a death's head and snored like a man. Kalchis hadn't awakened.

In front and in back, he could hear restless stirrings. Grandma was muttering something at the lump of the Marine's inert body. Two female figures in slacks slid by his seat. There was a flash of sharp yellow light as they parted the washroom curtains and opened its door, the sound of the baby, fretfully wailing. Across the aisle, Dr. Frankel was buzzing discreetly.

Elaine Weston crept out of her seat. She slung her coat over her shoulders, went up the aisle toward the curtains.

The car had grown cold. Yet, in spite of its chill, it was stuffy, fetid with flatulence, tooth and tonsil decay. He wriggled his arms into his jacket, buttoned it up, drew the shade down and again tried to sleep. After a half hour of trying, he knew that he couldn't. He climbed over the horseplayer's legs and went out to the platform.

It was chilly out there as well, but there was light from a small muddy bulb in the ceiling. He lit a cigarette, leaned against the wall and looked through the glass. Beyond the tracks, he could barely make out low, rectangular sheds and the circles of tree-tops. Thin lines of rain etched the glass.

A trainman came out of Fifteen, a stout man in blue. It was almost a shock to see him so neat, so wide-awake in this train of disheveled and sleeping. He unlatched the door opposite Corbett, gripped a handrail, a thin iron loop in the wall. Corbett crossed over, leaned with him. The rain swung in his face, pricked him with ice. He inhaled the pungence of pine.

"Where are we?" he asked.

"This side of Raleigh."

"What's holding us up?"

The man shrugged. "Hot box, I reckon."

"Hot box?" His voice must have held a note of anxiety, for the trainman said quickly:

"Nothing to get you fussed up. We get them sometimes."

"How late will we be?"

The blue shoulders again rose. "We made up some time. That's probably what did it. May make up some more after Raleigh. Cripes." His voice became petulant. "I'm as anxious to get off this train as you are." He paused, glanced at Corbett's uniform. "My kid's being shipped. He's home on his furlough. I got to get over to Lancaster before he goes."

A track-walker went by, swinging his lantern, a slight, lonely figure, plodding in the wet, alongside the long, slumbering train, the dull red glow getting smaller, dwindling down to a pin point.

The door of Fifteen banged open. A brakeman came through, stopped for a moment to murmur something to the trainman. Corbett couldn't hear what they said but he saw that their faces looked worried.

In the distance, the red pin point swung up and down. The trainman reached back for the door. "Okay, we're moving."

The signal tower lights in the distance blinked green. The Palm Queen shuddered, moved slowly at first, not quite sure that it dared. The trainman shut the door tightly, fastened its hasp. He remarked: "It's chilly out here. Steam's going on after Raleigh. You'd better go in."

Corbett went back to his corner and lighted a second ciga-rette from the end of the first. He leaned back, letting his body rock gently with the plummeting rush of the train. The coach door opened. Elaine Weston came out to the platform.

When she saw him, she took a step back, as if it alarmed her to find someone out there. She didn't greet him, nor did she show by eyes or expression that she knew they had ever spoken. She did something more subtle to show recognition. She looked at his hands.

He thrust his free hand into his pocket and in an attempt to be friendly smiled at her tentatively. "We're the night-walk-ers, the insomniacs."

"I'm used to not sleeping." She pushed the lank hair back from her forehead. As she raised her arm, her coat slipped from her shoulders. Corbett caught it and held it. "Put it on. Put your arms in. It's chilly out here."

She began to obey but stopped with her arms halfway into the sleeves. "It's strange to have a man help me on with my coat."

"A soldier and gentleman," he growled. He took out his pack. "Do you smoke?"

She took one and nodded to thank him. He opened his lighter. She stared into the flame and her face quivered. "Max had one of those. I bought him a gold one. A Dunhill. He said these were better."

He pushed the flame forward until it licked her cigarette and she had no choice but to draw in the heat. She coughed; her eyes watered.

He moved back in his corner, determined not to talk to her any more than he had to. She must have felt the same way for she moved to the opposite side of the platform and looked through the pane. The cigarette hung between her fingers, burning unsmoked.

After quite a long while, she exclaimed: "Why, it's rain-ing!" as though she had just found that out. Then she shivered and came back to his side of the platform.

"May turn to sleet before morning. Still winter up North."

"Still winter," she echoed.

"You should have stayed down."

"I should have stayed down."

The echo was becoming annoying. "Then, why didn't you?"

"She thought I should come back. Find a job. Take my mind off."

"Your mother?"

"Max's mother."

That surprised him. The older woman had seemed so placid, so pleasant, that you didn't connect her with this sort of trouble.

"She had no one but him," Elaine Weston said. She paused, added, "And me." Her face worked, trying for tears.

"She's right, perfectly right." He had to strain to make his voice carry over the clash of the cars. "Work's the best medicine. Just being useful. Doing something for someone." "That's funny," he thought. "That's a joke. *Me* telling *her*. The blind leading the crippled."

Again her limp hand mopped her forehead. "I've tried every other. Sunshine. Sea air. Vitamin capsules. Red pills and blue pills. Yellow pills. White ones. I've bought out the drugstore. Secconal. Amytal. Chloral. Nembutal. Phanodorm. Luminal."

She sounded hysterical and he thought: "I can't take it. I won't." He dropped his half-burned cigarette, stepped on it, moved toward the door.

She clutched his sleeve in a panic. "Don't leave me. Please don't go. I can't stay here alone."

He slouched back, feeling helpless, uncomfortable. Then he put his hands on her shoulders. "Look," he said, as though she were Joanie. "This is no good. You've got to behave like a grown-up. You've got to grow up." There wasn't a shade of response in her face. "You're not the first woman to whom this has happened. You won't be the last. God knows you won't be the last."

She kept still for a moment and then, with a slight lift of surprise, said: "Why, it happened to her!"

"To whom?"

"To Max's mother. Why, her husband died too." Her lips stayed parted, with sudden wonder at a fact that must have been hers for a good many years. She stared again and her stare was a kind of a cue. He began to feel as if she had chosen him purposely, as if there were things she wanted to hear said—things she already had thought out herself, that required reassurance.

"You know your husband died for a cause. He died for something so big, so important—"

"You think so?" The tone of her voice was almost flippant. "I wish I could be sure."

"You have to think so. You have to believe it. Otherwise nothing makes sense. You'd go out of your mind."

"Maybe I have."

He gripped her shoulders again. He said: "Snap out. You've got your whole life ahead." "Pollyanna," he thought. "I've come down to that. I've sunk so damn low."

"A whole *empty* life."

"Listen, you've got a family."

"My parents are dead."

"You've got friends."

"What good are they?"

He set his teeth. "You've got youth and your looks."

Again there was that listless gesture of brushing her hair off her brow. "I've nothing to live for." She was biting her lips. Her eyes shone with tears starting. "Nothing to wait for. Not even the postman. He wrote to me every day." Two big tears rolled down her face. "He sent me flowers for my birthday. They came after the telegram. He was so thoughtful; he loved me so much." The stream of her tears dripped off her chin.

His own throat filled with emotion and he shunted it off into anger. "Then don't be a pig," he snapped. "Nothing's for free. You pay for perfection. If you'd had less, you'd have had less to mourn."

"But why did it happen to us? There are plenty of people.

Mean people. Unhappy people." She was blubbering now, the sobs almost drowning her words.

"Stop that!" he cried. "Stop or I'll hit you, by God." He clutched her coat, gathering the black fur in his fist, as if he actually intended to hold her there until he could haul off and strike. Her blubbering stopped. Her mouth dropped open with shock. Then, lowering her eyes, in fear or in shame, she jerked her coat out of his grip, crossed the platform and once more pressed her face to the window.

From his side, he could see long strings of street lights, glimmering on rain-wet pavements, on telephone wires, on front porches. The rush of the train was abating. There were store fronts, the Christmas-tree colors of neon, before the Palm Queen eased itself into a train shed.

The trainman came out of Fifteen. He brushed against Mrs. Weston. "Excuse me, ma'am, we're making a stop." He opened the hasps of the door, swung it back, hooked it, barring the wide-open doorway with the length of his arm. The train ground to its stop. He stepped on the knob in the floor and turned down the steps. Elaine Weston watched him, following each detail of opening the car.

The henna-haired harridan with the coral earrings and blue slacks emerged from the car, a ratty fur coat over her shoulders, a valise in her hand. She blinked in the murky light of the platform. "Raleigh?" she asked.

"Raleigh."

"Thank God!"

Corbett crossed over the platform. "Want to walk? Stretch your legs." Elaine Weston shook her head numbly.

He swung off the Palm Queen.

The world was impersonal and solid and living down on the platform. People were walking on pavement, coming and going, carrying bags to the train and away, porters trundling their hand-carts, men doing work, in the dead of the night. Alongside the dark, sleeping train, a man dragged his hose to water the cars; another man crouched, lifting journal box lids.

Corbett looked at his watch. Two fifteen.

Down the platform, he saw the ubiquitous food cart. Two men from one of the coaches already were shopping. He looked over the layout: ham and cheese sandwiches, packaged cookies, coffee and milk. He bought a ham and a cheese, a container of coffee, laid down his change, reconsidered, added a cheese sandwich, a carton of coffee. He came back on the train. Elaine Weston was still on the platform, back in his corner this time. "Brought you some food." He thrust a cheese sandwich, a container of coffee at her.

She ignored his hand. "I don't want it."

"The coffee's hot. Do you good."

"I don't need it."

He said, with an upsurge of wrath. "Look, I can't force you to take it. If you just aren't hungry, that's one thing. If you're punishing yourself, that's something else."

She repeated: "Punishing myself?" with the querulous hurt of a child.

He set his own food down on the platform floor. "Oh hell, what's the use? Here." He took her hand, laid a sandwich, a coffee container on her palm. "I don't give a damn what you do with the stuff. Eat it or dump it."

Her face clouded. "I can't understand you. You seem to be giving me hell. Why, what have I done?"

He unwrapped one sandwich, crammed half of a half into his mouth, pried off the lid of his coffee and drank it. It was too sweet and too weak, but its heat stung his gullet and spread welcome warmth through his veins.

The heat of the coffee was apparently reaching her, too, for she shifted the cardboard container from one hand to the other, looked down at her palm, knotting her brows as if making a vital decision. Finally, she pried off the lid with her long fingernail and swallowed the coffee in thirsty gulps.

The trainman, locking the door up again, threw them a nod. "That coffee'll keep you awake. I guess you don't mind."

"It'll keep us warm," Corbett said.

"Steam's going on. You'll be warm." He turned and swung back to Fifteen.

Elaine Weston dropped her empty container. Corbett said: "Now, be a good kid and go back to sleep."

"I can't. I can't ever sleep."

He champed on his sandwich. "Well, hell, do something. Don't stand here like this. Go wash your face. Comb your hair."

She looked offended. "Why?" she protested. "Am I bothering you?"

He squirmed. "Yes and no."

"I am." Her voice rose, over the clash of the cars. "No one can stand me. I'm like a ghost. I haunt—"

He cut in with a gruff: "Shut up."

The tears leaped to her eyes. She whirled, gripped the knob of the door. The sandwich was still in her hand. She noticed it, then, turned full around and flung it at him. The wax paper flew open, scattering bread at his feet. She ran into the car.

He shrugged, finished his coffee and crumpled his cup, let it drop, lighted a cigarette, leaned back in his corner and stood with his back to the wall of the coach, watching the rain-lashed pines and the swift-moving darkness.

The Palm Queen was racing. He felt its speed vibrating from the wheels through the wall of the platform, heard it in the crash of the couplings. The Palm Queen was hurrying, in a rush to get home.

And what for? For my dough, it stinks, and all the Chanel Number Five—He commanded himself not to think of Nina. The girl who thought they were fighting this war for her glamour. The girl who had pumped and had pried, had led him on, kicked him out. He felt hot with anger and shame. All right, suppose she was a dish, suppose that her face was shaped like a heart and her hair was satin and her legs in their black-market nylons ... She needed a bombing to wake her up. Oh, she did? She talked through her hat. Through her silly hat. Forget her, by Christ! You made a mistake. You made a bum guess. There are plenty of women. Turn them all upside down ... That blonde with the lashes and diamonds. Thought he'd fall on his face when she talked about Powers and movie contracts. Sex and dough. That's all they think of. Well, what else is there, anyway? That Hastings kid. Come see me sometime. In lower—what was the number? He considered a moment. That skinny trollop! He decided the hell with that too. The things I got stuck with . . . That Weston woman. The worst of the lot. I didn't need her. Christ, one thing I sure didn't need on this trip was just that. Something warm, something sweet, something kind, understanding. Something soothing and gentle . . . I want mama. All right, I want mama. Not mama. Just someone who knows the score . . . The redhead knows the score. Hell, she knows too well. How can *they* know? Can you know pain till you have felt pain? Can you know fear till you've been afraid? . . . If we had just had one little bombing . . . Christ, forget about Nina. You'll never see Nina again. You don't have to see her. You'll get off this train. There are women and bars. New York's full of women and bars. Forget about . . .

He heard the coach opening, heard the swift swish of fabric, the quick tap of heels, and then the faint rattle of metal. He swung around.

Elaine Weston was lifting the catch of the door of the platform.

He plunged forward, his arms clawing wildly. He caught her. She struggled and kicked him: "Let me go. Let me be." She fought with the frenzy of madness, scratching his face, hammering his chest with her fists. He pushed her from him, toward the locked opposite end of the small corridor. His violent thrust sent him reeling back. The open door, banging, struck him, made him stagger, grapple for something to hold to. His hand caught the elbow of hand rail. He hung on for a moment, swinging until he could steady himself, and then, holding fast with one hand to the thin iron loop, he forced all of his strength into the other to push the door shut against the rush of the wind. He fastened the hasp, lay back on the safely locked door, drenched with his sweat, gasping for breath.

Elaine Weston came at him again, her face writhing, hair

flying wildly. She pounded his chest: "Let me go. Do you hear? Let me go."

He struck her then, a blow on the jaw, so hard, so stunning, that her face went white, her eyes glazed, her knees buckled. She dropped to the floor. With the lurch of the train she slid toward him, lay sprawled at his feet.

When he stood back to get over the shock of the thing he had done, he saw the three women, three blanched, wide-eyed faces, pressed into the glass of the door of the coach. He lifted Elaine's limp body and signalled to them to open the door. He carried her in. Betty Taylor held aside the green ladies' room curtain. The baby was fast asleep, prone on the settee, face turned from the light. He dropped Elaine into a chair. Her eyes were shut, her tanned face the dun color of ashes. Her head lolled on her shoulder, her lank hair streamed over her fur. For a moment, he stood in the circle of white-faced women and just gaped.

"Is she daiud?" The girl from Virginia was wringing her hands.

He knelt then and hunted a pulse, shook his head "no." He looked from one of the girls to the other and pleaded: "I couldn't help it. The damn fool tried to jump."

They nodded together. "We saw her," Betty Taylor breathed. "You had to do it . . . You were wonderful."

He felt slightly relieved. At least someone had seen what had happened. If you had been alone with her on that platform, nobody witnessing, you'd be behind the eight ball. What had happened in here? What had made them run out? He asked and the Southern girl shook her head dumbly: "Ah cain't imagine. We were jes' tawkin'. She was standin' here listenin', just about where ah'm standin'. Wasn't she, Mae? Jus' about heah. All of a sudden we saw her go wiut an' run like a shot."

He watched Elaine's face. "Christ," he thought. "She ought to snap out. I couldn't have hit her that hard." He said: "Give her water. Lots of cold water. On her face. On her head."

Betty Taylor filled a paper cup, dipped her handkerchief in it, tentatively dabbed at the dun-colored cheeks.

"That's not enough!" He snatched the cup from her, dashed the water into Elaine's face.

The Southern girl gasped. "Oh, her fu' coat!"

"Quick. Give me more." A second cup followed the first. He stood back and waited. A moan crept through the gray lips.

"She's comin' to. Lootenant, she's comin' to. She isn't daiud."

The redhead said quietly: "Hadn't we better find her a doctor?" It was the first word she had spoken. "She looks awfully sick. She looked pretty sick, even before this."

"Of course, get her a doctor."

The Southern girl's hands fluttered helplessly. "How can y'all fin' one on heah?"

"Wait." He frowned, trying to recall something that had gone into his ear and out of his mind. "There's one in the Pullmans . . . Glen Argyle . . . I think he said lower twelve. I'll go."

"You gonna leave us with huh? Lak thaut?"

"Just watch her." He was giving his orders as if he was the doctor. "If she comes out, give her water to drink. A few drops. Wet her lips. Don't let her move. In case something's broken." He raised the curtain, slipped out.

Coach Sixteen was restive, not quite awake, but stirring uneasily, as if it had heard something, an outcry, a bang, as part of its sleep, mixed with the noise of the train. He paused beside Elaine's mother-in-law's chair, tweaked her shoulder. He saw her white eyeballs, the spark of a ring as a startled hand fluttered up to her bosom. He bent down and whispered: "Your daughter-in-law. Not feeling well. In the washroom. She needs you."

She glanced quickly down at the sleeping child in the next seat.

He said: "Elaine needs you more. I'm getting a doctor."

"Oh, she's that bad!" The blanket of coat slipped from her knees as she rose.

He sped, ignoring the smart of the hurt when he stumbled
on luggage, through the dim aisle, out of the coach and into
the diner.

There, somebody tossed in the darkness. A drowsy voice
grumbled: "This ain't Penn Station. Stay outa here, boy."

There was a frail glimmer of light from the big mirror back
of the desk when he pitched into the lounge car and while the
door swung to behind him, he saw the reflections of shadows.
The stench of cigar butts was heavy and putrid. His thigh
struck an ash stand; his hip banged an armchair. He heard
sleepy mumbles of protest. He could barely distinguish the
outlines of figures, slumped in the chairs, hear the whisper of
breathing, the scuffle of feet. It was a relief to pause for an
instant in the murk of the platform. A train in the night, he
considered, is an inhuman thing.

He opened the door of Loch Lomond. Close to the entrance,
he saw the small fuzz of light from the washroom and then
the narrow black lane between swaying curtains. He heard the
noises of sleeping, the sighing and snoring and tossing. His eyes
sharpened for the plunge through the sibilant darkness. Ahead
of him, in the aisle, someone, something appeared to be moving, a shape, a human figure, a man fully dressed. It moved
very slowly, not with the purposeful urgency of a passenger
going to washroom, with the soundless, the watchful intentness
of hunter. It paused at one berth and another. It tilted its
head from side to side, listening.

Corbett stopped. The figure stopped, too, turned slightly
back. Some sound he had made, a footfall, an intake of breath,
must have come to its ears.

He stayed, rooted, tense. The figure moved forward. He
heard a light swish as of cloth. Before him stretched the
empty dark cave of the berths.

He went through the car. He saw no one, heard only the
faint yip of a dog behind walls.

He thought: "Christ, I'm off my nut. I'm seeing ghosts."

He crossed over the couplings and into Glen Argyle. It was
going to be tough to locate lower twelve in pitch darkness.

He pulled out his lighter. By the flickering flame he counted off curtains, counted to twelve, thought: "By Jesus, I hope this is right." He rattled a curtain, stage whispering: "Doctor Peck. Doctor Peck."

He heard the light buzz of a snore. "Doctor Peck. Doctor!" The snoring abruptly ceased. There was a thump of a body flipped over, the deep, drawn-in breath of a man waking up. "Doctor Peck, it's Lieutenant Corbett."

A pause, then irritably: "Corbett! What in hell do you want?"

He heard shiftings and turnings around them, a man's voice calling out: "Cut that noise. Have some consideration for others. Talk some place else."

"Doctor Peck, please. A woman's been hurt in my coach."

The curtains were moving. Behind them a light was snapped on. A head emerged through the slit in the curtains. "Oh, it *is* you. Hurt, did you say?"

"Please come right away. It may be serious."

The doctor sighed. "My vacation's over. Night calls again." He sounded disgustingly chipper. "Give me a minute. I'll put on my glasses and pants."

CHAPTER TEN

Elaine looked at him dully and asked in the plaintive whine of a child: "Did you hit me?"

The tip of her chin, magenta and swollen, was more of a reproach than her words and he shifted unhappily from one foot to the other, mumbled "I had to" and looked down at the floor.

The steam pipe was rattling and Elaine had probably not heard his low mumble, for her hurt chin tipped up toward her mother-in-law. "Why did he hit me?"

Dr. Peck whispered: "She doesn't remember a thing. Whatever happened, you knocked it clean out of her head." He stepped around to the back of the chair and delicately prodded the vertebrae at the base of her skull. "Try to turn, please. Easy now. Does that hurt?"

She whimpered. "My head aches. I've a terrible headache."

The dead ash-gray skin had turned saffron. Wet strings of hair plastered her forehead. Her nose looked peaked, sharp, Semitic. Her mother-in-law mopped the matted fur coat with a wad of brown paper. Then with the flat of her hand, she brushed back the damp hair, smoothing it tenderly, as if by trying to make the poor girl look almost human she could make her feel better.

A gawking gallery of females lined the walls, sat in the basins. Mrs. Taylor's baby had awakened and she held him over her shoulder, stroking his back to soothe him and keep him from crying. The girl from Virginia leaned on the mirror door to the toilet, her eyes on Elaine, big with fear. Was she seeing herself, Corbett wondered, herself in the future?

There were one or two new ones, ghouls who had wandered in, no doubt, on personal business, and had stayed to lap up the details of another's misfortune. They kept staring at him.

Dr. Peck asked: "Who has a match?"

Corbett took out his lighter.

"Good." Dr. Peck flipped it open. "Now look straight at this," he commanded Elaine. "Into the flame." She blinked. He peered into her eyes, said: "Good," again, and "Now, get up. Let's see how you walk."

Her mother-in-law steadied her arm, helping her up. Elaine took a few mincing steps, made doubly difficult by the sway of the train. The doctor asked anxiously: "How is it? Feel dizzy?"

"Just tired."

"We'll let you rest. Suppose all you clear out. Leave her alone. Her mother can stay. I'll keep her company a while."

Corbett touched the arm of the two girls in slacks. He said: "Come out to the platform. Let's light up a butt." He noted a flurry of alarm in their faces and he smiled grimly: "Take it easy. I don't go around smacking down women. Not as a rule."

The floor of the platform was littered with butts, with crumpled coffee containers and scattered, cheese-smeared bread slices. Rain ran down in streams against the glass of the doors. The girls glanced at the side door uneasily. "I locked it." He grimaced. "You're safe."

The red-headed girl shuddered. "Gee, I thought you'd never close that. You must be strong. Did you strain yourself?"

He shrugged. "Never did care about taking the jump without the chute." He took his cigarettes out and offered the pack.

The red-head took one but the other said "No. Mah stomach. It feels kinda queah. Ah bettuh not smoke."

The red-head drew in, let out the smoke very slowly. She said: "She looks awful."

"She does."

"She'll be all right?"

"I guess so. No bones are broken."

"What did he do that for—with your lighter?"

"Concussion. Possible brain injury. See how her eyes focus."

The girl glanced at the wings on his sleeve. "How do you know all those things? You're not a doctor?"

"The bombardier's first aid man of his crew."

"How funny!"

"A scream." He laughed his bitter, brief chortle.

The Southern girl cried: "You stop that. You give me the shivuhs."

The redhead was regarding him thoughtfully. "Too bad this happened to you!"

"You can't call your shots in this game."

"But you had enough. You rate a pleasant furlough."

He let his cigarette burn at his side for a moment or two, while they stood, all three, in a tense, waiting silence, rocking with the train. Finally, he took a deep puff, dropped the butt, said: "Now, tell me what happened. What made her do that?"

The redhead stared at him strangely, then averted her face. "I wouldn't know. I never spoke one single word to her. None of us did."

He shook his head emphatically. "Not good enough, sister. There was something. Something that gave her the push. What was it? I want to know."

She shrugged: "We thought she was queer the minute we saw her. She came in the room and didn't say one single thing to us all. Not even hello. She went in the can and when she came out she looked at herself in the mirror. Oh, a very long time. Not fixing her hair, though God knows her hair needed fixing, not powdering her nose, not even washing her hands. Just looking at herself in the mirror. We were talking. All three of us. Betty and Sue here and me. Sue, what were we talking about?"

"Ouah babies," Sue said.

"Oh yes." The redhead let out a mouthful of smoke. "Sue said she never took her kid on a train yet. But Betty and me, I guess we been living on trains. Good God, I bet I traveled ten thousand miles before my husband was shipped. This is the first time I left my kid home. I told them I used to give my kid that prepared baby food, straight out of the can, cold, like it was. My mother had fits when I told her. Never did the baby no harm. He's fat as a pig. And it saved me a fortune in tips to the porter."

Corbett cleared his throat impatiently. "Look, this isn't—"

She sighed. "I guess men aren't interested in babies. That's service wives' business . . . Well, I guess she wasn't interested, either. Betty was sitting on the couch with her baby. Sue and me, we had the two chairs. That's all there is, just two and the couch. She just hung around. Like she wanted to be where somebody was. I asked her once did she want to sit down but she said no, she was tired of sitting." Her forehead creased. "Come to think of it, that's all she did say the whole time we were there . . . Then she went out and after we passed Raleigh, she came in again."

"And you were still talking babies?"

"Why, no." The girl had burned her cigarette down. She stamped its fire out on the wall, broke the butt open, scattered the tobacco grains and rolled up the paper. "Learned that from my husband," she said. "One thing I learned from the Army." Then she went on, as though she had taken the brief interlude to gather her thoughts. "Why, no, we weren't talking about babies when she came in again. We were talking about what we did in Miami. Betty was just telling me about the place where she lived. The woman rented her one room, with kitchen privilege, for sixty-five dollars. Sixty-five dollars a month! Can you beat it? Said she was doing her a favor. She knew she could get eighty-five from the tourists. That wasn't the worst. She kept cats in the kitchen. Betty said she bet there were one dozen cats. It smelled something awful. Just turned her stomach whenever she had to go in to fix something for the kids. Then Sue here, she said—"

Sue paled, her eyes slightly bulged. Corbett saw her lay a finger over her lips. The other hadn't noticed the warning or didn't want to. She went on: "Sue here, she said, Saturday night she went out with her husband to see all the sights in Miami. They went out to the Beach. They walked down Lincoln Road, that street that has all the swell stores—"

"Mae, Ah don't really think the Lootenant's interested in that."

Mae paused, raised her eyebrows.

Sue braided her fingertips, faltered: "Ef y'all don' min', it's chilly out heah. Ah think Ah bettuh go in."

The redhead's lips thinned. "You go in if you want to. I'll tell."

Sue had her hand on the knob. She looked back, unsurely, from the redhead to Corbett. She quavered: "Ah'm gettin' off, anyway. Ah have to get mah things all together."

Mae nodded, frigidly. "Go on in, if you want to."

"Ah'll see you befo' I git off?"

"I'll be on the train. I'm not jumping."

When the door had opened and shut behind Sue, the redhead moved over to Corbett. "I know what ails her," she said. "She thinks she made that woman do that." She wagged her head somberly. "I just caught on. She *knows* she did. It was what she said about Miami. She said when she and her husband walked down that street and saw all those women in fur coats and diamonds, she said to her husband: 'That's what I sent you away to fight for.' " She tried to mimic the Southern accent but it didn't come off. "And he said to her: 'Honey, don't worry. Don't worry your pretty head. After I finish the Germans and Japs, I'll come back and get *them*.' "

So that was it. The plague that had poisoned all Europe was festering here too, growing and feeding on war.

"I tried to tell her Christians wear diamonds, Christians wear furs, Catholics and Protestants, they're all making money and spending it just like water. I've seen them do it, not only Miami. All over the country . . . Say, you're not a Jew?"

"Presbyterian. Way back. Not that it matters."

She let out her breath. "Well, that's a relief! You know how touchy they are. Even when you try to show you're on their side or you're trying to be honest and fair, they blow up — Well, Betty, I don't know just what she thinks but she tried to sort of be in-between. She said I was right but Sue was right, too. Jews ought to be extra careful what they did now because it was all on account of them we were having this war. It was all on account of them the government took our husbands away and we were living like this, traveling in pigsties of coaches, no home for our kids, worrying and working ourselves to the bone. And if her husband was killed, why she guessed she'd just go out herself and kill every one she could find. When Betty said that, that girl made some funny sound, like a choke. And went out like a shot."

"That woman's husband was killed. On the Anzio beachhead."

"Oh no!" Mae clapped her hand over her mouth. She looked white and stricken. Tears gushed into her eyes. "Oh no. She never said. How could we guess?"

"She's Jewish," he said. "Couldn't you even guess that?"

Mae didn't answer at first. Then, very slowly, she said: "I guess maybe Sue did hope she was and she was telling her off for the others." Her face turned up to his, white and grave. "That's what did it, I guess."

"I'm ashamed of my country," he said. "People like this aren't worth fighting for. They aren't worth dying for. Aren't worth killing for."

"Oh please!" She touched his sleeve. "Don't blame me. I don't hate them. I don't want to get even. I just want Mike back. I got no prejudice against anyone. They all believe in God, same's you and me."

He stiffened against the wall and said sternly. "Jews are *fighting* this war. They're dying. Like Catholics, Protestants, Mohammedans, Atheists. To make a safe world for your kids. And they've taken the beating. The very worst beating. The first. From Hitler. While you and I sat on our fannies and said it was none of our business. Tell Susie that!"

She kept still again, looking down at the floor. "She don't know. *They* don't know," she finally said. "Nobody teaches them. Nobody tells them those things. They're like kids. They don't understand. Nothing's happened to them, don't you see? Nothing important, I mean. It'll take something terrible, something to shake them out of their mean little lives." She looked up at him earnest-faced. "Something like bombing, I mean." She stared, her mouth dropping open. "Why do you do that? Rubbing your hands?"

He pushed his hands out of sight, behind his coat-tails. He felt himself flushing. He bit his lips. After a wait, he said: "Go in and see how she is."

She went in and came out in a minute. "She's sleeping. She's asleep on the couch. Her mother's there with her."

"Her mother-in-law," Corbett said. "A soldier's mother. A dead soldier's mother. Tell Susie that, too."

He held the door for her and they went into the coach. Betty Taylor had come back to her chair with her baby. She whispered: "Is she all right?"

"She's sleeping."

"That's good."

He tried to crawl over the horseplayer's knees. Kalchis jerked back his legs. "Where you been all this time?" His voice was sharp with suspicion. "What in hell's goin' on?"

Corbett stretched his legs to the footrail of the chair in front. His muscles ached. His armpits and shoulders felt sore. Weariness poured through his body. He closed his eyes, tried to sleep. In a few moments he knew that he couldn't and wouldn't.

Beside him, Kalchis was shifting and scratching. Beneath him, wheels grated the rails. He felt the speed of the train. The Palm Queen was making up time, racing toward the North. Thank God for that. Let this long night end, this trip be over. The sense of repetition struck him again, the feeling he'd had in that Miami alley, of something done over and over. Now, measuring time. Waiting and praying and sweating for time to be ended; the hours of fighters and flak till the target was reached; the minutes till the bombs were away; the counting of missions, so many done, so many more till the furlough back home . . . Back home to sweat out this journey. Life repeated itself. It never left you alone. If you kept your mind open, if you left your heart open, it came at you . . . It threw the book. And you took it. Or tried not to take it. That was best. Don't take it. It doesn't mean me. Stand off and duck. Watch the other guys get it. Hurts less that way. Hurts them. Not me. "God—" He heard himself praying—"Teach me how to close my eyes, close my mind, close my heart. Deliver me from evil and pain. If you push me, keep on crowding me any more, I'll jump off a train . . ."

Elaine Weston's sombre figure moved into the nub of his mind. It moved in, whirling like a black dervish, fighting for death. Gradually, it quieted, faded, dwindled and changed. It had a new face and new form. Why, that was Nina! The sleek, dressed-up pretty. She was wriggling and squirming, fighting off something, a hand, the touch of a hand on the careful arrangements of fabric and paint that made you think she was a woman . . .

Kalchis was mumbling at him. Kalchis was trying to get him to answer a question. With an effort he brought his attention around.

"What time is it? Know the time?"

The time? Oh, the horseplayer hadn't a watch. Dr. Peck had told him the time from a platinum turnip. He thrust out his wrist. On the luminous dial they made out ten after four. This side of daybreak.

Kalchis yawned. "Cripes, I'm tired. I can't never sleep in these cars."

"I saw you were sleeping all right."

The man's head turned. He could see the bright sheen of the coal chips. "Yeh," Kalchis said. "I was sleeping. I was sleeping awright until you come in."

Why had he said that so quickly, emphatically? Christ, he *had* slept. "I saw him here snoring." Corbett sat up with a start. He thought: "If he's been up to some lousy trick." You were helpless on trains! If you slept in a sleeper, you had to have trust in mankind. "Christ, I'm like Christ. Between thieves. One thief. Hell, give the poor crumb charity. Benefit of a doubt, anyway."

Back in the coach there was fumbling with luggage. A porter's white coat zig-zagged down the aisle toward the exit.

Kalchis asked: "We stoppin' again? Is it Richmond awready?"

"Thank God!" He remembered the frizzy-haired hag who had stepped off at Raleigh. Thank God for each station achieved.

A valise bumped the seat. Who got off at Richmond? Oh yes, the sweet little pixie from Dixie. Too bad her stop wasn't Raleigh. Might have saved Elaine Weston a sock on the jaw. "I'll talk to Elaine," he decided. "After breakfast, I'll sit down with her. I'll try to make clear— Make what clear? That the right to hate belonged to democracy . . . That you fought for the right of people to say what they pleased, to think as they pleased . . . Even destroy one another? Hell, no . . . All right, then what? About tolerance. I hate that word. It's snide.

I'm better than you but I won't push your face in. Equality? You can't have equality except between equals. Where's there equality? Only in death . . . Tell her that? She'll get a hell of a lot of comfort from that one. I'll tell her she ought to be glad her husband died as a victor, not victim. Died like a man. A free man. *Died*. That was the point. That was all she knew, wanted to know . . . I'll talk about what we're fighting for. For a cause that's bigger than people. For country. But country is people. It's Kalchis and Hastings and Sweet Sue from Virginia and Voorhees . . . And nothing! . . . If you can only stop thinking of individual people. Think of movements, ideas and forces. Life has more meaning without faces and voices. Christ, I'm mixed up . . . Who the hell isn't?"

He felt the train slowing and let the window shade up. The pane was opaque with car heat on cold glass, and ploughed by the furrows of rain. Yellow lights twinkled through the rushing slate fog.

The Marine was reaching up to the rack for his bag, coat and cap. Corbett heard grandma's voice, fretting: "What you look for?"

The Corporal answered her patiently: "It's my station. I change here for Quantico."

"Quantico? New York?"

"Virginia."

"Oh. You live here? . . . I'm sorry I make you so much trouble all night. You're a fine boy. I wish you good luck."

"That's okay, grandma. You're okay, too. You just tell the kiddies you been sleepin' all night with the U. S. Marines. So long. Get home safe."

All through the coach, people were stirring, aroused by the voices and change of pace of the train. Joanie wailed: "Mommy, it's dark. I'm scared."

"Hush, darling. It's all right, darling." Betty Taylor was hoarse with fatigue. "Go back to sleep, sweetie-pie."

"My foot hurts me, mommy. My foot is all tired."

"Hush, baby. Hush, darling. You'll wake brother up."

"Mommy—" Her whimper trailed off. The baby made sounds, a soft throaty coo, like a croak.

Dr. Frankel was rootching around. He whispered gutturally: "Where are we? Where's Mrs. Weston?"

Corbett muttered to Kalchis. "Let me out. Don't you want to walk? Stretch your legs?"

"Me? Nope. Not me. I stay in my seat nights on a train."

As Corbett slid through the passage, Dr. Peck thrust aside the washroom curtain. "Well, Lieutenant. I'd been wondering what happened to our Good Samaritan. Remember what *he* got, don't you?"

"How is she?" he asked.

"Still asleep. No obvious damage. Her mother and I have been talking. Her husband's mother . . . That's a fine woman. Strong as a tree. An oak, I should say. Deep roots. No matter what storms. Lord knows she's had plenty to take in her life. If our younger generation had just a small bit of that wonderful faith in the wisdom, the ultimate justice of God." He put up his liver-flecked hand to stifle a yawn. "Think if I went back to my berth, I could still get some sleep?"

"You might try it, sir."

"Where are we?" He leaned across Corbett and tried to see through the steam-frosted glass.

"It's Richmond."

"Fine. Almost home. What time is it now?" He fumbled sleepily for vest pockets and then realized that over his trousers were only the top of pajamas. "Oh damn! Left my watch and my wallet in there."

Corbett felt a twinge, but he hastened to reassure Dr. Peck. "They'll be safe. I'm certain they will."

"Of course they will. You do have a watch. What time is it now?" Corbett stretched out his wrist.

"Four-fifteen, eh? Practically on the nose, isn't it?"

"Made up some time over night. We were riding like crazy."

"Too busy to notice . . . Well, see you some time. After Wilmington . . . Philadelphia."

Mrs. Weston's gray hair and drawn, haggard face came

around the curtain. "Doctor, Elaine's waking up. Will it be all right for her to get up?"

"As long as she feels well enough. No vertigo. Nausea. I'm quite sure there is no concussion. I'd put a cold compress on that jaw. Ask the porter to get you some ice and a towel. Assure him you won't sue the railroad." He winked at Don Corbett and patted his shoulder. "You're okay, my boy."

Mrs. Weston said: "You saved her life. I want to thank you." She extended her hand. He took it, scuffing his feet like a schoolboy.

"Elaine will thank you herself some day. Poor girl!" She sighed: "She has nothing. That's what it is. You have to have something to live for. I always had something. Max. Now Elaine . . . If she could find something."

Corbett said. "The train's stopped. Who wants some hot coffee?"

Dr. Peck shook his head. "None for me, thanks. I need my sleep. Bring some for them. Make your peace."

The train shed at Richmond was night-gloomy and chill but here, as at Raleigh, was that incredible bustle and stir of life and work going on in the dead of the night: trucks rolling, piled high with cartons, bales, trunks and duffles; sullen-faced workmen, shuffling along with hose nozzles and oil spouts; people arriving, departing, and, way down the track, the refreshment stand. Two men were buying stacks of sandwiches, cartons of coffee, so many it seemed they were stocking a party. Corbett made his own purchases quickly: three cartons of coffee, a package of cigarettes. He handed two coffees in through the washroom curtains, returned to the platform to drink his own coffee before the train started. The porter locked up the door, scowled at the litter of butts, bread and coffee containers. "Jus' pigs," he mumbled. "Jus' pigs in a sty."

The platform was cold, a raw stuffy cold, but you could see through the rain-slathered windows, watch the black sky dimming to slate, see houses and trees taking form, street lights of towns looking wan in the misted dawn. For some distance he followed the white headlights and red warning lamps of a huge truck with a trailer, racing the Palm Queen on a highway parallel to the track. The guy was traveling but the Palm Queen was beating him out. "We're doing better than sixty," he thought. "The rain slows him up. We can make time but he can't."

He felt the drumming vibration of iron, the ear-splitting clash of the cars. It plucked at his nerves. He crossed over the platform. He saw a broad stretch of wind-whipped water, shimmering steel beneath the lowering sky. The heavens were cushions of rain bearing clouds, round, fecund, dark . . . like the flak. He crossed again to the side he had come from. There were freight trains on sidings; long strings of red, yellow, brown.

The trees here looked barren. They had only the palest of timid green feathers on wet, shiny branches. The dooryards were muddy. In one a forsythia bush was bowed to the ground by the wind, dragging its gold-yellow flowers in the mire. When you whizzed through a town, you could see people in raincoats standing on corners, beneath dripping umbrellas, waiting for busses.

It was full seven o'clock when he finally saw the fawn-colored tower of the Masonic Monument at Alexandria, and then the sprawl of the Pentagon, the pewter Potomac, pock-marked by rain, the shimmering black cars whizzing over its bridge, the network of rails and overhead power lines, and finally the Monument, a slender white pointer, tip lost in the mist.

When the train slid into the Washington shed, he went back to his car. Sixteen was by now fully awake. Its shades were all up. It was vocal and busy, digging under the seats for its overnight cases, climbing up on the chairs to get boxes and bags from the rack. The middle-aged couple in one and two were already peeling their oranges, shelling hard-boiled eggs.

Kalchis had moved over into his seat and was moodily doodling the pane. He muttered: "You want to sit down?" but made no move to get up. The man looked white, drawn, exhausted. Corbett climbed on a chair to get down his bag from the rack. He was teetering there, precariously balancing himself, when Elaine and her mother came up the aisle.

Elaine's hair had been combed, her nose powdered. There was rouge on her lips. When she saw Corbett standing up on the seat, her slate eyes grew cloudy and fearful. She swayed, reached toward a chair. Her mother-in-law's arm went out quickly. "I'm all right, mother. I really am." She managed a smile.

"I'm sorry we took your seats," Betty Taylor said anxiously. "I'll pick Joanie up. I've got to wash up the children and give them their breakfasts."

This time Elaine Weston's smile was more sure of itself. "I'm sorry we dispossessed you from the washroom."

"Elaine had a nap," her mother-in-law offered. "It did her good."

"I'm glad." The gunner's mate's wife touched Elaine's sleeve timidly. "I can't tell you how sorry I am," she began. To hide her embarrassment, she reached over for Joanie. "Come, darling. Let the lady sit down."

"Please let me." Elaine Weston slid into the space, lifted Joanie into her lap. "Let me hold her a while. Till you're done with the baby."

Joanie eyed her, suspicious, still sleepy, and then snuggled her pigtails against Elaine's breast. "You smell nice," she announced. "Like mommy's powder. I like your smell."

*   *   *   *   *

The men's room was full of stretching and yawning and groaning, of men stripped to their undershirts, sputtering like porpoises as they slathered their faces with tepid, rusty water, rubbed neck and armpits with rough paper towels; shaving with tortuous slowness; struggling with shoes that wouldn't go on; griping incessantly: "God what a night! First you freeze; then you roast." . . . "Those seats. Made out of cast iron." . . . "Took off my shoes. My feet are so swollen, I can't get 'em on." . . . "Did you see how it's raining! Bet they got snow in New York. We come back too soon." . . . "Say how late are we?" . . . "Not much. Made up some time." "Oh yeah! What was that long stop?" . . . "Hot box, they say." . . . "Hot box, hey? Believe me, it feels like a hot-box in here, right this minute." . . . "Say what was that noise on the platform?" . . . "Some woman fell down." . . . "Dumb dope. Who tells her to walk around on a train? Could she sue?" . . . "Some dope in the car kept walking all night. My wife wanted to sock him." . . . "You got no kick. I hear they had a poker game on all night in Fifteen." . . . "Say, why don't nobody tell me these things? I might of made me some change. If my luck is still running. It was running awright in Miami." . . . "Miami? Where's that? Never heard of the place." . . . "Couple more hours and we're home."

CHAPTER ELEVEN

Nina stood in the passage at the far end of the diner and Corbett tried to deny to himself that his heart skipped a beat when he caught sight of her there.

There were two empty tables, both fours, at her end of the car. She could have been seated if she hadn't obviously been waiting for someone. "Me," he thought first and quickly amended his thought. "She's waiting for one of her pals . . . Forget her. By Christ, put her out of your mind."

He sat down at the large table nearest his entrance with his back to her doorway, picked up the menu and busied himself with the choice between prunes, oatmeal, rolls, coffee, sixty cents; or fruit juice, bacon and eggs, toast, coffee, eighty-five.

Without looking up from the card, he knew she had taken

the opposite chair. The scent of Chanel Number Five crossed the cloth.

He kept his head down, writing with painstaking slowness: "Orange juice (double); two eggs and bacon, toast (buttered); coffee (pot)." When the waiter had ripped off his order blank, he looked through the broad window pane.

Delaware's flat fields slid past. The rain seemed to have thickened and was probably sleet. The few cars you could see on the highways were crawling along. He wondered idly what railroads did about ice on the tracks. Sand the rails? Reduce speed? Probably nothing. Trains held the track regardless of weather. Trains didn't skid, collect ice on their wings. Oh, all right, they had rear-end collisions or washouts or signal switch failures, splayed rails. But not on these main lines. On crack tourist trains like the Palm Queen, you were safe as a babe in its cradle, snug as a bug in a rug. Warm, dry, fed on linen and china.

He heard Nina say softly: "Hello, Don."

Without shifting his gaze, he answered, with cold politeness: "Good morning."

"It isn't. It looks like I feel."

The waiter placed his whole breakfast between them; a vial of yellowish fluid, two grease-swimming eggs, two underdone strips of bacon, a plate of charred toast, a scabrous coffee pot, a thick cup and saucer, and he had no further pretext for just watching rain.

He drank his fruit juice. It was watered. He thought: "That's a laugh. On a Florida train you can't get good orange juice." He kept his head down while he tackled the bacon and eggs.

Her voice and perfume came at him. "Look, Don. We have to talk this thing out. I can't let you think I'm only a ——"

His lashes flicked up. "Ladies don't use four letter words at the table."

She was scribbling her order. Her pencil had stopped. "How would you know about ladies?" The sarcasm was only an act. A tremor in her voice gave her away.

While he swallowed a forkful of bacon and eggs, broke off a corner of toast, he heard Joanie's squeal: "Ooh, it's a restoo-runt!" He looked up, past Nina's shoulders. The Westons were leading the child in for breakfast. Elaine held Joanie's hand. She saw him and averted her glance when she went by the table. Yet he felt he had to say something. But what do you say to a woman whom you've socked on the jaw? "Oh, have we met? The bruise is familiar but the hairdo is different." He said: "Good morning. Hello, Joanie." Neither one of them seemed aware he had spoken.

The older Mrs. Weston, just behind them, paused at his table. "Elaine thought she'd like to give Joanie breakfast. When we get through, we'll take care of the baby, let Mrs. Taylor come in for a change. Poor thing. She's had nothing but sandwiches since we left Miami."

When they had passed to the four further down, Nina asked: "Who're your friends?"

"No one you'd know."

"I might like to."

"You wouldn't. They aren't your kind."

The waiter set down her breakfast: tomato juice, unbuttered toast, coffee. After he'd gone, Nina said: "You're not fair. You won't even give me a chance to set this thing straight."

He rested his fork on the rim of his plate. "If you don't mind, I don't feel like discussions this morning. I'm hungry. I'm tired. I've been up most of the night."

She came in at once. She'd been apparently waiting for just that lead. "I didn't sleep either. Didn't shut my eyes all night long."

There *were* mauve shadows beneath her eyes, but insomnia hadn't changed the heart shape of her face or the sweep of dark, wonderful lashes. Her full lips were crimson, her hair sleekly brushed, not one strand out of place, the filigree shells on her ears. His eyebrows rose skeptically. "You look fresh as a daisy."

"It's a trick. All done with mirrors. Women have ways." She talked fast, seemed to be fearful that if she let the dialogue lapse she'd lose his attention forever. "A little skin freshener. Stuff out of bottles. Cold towel on the eyes. Rouge and lipstick." She showed her fine teeth in a smile, too gay, too flirtatious, too plainly hopeful he'd pick up that line and go on to casual banter. But when he merely went on, methodically slicing fried egg with his fork, crunching on toast, she erased the smile and bent over toward him. "Look, Don, I know I behaved very badly. I didn't intend to. I wanted so much to help you, to be understanding. . . . It isn't easy. You seemed to feel, to expect. . . ."

His fork clicked on his plate. "Expect what?" he asked coldly.

She took a sip of tomato juice to gain courage, gulped, dabbed her lips with her napkin. Not daring to look at his eyes, she began again: "Don, I knew what you wanted, how badly you needed it, too."

How badly! Christ, how badly! A door had been slammed. Let it stay.

"Don." Her face was so desperately earnest it was almost convincing. "I'm ashamed of myself. I bawled myself out all night long. 'Why couldn't you give that poor guy what he wanted?' I kept asking myself. 'It's so little compared to what he has already given.' I felt like a crumb."

His brows rose again. He speared his last curl of bacon.

That was new, a hell of a note, a girl apologizing because a guy couldn't make her.

She finished her tomato juice before she started once more. "But I couldn't. Really, I couldn't. You see, I'm not—Oh, I sound like a girl-about-town. But that's not the real me. Just the surface. The veneer you need in my business." She was feeling around for her words and trying to smile while she groped. The smile was insurance, to stiffen her backbone. "You see, well, it's simply, I'm just not a Victory girl."

His mouth twisted. "And why not?" He went on with his breakfast.

A blush mounted her cheeks, turning the tan into Virginia red clay. She said: "Oh please!" set down her glass, opened her handbag, took out the gray box of *Parliaments,* pretended she couldn't find matches and waited for him to bring out his lighter.

He didn't. Instead, he inspected the diner. The grande dame with the feathers was having waffles with syrup and butter opposite a gaunt man who was taking stewed prunes. Mrs. Hastings and Pat were eating alone at a two. Rauchmeyer sat across from Captain Metzger. The young Captain seemed far more concerned with the landscape than with the head of the Rauchmeyer chain. At the far end, the coach entrance end, the faces were new, probably out of Fifteen and Fourteen and Thirteen and back of that. He turned from the car to see what there was in the varying vista. There was brown and red brick: Baldwin Locomotive. There were words on a sign: WHAT CHESTER MAKES, MAKES CHESTER. There were ice-coated pavements and overhead wires. There was steady rain.

Nina's smoke blew in his face. "Lieutenant Corbett!" She wouldn't give up. Well, they can't shoot you for trying. He poured himself coffee. "Yes, ma'am," he said, breathing a long-suffering sigh.

"Miss Gilmore to you!" She was trying a new tactic, the kidding around with which they had been most successful before. "Lieutenant, if I might suggest, some evening when we're both in New York. At my apartment, for instance. My liquor is good. My cook is first rate. When we're not so sleepy, so much under strain, we might hold a symposium on whether or not it's every girl's duty—her patriotic duty—to give every soldier who asks what he seems to want. It should be talked over, gone into thoroughly. What do you say we start tonight?"

"I'm busy tonight."

Her smile faded. "A date?"

"You bet. With a bartender I know."

"Oh! Tables for ladies?"

"You stand at the bar."

"It's a date."

He shook his head. "Oh no, my beauty. You're a smart operator but not on Don Corbett. One kick in the pants is enough."

She lowered her head while she poured out a cup of black coffee. He saw tears on the rims of her lashes. His heart betrayed him again. He felt it melting, even wanting to comfort her and steeled himself to resist. He poured out his coffee and generous cream, stirred in the sugar.

The glass beads on her eyelids trembled with the Palm Queen's vibration. They were going to fall off. He said: "Look, if you prefer salt in coffee—"

Her chin came quickly up. The beads jumped. They dropped on her cheeks and rolled down. She bent over her handbag to hunt a handkerchief. It gave her a chance to conceal the short struggle to steady herself.

He drained his coffee cup and refilled it, lighted a cigarette.

She gave one final dab at her eyes, sipped her black coffee, pushed back her half-emptied cup. "Don, I must make you see—"

"I see well enough." Behind the smoke his eyes were unblinking agates.

"I can't let you think that I'm just a—"

"Why not?" His voice was chipped ice. He flicked off his ash in his coffee-wet saucer. "Why should you care what I think?"

"Oh, because—" She commenced to play with her spoon.

"Don't tell me I picked New York's only virgin."

She blushed to the roots of her hair. "You can be cruel." She took another mouthful of coffee. "Look, Don, please don't be sarcastic. Maybe I deserve what you're doing to me. And maybe I don't. It wasn't a question of morals or virtue . . . I'm a grown woman. I can do what I please with myself. That's why I'm ashamed."

He felt himself reddening too and puffed out some smoke to veil his flushed face. He said frigidly, "There are a few words in the language I hate. One of them's charity. Another one's pity."

That stopped her.

She twisted the napkin, pleating it between her scarlet-tipped fingers, and desperately trying to think of how to go on.

The Palm Queen had halted. On the long, bleak platform, travelers were gathering their baggage, striding toward exits. He saw a pretty young WAC, brisk and soldierly, stride down the platform, rush into the arms of a middle-aged man, get a kiss on each cheek.

He doused his cigarette in the dregs of his coffee and looked around for his waiter. "If you'll excuse me, Miss Gilmore," he said, "we'll call it quits. A mistake all around. I guessed wrong. You guessed wrong."

She said: "Please!" and stretched her arm over the table, her hand on top of his. "Don't say good-by like this . . . Don, let me try to explain. Don't look like that . . . There was a sort of hysteria yesterday . . . It got both of us. It was wrong. It was ugly."

He drew his hand back, folded his arms on his chest. "Since that's so, why go on?"

"Because I want to go on. I want to set this as straight as I can. My conscience means something to me. . . . Each time before—Oh, New York's not a nunnery—there was, well, let's call it romance." She was stammering and stumbling. "You look for, expect, well, to be courted, to feel you're something special, not just a—a convenience."

It was hurting him as much as it hurt her. He looked away, hoping that something would happen, someone would come and make her stop talking.

Two men at the table for two across the aisle dropped their tip coins on the cloth, rose and went out toward the Pullmans. An old couple, both white-thatched, thin, threadbare neat, came down the aisle from the coach entrance and timorously sat at that table for two.

Then Mrs. Forsythe came down the car, her face pale, eyes distraught. She saw Corbett and the two vacant chairs at his table and dropped into the seat next to him. She said: "Good morning, Lieutenant," and seemed glad he was there. Nina examined her covertly, took out her compact and began to powder her nose and do up her lips.

He gave Mrs. Forsythe his friendliest smile: "You're almost too late for breakfast."

"Am I?" She seemed more distressed than mere missing of bad toast and coffee would warrant. "I waited for Mr. Voorhees."

"These elderly men—" he suggested.

"Oh no, he mentioned particularly that he was an early riser. That I should be ready for breakfast at eight."

He shrugged, smiled again. "Overslept. His watch stopped. Did you ask the porter to call him?"

"Why no." Her blue eyes grew larger. "Does one do that?"

"Porter will probably do it himself. Give the man time to get dressed."

"But he was quite definite—I couldn't have misunderstood —about breakfast at eight. I woke at seven myself . . . As a matter of fact, I scarcely slept all night long."

Nina coughed. He knew she was trying to come into the conversation.

Across the aisle, the elderly couple were having trouble. "But we only want coffee," he heard the man say.

"Cain't serve you jus' coffee."

"But he—the headwaiter—said we could have coffee."

"With somethin' else."

"Arthur." The woman nudged her husband. "How much is toast?"

"It's all right, mother." He stroked her arm reassuringly. "Waiter, bring us one order of toast. Whole wheat toast."

The waiter came over to Mrs. Forsythe, picked up her blank card and scowled. Corbett asked: "Shall I write out your order?"

"If you please. I'm so frightfully nervous this morning. I'm afraid I can't write. Why, my hand shakes! . . . Grapefruit and porridge and tea."

"Good Lord," Corbett thought. "She means business. She's

worried about that old man." He began: "Oh come now, come, come," but she interrupted: "You see, during the night—I had the upper, you know, over him. He did suggest changing but I wouldn't consider—he seemed so restless, thrashing about, making strange noises." The fear in her eyes grew as she talked. "Almost as if . . . Lieutenant, have you ever heard a death rattle?"

He said sharply: "Stop that!"

Across the table, Nina asked sweetly: "Is anything wrong? Can I help?"

Mrs. Forsythe glanced at her quickly, startled at first and then relieved, visibly eager to draw Nina into her circle of trouble. She gave Corbett no choice but to mumble their names to each other. Nina promptly took over: "You seemed so distressed I had to barge in."

"Oh, but I am. My friend,"—Her tongue tripped on the word—"Mr. Voorhees, he made a definite engagement for breakfast but he hasn't—"

She fell silent as Dr. Peck slid into the one vacant seat at the table, raised his hand in a hint of salute. The doctor looked weary. His smile was abstracted. He nodded at Mrs. Forsythe and at Corbett and picked up a menu.

Corbett jerked his head backwards: "Seen your patient this morning?"

"How is she? . . . Anything happen after I left?"

"She's fine," Corbett said. "Eating breakfast and feeding a kid. Back there. You passed by her table."

"Good." Dr. Peck didn't look. Corbett thought that was queer. He asked: "Why, what's wrong?"

Dr. Peck glanced uncertainly from Mrs. Forsythe to Nina. Nina said: "Don, you know *more* people. Do you have to be told you should introduce—"

"Miss Gilmore, Dr. Peck."

"Glad to know Dr. Peck. Aren't you in my car?"

"Glen Argyle?"

Of course. This is just like New York. We sleep under one roof, yet we've never met."

"If we sleep under one roof," he no longer tried to be off-hand, "you may as well know, we've a thief in our midst. Corbett, my wallet was stolen last night and my watch. Probably while I was out on that call."

Corbett moved back in his chair. He thought: "So I wasn't crazy . . . I saw it. By God, what I saw must have been a thief." Then his mind leaped, without prompting, to the nervous man in Sixteen, doodling designs on a steam frosted window. "Reported it, sir?"

Dr. Peck shrugged. "Just discovered my loss. When I dressed. Oh, I'll report it. When I find the conductor. But what good will that do? Will they search every passenger? Will they know who got off at Richmond, at Washington, Baltimore, Wilmington? They will not. However—" He raised his shoulders. "Who steals my purse just steals trash. Fourteen dollars. My watch. That's different. But I trust the police. They'll find it eventually. It's inscribed, you see: 'Presented to Dr. Amos Corydon Peck by the staff of—' The usual. It will be traced."

The waiter set down Mrs. Forsythe's fruit, oatmeal and tea, pushed the order slip under Dr. Peck's hand. He began to read the menu, suddenly stopped, thrust his fingers into his pocket and brought out a handful of coins. "Forty-four, forty-five, forty-six, fifty-six. . . . Is that a dime or one of those silly steel pennies? . . . Can I eat for this much?"

"Put it back," Corbett said. "You're eating on me."

"Oh, I couldn't. Not from—"

"We get paid," Corbett said. "Cash money. Big risks. Big dough."

The doctor juggled the coins on his palm. "If that's the case, you must lend me a dollar besides. I have to get home." He grimaced sourly. "Good Samaritans, both of us. What was it they did to the Good Samaritan? Beat him and robbed him. Oh well, we've one break. We divided the punishment."

"I wish you two would be serious," Nina broke in. "You say you were robbed?"

The doctor put back his coins. "I've learned to reserve diag-

nosis until all the data are in. My possessions may well be mis-
laid. In any event, I can't say this junket was dull. Madam,"
he leaned over the table to Mrs. Forsythe, "I beg you, don't
look so distressed."

"But I am. First, Mr. Voorhees, then you . . ."

His head came up sharply. "What happened to Voorhees?"

She stammered: "Why, I don't know. He hasn't awakened."

"Shall I see?" Dr. Peck started to rise.

She put her hand on his arm to detain him. "Please. Do
breakfast first. The Lieutenant is sure he's just oversleeping."
She smiled wanly and added: "Old men do."

"They don't." Dr. Peck's tone was brusque. "They get up
with the birds."

The waiter pranced to their table, scooped up the soiled
dishes from in front of Nina and Corbett, flung down two
checks. Nina opened the catch of her handbag. Corbett picked
up her check, gave it with two single bills to the waiter. She
had taken a bill from her wallet and she registered surprise
when she found her check gone. She protested, although she
seemed pleased. "Those War Bonds you bought," Corbett
said. "Dividends."

The waiter rested the heel of his hand on the table, balancing
the crockery-laden tray shoulder high, while he waited for Dr.
Peck's order, bracing himself against the convulsive jerk of
the train. "You bes' ohduh up. We pas' No'th Philadelphia."

Dr. Peck frowned as he started to write out his order. The
table had St. Vitus' Dance. He scowled, clutching the pencil,
trying to steady his writing. "Stop that," he grumbled. "Somebody hold down this table."

Across the aisle, the old woman's voice rose, shrill with
panic: "Arthur, this train's shaking so. Arthur, something's
wrong with the train! Arthur-r-r—"

It began with the screech of a name.

It began with a look of surprise on the waiter's bland, chocolate face, with his mouth dropping open, white eyeballs bulging. It went on to his crazy cake-walk in a zig-zagging aisle,
and the wild leap of the tray from his hands.

It began with the spatter of coffee in their faces, with hail of silver and crockery around their skulls, with Nina's outcry of dismay, Dr. Peck's "What's going on?"

It happened in seconds.

The table slid from the wall. The car jiggled and quivered and trembled as though some giant hand was jerking a toy on a string.

The waiter's huge, white-coated body, his brown face, towered over the table one instant and the next one was gone.

Corbett gripped the rim of the table, felt it glide through his fingers. He said to himself: "This can't be so. This is the Palm Queen. Nothing happens to it." He hung on to the thought, hung on for his life. Mrs. Forsythe's hand clawed at his arm, fell away. Nina's face loomed over the table, all of it eyes and hair that gleamed through a haze and dropped out of sight.

The car had gone crazy. It was banging and crashing and grinding and ripping.

Soot streamed through the diner, a black torrent gushing out of the galley.

Corbett forced himself back in his chair. His feet hooked the rungs; his whole body tensed, in one frantic effort to hang on to something, and then he slumped, letting go, to roll with the inevitable crash.

It came almost at once. Before you could scream. Before you could will one single move. It came in an incredible leap and a monstrous smash of furniture, dishes and glass, of iron and steel. Before he plunged from his chair, he saw Joanie's body sail through the murk, a rag doll, limp, without joints.

In that final moment, he was aware, with a sharpness almost like pain, that in the entire car there was not one human sound. Then everything stopped; the fantastic movement, the ear-splitting din.

He lay stunned.

Slowly, his senses returning like goads, he felt the thick smoke, filling nostrils and throat. All about him was silence, so total, so strange that for an instant he thought he was entirely alone in this world. He opened his eyes. Smoke stung his eyeballs. He was aware of pain in his back, in his legs. He shifted his body with instinctive caution. The pain wasn't bad. "I'm not hurt," he thought. The relief that flooded his veins was reviving. "Nothing's happened to me." His hands moved back carefully. They met the texture of wood of a wall not the soft fuzz of carpet on floor. He was sitting, not lying, with the legs of a chair on his chest, with his back to a wall and his feet stretched straight out on a carpet that rose perpendicular.

The back of his head hurt; his groin sent up pain. Yet it was the smoke that bothered him most. It smarted and strangled and blinded. It fogged mind and vision, finally drove through his mind and pushed in the dread that spurred him to motion. "Christ! I won't die in fire! No. Not fire."

He forced himself up and over, groping on hands and knees, on the wall of the diner, past upended tables and chairs and soft human flesh. Jagged glass knifed his hands. Through the haze he saw moving figures, shadows, unsubstantial and soundless. Nothing was real save the smoke and the absolute silence.

On all fours he scudded, through a hot tunnel, with the delirious speed of an infant who has just learned to crawl. Finally, at the end of hours, days, months and years, he went through a door that was wider than tall and felt a cold wind on his face.

He tried to stand up, bracing himself against metal walls that slanted crazily up. He was out on the platform. He tore at the hasp of the door. It flew back with a rush, as if it, too, was glad to be freed. He jumped. A handful of ice was flung in his face; sleet needled his eyelids, his cheekbones, his neck.

He stood motionless, savoring the triumph of safety. Still stunned, his mind and instinct could travel no further than self. "I was in peril. I am alive." With the aloofness of man looking at distant pictures, he saw steel rails twisted like ribbons, wooden ties torn to matchsticks. The diner lay on its side, a drunk at the end of a spree, nudging a mass of dark metal, crumpled against a slanting steel tower. Wires dangled like black snakes above it, dipping their noses in puddles, festooning the glistening torn rails.

As far as he felt anything at all, he felt indignity, a sense of enough is enough, you can push a man only so far. This was the too much. The final insult of peril.

He shivered with cold. The sleet showered his jacket. Yet he stood rooted. Dully, objectively, as if it was something on a cinema screen, he looked at slickers and ponchos scrabbling up an embankment, a horde swarming, stampeding over icy wet cinders. Resentment edged into his mind. It was somehow indecent for spectator eyes to look on the mangled Palm Queen.

A figure crept out of the wreckage, a heap of clothes streaming blood, crawling along, inch by inch, across the ripped rails. It tried to stand up. It staggered and stumbled over a rail into a pool and a wire and sprawled with its face in the pool. He saw a blue flash of flame, a spiral of smoke. The stampeding crowd stopped. He heard murmurs and shouts and then the clanging of bells and the wailing of sirens.

Out of somewhere, a man stood before him, a man in work clothes, yelling: "Stay away. The power's on." It took him a while to become aware that he was out of the shock of destruction, that the man was screaming at him: "Holy Christ, it's a mess."

"Holy Christ! Look at you! Anyone killed in your car?"

"I don't know." It was seeping in: the knowledge of horror and dread: "Why, Nina was there! Nina and Joanie. Dr. Peck." People he knew. People with names. Acquaintances. Friends.

He gripped the high-tilted edge of the platform, pulled himself up and crawled into the diner, crying: "Nina, Nina." His voice sounded strange in his ears, crying that name. He heard a melee of whimpers and moans, of hoarse calling of names and directions, of smashing of glass. Panic swept over him. He tried to stand up and run and he stumbled.

He felt a hand on his arm, heard Dr. Peck's voice. "Corbett? You're all right? I've got Mrs. Forsythe."

Through the murk, he saw faces, a man and a woman, blackened like minstrel end men and ribboned with blood.

"Miss Gilmore?" he panted.

"She's—" Dr. Peck's voice wavered and Corbett's heart stopped. "Your friend? I think I saw her. I believe she got out. . . . Yes, she got out." He pointed back toward the Pullmans.

The lounge car still clung to the couplings that held it fast to the diner. Its glass door was shattered, swinging wide to a shambles of overturned chairs and broken ash stands.

He climbed over the wreckage and raced toward the Pullmans. A horrible figure and face flashed before him and as he ran he was vaguely aware that what he saw was himself in the shards of the mirror, blackened and bleeding and wet.

Loch Lomond stood straight, its door primly shut. He pushed the door open.

CHAPTER TWELVE

Afterwards, when he tried to recall the details, he was sure he had passed through Loch Lomond in nightmare.

First there was wall-muffled cursing and scuffling and crashing and clanking that burst into an orgasm of violent noise, as a door was flung open. A head loomed before him, a livid face, spurting blood, bulging eyes, corded throat making animal noises of strain. Shoulders blocked his path. He struck out with his fist, heard it thud upon flesh, saw the eyes going glassy, the face fading green. He shoved with his body to get the thing out of his way. From behind, the blue-black of a pistol butt rose and descended. Hands reached from a room. The shoulders were pulled out of sight. A door slammed; its lock rasped. An instinct, faint through the shock anesthesia, tried to tell him that this was the prisoner of war, that he had struck at his enemy, had helped to prevent a mad, futile attempt at a break. But he was only impatient because this had delayed him in getting to Nina.

Just as much as the curled, yellow toenails on the wax feet of a man who lay sprawled in the aisle, flat on his back, night-shirt rolled up over bare, skinny thighs, almost to the navel. The passage was blocked. He had to step carefully around, over an outflung, rigid arm, and he was annoyed that no one had picked the man up. Yet a car full of passengers seemed quite unaware that an indecent corpse lay in the aisle.

People just sat there like statues, frozen in poses of staring. They watched Corbett go by, yet no flutter of eyelids nor change of expression proved they had seen him. Their breath iced the windows. In that white cavern of Pullman, the silence was absolute, awful.

At the end of the car, he heard the whining and scratching of a terrified dog shut up in a room.

He ran through Glen Argyle. It was the dream, the one where you run down an unending carpet strip, seeking a person, a place, an escape, but the carpet goes on and on, like a rubber band, till you pant with exhaustion, cry with despair.

At last he came to the small room at the end of Glen Argyle.

Nina stood at her basin, scrubbing her face, and of all the fantastic sequence, that shocked him most. At such a time, she thought first of her looks.

She made a small startled outcry when she saw his black, bloodied face in the mirror over her washstand, a fluttery, in-drawn "Oh."

His anger flared. "What in hell do you think you're doing?"

She gestured with her washcloth. It plopped in the water. "Why, I'm washing my face. My face is dirty. That terrible soot. Oh, look at my hair. It's a mess!"

The black wings lay flattened, dirt-dulled; the snood trailed in torn string, with straggles of hair, down her back. One ear-ring was gone; there was a rent in her jacket; her stockings were ripped and dappled with blood.

Exasperation curdled his anger. "You dumb women! You idiots!" he shouted and then, with that out of his system, he eased down and asked: "Are you hurt?"

"Hurt? Why, why . . ." She gaped. The notion had reached her at last that she might have been injured, might have been killed in the crash of the Palm Queen. "Why I could have been *killed!*"

He gripped her shoulder roughly, turned her around. She squirmed, pulled away. "Don't! You'll get blood on my clothes."

It was hard to believe she remained Nina Gilmore, concerned about looks, about clothes. The rut of her life ran so deep that it took more than a train crash to jar her out.

"Sit down on that stool," he commanded.

She obeyed him unquestioningly, yet with a wondering look in her face. He knelt before her. "Your stockings are torn."

"Oh, my precious nylons!"

He bit his lower lip to hold back his rage. He wanted to slap her, beat common sense into her head. Instead, he said briefly: "Your leg is cut." He snatched a clean towel from the rack, soaked it with water. She didn't protest when he reached up her thighs, unhooked her garters, rolled down her stockings. While he mopped clotted blood and dirt from her shin, she gripped both sides of the stool, holding her breath like a child who's afraid the cold water will sting. Then, suddenly, she let out her breath in a long susurrus. Her face blanched beneath grime and suntan. She swayed and fell toward him.

He cradled her head on his ribbons and then lowered it gently between her bare knees. When she finally looked up, some pink had returned to her cheeks; the glaze had gone from her eyes. For a brief moment, she stared at him and then burrowed her head on his shoulder and started to cry. "Oh, Don," she sobbed. "Oh, Don . . . Don . . . Don . . ." repeating his name as though it stood for salvation. After a

while, a long while, she sat up. She had a new face. It was
tear-stained, but grave. It was almost the awed reverent face
of a woman at prayer.

"Don, it was a wreck?"

"It was."

"People were killed?"

His teeth came together. Between them he ground out a
"yes."

"In our car?"

"I wouldn't know."

"They were! We escaped! How'd we escape?"

He forced a grin to his mouth. "That angel who rides on
my shoulder."

"But you're hurt!" She touched the back of his hands. He
jerked them away, turned them palms up. Blood had caked
with the soot over cuts but the wounds didn't look deep. He
pressed the spigot, let water run over them, rubbed soap on.
They were nothing, just scratches. They still oozed a little.
He patted them dry with the towel, held the cloth on them a
moment. He moistened the towel, ran the clean edge over
his cheeks and nose, wiped the dirt from his eyes. She sat
watching him somberly, holding her face between her hands.
"Don, bombing's like this!" There was a naive surprise in her
tone. She halted to let her own thought sink in and then stood,
pulled up her torn stockings, hooked on her garters, swirled
the loose ends of her hair all together. "What are we doing
here? They need us out there."

She began to go out of the room. He drew her back. She
thought he meant to prevent her from going, and she cried:
"You can't stop me. I have to help."

"Put on your jacket. It's cold on the tracks." He slipped
the fur coat from its hanger, wrapped it around her, bent over
and kissed the top of her head.

Glen Argyle had come out of the trance of its jolt. Passengers were gathering in clusters in the aisles, on the arms
of the seats, at fogged windows, talking in muted funeral tones.

One woman noticed them, asked: "You were up there, weren't you? Were many hurt?"

Nina snapped: "Hurt? Many dead."

"Oh, my God!"

A few of the people looked at them queerly, with the mixture of horror and awe that the populace must have given to Lazarus when he rose from his grave.

It was cold in the car. The steam had gone off. Corbett said: "It's cold. Nina, wait here for me while I pick up my coat." He took a few steps and stopped in the aisle. His coat and his cap and his bag were up on the rack of Sixteen. That coach was a junk pile of metal, flung at the base of a slanting steel tower. The sense of personal loss left him for the instant bewildered and empty.

A trainman, his blue uniform dirtied and ripped, his face paper-white, came into the car and ran through, calling out: "Women please stay on the train. All men come out and help." A man in a sport suit got up. His wife seized his coat tails. "No, you stay in here. It's raining out there. You'll catch a cold."

He protested: "You heard what he said. They need men."

"They'll do without you. Your sinus trouble. You can't come home sick."

"Look." He jerked his coat-tails from her grip. "I got to go out. I got to see what it is, anyway."

His wife settled back in her seat. "Go out and come back and tell me. Find out how long we'll be here."

Loch Lomond was different. Loch Lomond knew what it all was about. Even the Peke seemed to know. In a compartment at the end of the car, the fat woman lolled on her sofa, fanning herself with her feathers. The dog cowered under the washstand, shaking all over, wisely keeping out of her way. It gave one feeble yip as Corbett and Nina passed by.

The car was crowded with people who had been in the diner, blackened and bloodied, their clothes hanging in tatters, and all with the same drugged look on their faces. It was a look

Corbett knew: the look of the people of Europe when they crawled from their rubble after a bomb hit.

"Don, bombing's like this!" Nina's voice echoed in his mind and it reached further back, completed the thought with a few other words she had spoken: "If we'd just had one little bombing to wake us up . . ."

"Wake us up!" They looked like somnambulists. Paralyzed. Petrified.

"The people whose faces were clean were twittering and fluttering around them, squeaking excitement, wanting to help and not knowing how.

One green curtained berth stood in the middle of the car, unmade and unnoticed.

A queer smell filled the Pullman, the musky, sweet odor of death.

He heard Joanie's voice, crying "Mommee . . . Mommee. I want my mommee," and he looked for the child. Elaine Weston had her, was hugging the kid with a resolute tightness, as if she believed the pressure of her woman's body would give Joanie the comfort one got from a mother. Her mother-in-law was mopping the little girl's face with a towel. The kid's face and hands had some scratches, her forehead the round welt of a bump.

"Hush, baby doll," Mrs. Weston was saying. A twist of silvery metal hung over one ear, the remains of lost spectacles. "In one minute the doctor will come and make you all better."

Joanie's legs thrashed. "I don't want the doctor. I want my mommy."

"All right, little darling, all right. Just as soon as the doctor fixes you up, we'll take you to mommy."

A chill ran down Corbett's spine. He bent to Nina: "Here's your job. Take these people back to your room. Take care of them. Make them comfortable. Give them your best. I mean your *best*." He touched Elaine's shoulder. She looked up. Instantly, fear clouded her face. He felt a twinge of annoyance that with all that had happened, her nerves still reflexed the impact of his fist. He said: "Go with my friend. With Miss Gilmore. I'll send Dr. Peck when I find him." He took Joanie's hand between his. "Joanie! You remember me, Joanie?"

The little girl blinked at him through sooty, wet lashes and whimpered "Yes."

"Joanie, you go with these ladies. They'll make you all better."

Her dirty fist dug her eyes. "I want my mommy."

He pulled her hand off, held it, swallowing the lump in his throat. "Joanie, they've got candy and things." This was how you began. With petty distractions. Inconsequentials to fill the great gap of one major bereavement. If it had happened . . . He stretched his arms to lift the kid from Elaine to Nina. Elaine shook her head. "Let me. I can carry her in."

He patted the little girl's back, tried to sound jocular. "Take my word for it, Joanie, you'll have a wonderful time. Nina'll let you try on her hat. She'll show you her toilet."

The kid's sobs tapered off. She let Elaine lift her. When they had gone up the aisle, he looked for the others he knew and saw Pat Hastings. She sat on the arm of a chair, fever-flushed, daggled, and after a fashion, consoling her mother. The Senator's wife was a witch. Her gray-blonde hair streamed to her shoulders; channels of tears striped her sooty, plump cheeks. She kept jabbering: "Pat, wire your father. Tell him we're safe. Pat, get me some water. Pat, my arm must be broken; it hurts me so. Pat, it's so terrible. I'll never get over it. I'll never get the sight of that out of my mind . . . Oh, why did it have to happen to us? Why couldn't we have got off with your father?"

Pat noticed Corbett and tugged at his elbow. "Help me with her. Help me do something for her."

He stopped.

He touched her mother's arm gingerly. She screamed. "Oh don't!" and moved it away. It wasn't broken, he saw. She flexed it too readily.

"She'll be all right. More scared than hurt. Get the doctor."

"Your father was lucky. That was God's mercy. That was God's way. He'd have been in the thick of it. He always is, it's his nature. He'd have been killed. Pat, your dear daddy would have been killed, crippled for life . . . I will be too. My arm. I'll never be able to use it again. The table fell on it. The whole table fell on it."

Corbett asked: "Where's Dr. Peck? Have you seen Dr. Peck?"

Pat Hastings gave him the blank stare of numbness. "Dr. Peck?" Then, she forced herself to start thinking. "Why, he's in there." Her head inclined toward the green curtained berth. "Mr. Voorhees is dead. Don't you know?"

His forehead wrinkled. Of course he knew. He had known all the time. It had even been mentioned at breakfast . . . long, long ago . . . Mrs. Forsythe had heard the death rattle. Why, he had seen the dead man, the yellow toenails, the rigid limbs in the night shirt, just a short while before. Then nothing had registered, nothing had come through the stone wall of shock. Now everything did, every word, every scene, every motion. You tried to see everything at once. Each person's experience was something in which you had a share.

"Pat, that old man's been murdered. Pat, that sweet old man has been murdered."

He stared, open-mouthed at the Senator's wife.

"You can't tell me, I know. And I'll tell you who killed him. Those dreadful New Dealers. They killed that old man. When they took his gasoline. When they made him ride on this train, they killed him as surely as if they'd driven a knife . . ."

It was a talking jag, that's all it was. Why, the same thing hit some of the men after tough missions. They couldn't stop talking, said all sorts of fantastic things. Accusations, abuse, recriminations . . . But you got over that . . . You got over everything . . .

Pat Hastings plucked at his coat. "For God's sake, give me a cigarette. At least you can do that much for me." Automatically, he reached for his packet and lighter. While he held the flame, he heard a female scream: "Oh, it's gone. I've lost my bracelet. I've lost my new diamond bracelet." He heard running footsteps. The fur-jacketed blonde bumped against him as she ran through the aisle. Pat Hastings said wearily: "That dumb bitch! She ought to be glad she's alive."

He snapped down the lighter and went toward the green-curtained lower. The closed curtains bulged. Beneath them he saw three sets of heels, two men's and a woman's. The sidelights were on in the dim vault of the lower. Dr. Peck and a porter stood alongside the berth and in the far corner, down at the foot, Mrs. Forsythe crouched, the palm of her hand pressed on her mouth to hold back a scream or a vomit.

Without looking up to see who was there, Dr. Peck began irritably: "I thought I had ordered everyone to stay out." He peered, myopic without his eyeglasses and when he saw it was Corbett, altered his tone: "Oh, so it's you. Well, do me a favor. Take care of the lady. Just take her out."

Corbett stood rooted, staring at the face on the tumbled bed-clothes.

The Puritan face was serene, almost gentle. White eyebrows smudged smooth yellow tallow. The thin lips, relaxed in death, seemed almost to smile, as if at the end when the Pullman mattress at last was a bier, Voorhees had lost all his terror, was finally at ease on a train. The decencies of death had been done. The eyelids were down. A sheet had been drawn over the toenails, the skinny legs, the ludicrous nightshirt. Only the plucked rooster throat was still bared.

When Dr. Peck saw that Corbett was not moving, he turned to the porter. "Find some place for Mrs. Forsythe to stay, some quiet spot where the lady can rest."

"Yes, suh." The Negro extended his hand. "Please, ma'am." His voice and hand shook.

Mrs. Forsythe's pupils contracted. She shrank into her corner. "Don't touch me," she quavered.

"No, ma'am." The colored man took a backward step toward the doctor. "Ah won' touch you."

"Why, he's more scared than she," Corbett thought. "Why —Holy Christ, she thinks he did it." His mind stopped and began to go back. He looked at the Negro again, and felt his blood chilling.

"Doctuh, she won't come wif me. Doctuh, ah cain't stay in heah." The man's eyeballs were rolling. "Ah, got things to do."

Dr. Peck's voice rose, testy with weariness, sharp with authority. "You'll stay here all right. *I've* got things to do. It's a coroner's case. Someone has to stay here with him. Till the authorities come."

"Not me, boss, not me."

"Why not? He can't hurt you." His fingertips touched Voorhees' throat with the professional casualness to which all human flesh, quick or dead, is merely tissue. "He's been dead a long while. At least eight hours, I'd say. Full rigor's set in."

"He don' die fum the wreck?"

"Good heavens, no. Gone long before. They'll have to do an autopsy of course. I'll wager they'll find coronary occlusion. Simple heart failure." He pulled the sheet all the way up. "No use wasting more time on the dead." He paused. He turned, he looked thoughtfully at Mrs. Forsythe. His pause stretched out by seconds. "You can't stand here, ma'am." His tone was the doctor's, firm and no nonsense. His forehead creased. "Mrs. Forsythe, what was this man to you?"

At first she returned only a dazed, wooden stare. Then her brow furrowed like his and her hand came away from her mouth. Her shoulders drew together in the involuntary action of straightening herself. "Why, nothing. Why, nothing at all."

His scowl deepened. He glanced down at Voorhees and once more at her face.

"Why, he was only someone I met on this train. A casual acquaintance. Someone you meet on a journey. Talk to and eat with. Why, you must believe me." Her head pivoted from one to the other. She had begun to sound frantic. "You must believe me, he was only a stranger. I have a husband in London. Why, I'm starting back. They mustn't know, mustn't think. Oh, I can't be involved in any . . ."

Corbett cut in. "Dr. Peck, there's a child in the next Pullman. She needs you more. In bedroom C. I promised I'd send you right in. She's with Mrs. Weston."

"Mrs. Weston!" The doctor's repetition was like a bell ringing, a bell that belonged in Sixteen. Betty Taylor was there with her baby. And Frankel and Kalchis. And grandma whatever her name was . . . And Chuckie and that red-headed girl with a one-legged husband. People you knew. People you'd sat with and talked with and slept with . . . So old Voorhees was dead. One old man was dead. Old enough to shove off.

"Dr. Peck," Corbett said, "I'm going out there. They need men. Please take care of the kid. Will you take care of the kid?"

When he went by, he saw that the door of Drawing Room A was ajar, the room vacant and littered with wreckage. In a welter of dishes and glasses, a thermos jug lay dented and bloodied. The torn shade hung askew. The window was cracked, the towel on the sofa-spattered with gore. He stopped. What had happened in there was written in shards of china and glass. "The bastard put up a fight. Tried to escape."

Through his mind flashed the thought that perhaps this had been planned, just this way. Those swine might wreck a train, kill civilians, just to save one of their own. "Christ!" he thought. "I'm not working for U.P. That was two years ago." Yet, while he stood there, impatient with himself for stopping and gawking, his mind wrote the scene out in a newspaper lead: "Sabotage was hinted today as the cause of the wreck of the Florida express, Palm Queen, when it became known that a Nazi prisoner of war in the custody of F.B.I. men in a drawing room on the train had attempted to make his escape during the excitement attending the crash . . ." He thought: "I ought to be phoning a story. I ought to be in a booth, calling up someone about this . . ."

For a long moment he stood in the drawing room doorway, hovering between the man he had been and the man that he was. "Hell," he concluded. "I'm *in* this. Let someone else write it up."

And as he crossed over the couplings between the Pullman and lounge car, for the first time since Pearl Harbor, his mind was perfectly clear. He was a man going forward to do a job, to do what he had to. He was in it, all the way in. He was rid of confusion and doubt, of the questions, the two that had harrowed him after each flight: *"What is it for? Why did it happen to me?"*

That was the torment. Not fear of death. Not guilt of killing. But that he hadn't crossed over, out of himself into life. Now, in the chaos of a wrecked passenger train, he had come unexpectedly, stumbled, through three little words, on his answer. *"I'm in this."* Suffering was life. Struggle was life. Destruction was life. Even death was. You're alive. You're in it. You take what it gives. You do the best that you can.

There was a man in the lounge car. Corbett recognized Rauchmeyer, wandering from one overturned chair to another, fussily trying to set them up straight in their rows. When he saw Corbett, he complained pettishly: "I can't find a chair to sit down on."

Corbett laughed. His laughter, he knew, must sound mad in that shambles. He said: "Why don't you get off, Mr. Rauchmeyer? There's a hell of a story out there."

"You blasted fool! What do I care for a story? I'm in this. I'm tired. I'm hurt. I need someone to take care of me."

CHAPTER THIRTEEN

At first you couldn't see the wreck for its spectators. As far as Corbett's eyes ranged, phalanxes were solidly massed under umbrella mushrooms:

school kids in mackinaws, carrying briefcases, housewives with old sweaters on house-cleaning dresses, men with coat collars turned up to hat brims.

They stood silent, except when a stretcher went through. Then a weird sound, part squeal, part sigh, broke from the people in front, rippled back through the crowd.

Where they'd all come from God only knew. The crash had occurred just outside the city. Below, beside the tracks, were occasional tenements, yellow brick "tax-payers," the dingy red brick and grayed glass of a factory. The road was congested with cars. Corbett caught the white streak of an ambulance, heard the wail of its siren.

The people kept coming as though the city had opened and spewed them all out. He could see them down in the street, gesturing "hurry-up, here-it-is" to others behind them, climbing the embankment, mashing the mire into wax, lifting their muddy galoshes over the rails.

Policemen in glistening slickers kept them back from the Palm Queen, clearing a lane for the stretchers, a semicircle for cameramen and reporters. A tall priest, black hat brim soaked down to turned-up black overcoat collar, pinched nose blue with cold, cut through the crowd and strode toward the train.

Half of the Palm Queen—the uninjured part with the Pullmans—snaked on its track, inert and erect. Almost at right angles to it, the dining car sprawled, straddling the twisted, torn rails. Pulled two ways at once—by the racing engine, the careening coaches—the diner had gone its own way, had heaved almost over, come to a halt on its side. Behind it, shattered coaches were piled at the base of the tower.

They were still taking people out of the diner. Corbett could see the bent double figures of men at the rim of the upslanted platform, maneuvering a shrouded figure down to a stretcher.

A thin, white-haired old man stood just under the platform, shivering and wringing his hands. "Is that my wife? . . . Haven't you found my wife yet? Oh, please get my wife . . . She's in there . . . I know she's in there."

This was England again, the people outside the wreckage and cinders and dust that had once been their homes and their households. The barbaric violence that chose victims by chance. The bomb that was labeled: "To whom it may concern."

It was the cook who was hoisted down and laid flat on the litter. The massive brown man of the horn-rimmed spectacles and jaunty cigar was rolling and screaming in agony. The blanched flesh of his cheeks hung in strips. A young man with an interne's white coat beneath a poncho, bared the cook's arm, shot in morphine, signalled three bearers to raise the stretcher with him.

The dining car steward, sooty and bloodied from hair-line to shoes, noticed Corbett, called down: "You okay, soldier? Give them a hand with that stretcher," and the interne transferred his handle to Corbett.

A stout, bronzed man in warm winter coat and fedora, a man in a trackwalker's sweater and cap, and a Naval Ensign held the three others. The Ensign had on his raincoat and the cellophane shield for his cap.

The man in the overcoat said: "Hi! We need you" and "Is Nina all right?" to Corbett and he saw it was Stengel, who had almost bought a Miami hotel, who wanted to make Valor Fabrics. Stengel seemed to be bossing this show. He gave the orders: "Take it easy. Short steps. Don't jar him," the voice of experience, cool, competent and remotely officious.

Under the morphine, the cook's screams were ebbing to moans. By the time they'd got through the lane in the crowd and down the embankment, the cook had grown quiet, had closed his scorched, lashless eyes. They slid the stretcher into the ambulance. A nurse pushed out an empty, tossed down a folded clean blanket and they plodded back, shoes weighted with muck.

Stengel moved up to Corbett. "Where's your coat? You shouldn't have come out here like this."

"I'm used to cold."

He slapped Corbett's shoulder. "You boys are tough. We civilians still got to take care of ourselves . . . I've got a son in the Navy. Younger than you. Lieutenant, Jay Gee. That's the same rank as you, isn't it?" He passed Corbett, caught up with the Ensign. "I've got a son in the Navy. Lieutenant Stengel. You ever meet him?"

Captain Metzger was waiting for them, stretched out on the platform in that crazy slant of the wreck-tipsy car which made a man lying down appear to stand up. His eyes were shut, his face gray. When they hoisted him over the edge, an arm dangled, and splintered white bone stuck out through pink flesh. The interne felt his pulse, glanced at his pale lips. "Plasma at once," he commanded. "In the ambulance, please. Before they get going."

Automatically, Corbett replied: "Yes, sir, I'll give it."

"You'll give it?" The interne's voice and brow-lift reflected surprise. "It's a hell of a thing for you to come home to," he said.

Stengel repeated the interne's remark while they bore the young Captain back through the crowd.

"I'm home," Corbett said. "Don't feel sorry for me. Feel sorry for *him*." He nodded down at the stretcher. "He has a wife and a kid."

Stengel tsked sympathetically, waited a moment, then asked: "Where were you when it happened?"

"Back there in the diner."

"Boy, you were lucky!" the Ensign whistled.

"I saw you jump out," the trackwalker said. "You were the first one jumped out. Remember, I told you stay away from the wires? I saw the whole thing. I saw how it happened . . . I see her comin'. I says to myself: 'There's Ninety-two. There's the Palm Queen.' She goes whizzing by me. I see sparks comin' out from the wheels of one of them coaches. Then—zingo—I see her crack up in the middle, begin to go crazy, smack right into the tower."

Stengel could scarcely wait for the man to be done. "I was up there," he began. "In my room. Packing my bag. I felt the jerk. I guess that was when the diner pulled off the track. I couldn't imagine what happened. First I knew what it was when a trainman ran through and asked men to help. Believe me, I'm glad I can help. It takes a strong man."

"You bet," the trackwalker said. "It takes a strong stomach, too. You ain't seen the worst."

"What did it?" the Ensign inquired. "Ice on the rails?"

"Naw." The trackwalker's voice dropped, became confidential. "A wheel come off."

Corbett began: "There was a Nazi. Prisoner of war—"

"I saw him on the train," Stengel cut in eagerly. "With two F.B.I." He spoke with a strange kind of pride—both he and the trackwalker did—as if being eye-witnesses, being part of this horror, was something that set you above the rest of mankind.

The trackwalker's voice preened itself. "I seen him come off. They took him right off. First thing. To the clink."

The Ensign asked diffidently: "Do you suppose—could those Germans have done it—for *him*?"

Stengel's jaw came up sharply. "You mean sabotage?"

"Naw." The trackwalker shook his head sagely. "They don't needa do it. Rolling stock's shot to hell. That's what it is. Shot to hell."

They slid in the stretcher next to the cook. "Plasma," Stengel said to the nurse with his air of importance. "The Doc says give him plasma before you get started."

The form on the sloping platform was tiny this time and the white-thatched man had to stand on his tip-toes to stroke its cheeks. When they lifted the battered old woman down to the stretcher, they saw that its bloody, bruised face was stamped with the imprints of heels.

The interne moved around to Stengel's side as though he were the man best equipped to hear bad news. "Put her in the ambulance anyway," he whispered. "Let him go along. She's finished. Nothing they can do for her any more, but I'd rather he didn't find that out up here. We've got plenty without him caving in."

The old man plodded after them through the crowd and down the slope, anxiously twittering. "Carry her easy . . . Do you want me to help you? . . . She's not much of a load. Weighs ninety-five pounds. She's so tiny. Eats like a bird . . . They'll give her good care in the hospital? They'll get her good doctors, won't they? . . . She's just stunned, isn't she? . . . She'll be all right? Won't she be all right? . . . She'll be a good patient. Never complains . . . See how quiet she is . . ."

When they came back with an empty, the steward called down from the platform: "No more in here. We got 'em all out. Pick up that guy on the tracks. Cripes, you can't leave a dead man out in the rain."

"About time," the trackwalker said. "I seen him get killed. Before the juice was turned off."

"Poor bastard must have been in a rush," Stengel said.

"They seen he was dead," the trackwalker said. "They said leave him lay. Get out the living ones first."

The face of the corpse drowned in a black pool of water. His torso lay on the track, arms flung up. His shoes were toward them, black and white uppers, worn-down heels, round, ragged scars on the soles. Rain plastered his clothes to his ribs. The suit, the shoes, the glistening black hair, gray-salted, looked familiar. Before they had turned and had lifted the man, Corbett knew it was Kalchis. He felt a slight pang of pity. It was, after all, someone he knew.

When the Ensign and trackwalker seized Kalchis' arms to raise the body, the cable moved with it. The fingers of one hand were coiled, were drawn, stiffened, around the loose end of a broken high tension wire. There were charred holes in the knees of the trousers and the legs that had lain on steel rails were burned through to the bone. As they turned him, a shower of trinkets fell from his pockets, splashed into the puddle. Corbett and Stengel stooped simultaneously and roweled the muck. They looked down at their hands and then at each other.

In Corbett's fist lay a chunk of white metal, melted around the dial of a watch, and pebbles, gray, lustreless, almost like coal chips, wadded together with wisps of black metal. Stengel held a half dozen squares of soggy, singed leather.

"Whee!" The Ensign gasped. "Imagine that heat! It burned up the stuff in his pocket."

"Put it back," the trackwalker said. "Don't let 'em say we robbed the dead."

"He robbed the living," Corbett said grimly. He took the leather squares from Stengel's hand, pried one open. The name was unfamiliar but it wasn't Kalchis. He opened another. Under a glassine strip he made out the blurred letters of Amos C. Peck. He opened a third, a fat billfold of brown. He saw Voorhees' name.

The Ensign looked bewildered. "He robbed 'em? Now? In the wreck?"

"During the night," Corbett said. "He robbed the berths." He saw Stengel glance at him, eyes suspiciously narrowing, heard the man ask: "How'd you know?"

He answered impatiently. "I saw some of those things on the people that owned them. You won't find *his* name in those wallets."

"What's his name?"

"Benny Kalchis."

"Is that so?" He was aware that Stengel didn't quite trust him. The man was flipping the wet billfold covers and glancing at him out of the corners of his eyes.

"I saw how he acted," Corbett began to explain. "He had the seat next to mine in the coach."

"In the coach? In what coach?" The trackwalker looked toward the tower.

"In Sixteen."

"Holy cow! Your seat was in Sixteen!" The trackwalker took off his cap, held it up to his chest in the reverent posture of men in the presence of death, "Say your prayers. Get down and pray."

Corbett's tense fingers bunched the man's sweater. "All killed in that coach?"

The man pulled away. "Wheel come off Sixteen. Fifteen and Sixteen they got it worst."

Corbett's hand opened slowly, releasing the sweater. The Ensign shuffled his feet. "Whatever he is, we can't let him lie in the rain."

"Let who lie?" Corbett stared at the rain-slashed corpse on the cinders. He couldn't remember what had happened a half minute before. Without saying one word to the three who were with him, he turned and raced toward the slanting steel tower. He passed a blur of white faces, bug-eyed, streaming with rain. Glass crackled under his shoes.

In two giant piles, hugging the base of the tower, lay twisted scrap iron, broken valises, spilling out clothes, squashed golden oranges and pieces of people. The rubble heap screamed, moaned and whimpered, cursed and prayed. His futile fingers clawed at the pile directly back of the diner.

Someone touched his arm. "Sorry, soldier. Got to wait for equipment to get this stuff off."

The priest with the dripping black hat moved up to him, put an arm across his shoulder. "Have you some one in there?"

"There's a woman and baby . . ."

The priest's arm tightened around him. "Can you give us a description?"

He tried to remember what Joanie's mother looked like and finally said: "She was young. Just a kid. Long brown bob. She wore a red coat."

"How old was the baby?"

He frowned. Why were they asking all this? "The baby?" He could hear her voice at the depot and he spoke with her words: "You wouldn't believe he was only nine months. He looked like a year and a half . . . big, fat baby. Blonde hair. Kewpie doll."

From the way he talked, intimately, with affection, they were sure it was his. He watched the priest trading commiserating glances with the man who first had addressed him, saw the priest signal the man to leave Corbett to him.

"Son, you are a soldier. You know what it means to be brave. God takes whom He loves . . ."

The other man—he was a passenger, you could tell by his clothes and his tan—said: "Take it easy, soldier. We got them both."

He breathed: "And?" He wrenched himself free of the priest's arm, looked into the passenger's face. The man shook his head. "I know it's a tough one to take. Your wife and your kid."

"They're not mine. They're people I knew. People I met on this journey."

"Oh!" Relief was plain on their faces. Now they could tell him without wasting time or emotion. "Flung clear," the man said. "Through the window. The girl had the baby. Hung on to it tight. They thought the kid might be saved. It died on the stretcher."

At the rim of the huddle, a new voice asked: "You don't mean the boy?"

"I don't mean him. He might be all right. You can live with only one arm. Christ, did you see how that glass cut that clean? Like a knife."

The ground waved under his feet. The daylight turned black. He staggered away, leaned against something and covered his face, to shut out not only sight but all thought and feeling. It was a long while before he became aware of the hard, round wheel of the diner, pressing his spine, the ice of the rain on his skin and the rhythm of hacking.

Then he went back to the junk pile and in a fever of doing, helped to uncover the living and drag out the dead. He closed Kurt Frankel's eyes; he sent grandma on her last journey; he gave Chuckie's father a comforting word, not certain whether the man could hear what he said: "Your boy's safe. They got him out."

Now and again, in the welter of people and tools, he glimpsed Dr. Peck, drawn-faced, waxen yellow, climbing over the rubble, saw the priest, weaving in and out of the throng, kneeling, dangling a rosary from shivering hands.

The last person he saw was the red-headed wife of the soldier who had lost his leg. He watched her white face, cinnamon-freckled, while the acetylene torches spat at the metal that pinned down her limbs. She was conscious, biting her lips to silence her pain. Blood trickled where her teeth had bitten her mouth.

An interne crawled over the wreckage, shot morphine into her shoulder. Before her eyes closed, she had recognized Corbett, had managed a ghastly small smile: "Hello, Dempsey, did you knock me out?" . . . and "Say, give me a butt."

His cigarette package was soaked. In the middle of the pack, he found one that was partially dry. He broke the sodden end off, lit it, placed it between her lips. She murmured: "You'll have to hold it for me. Can't use my hands." She drew in just once and then her mouth sagged and it dropped from her lips.

When they finally lifted her out to a stretcher, her eyes opened wide. She struggled to sit. A nurse wrapped a blanket around, held its sides to restrain her. The blanket fell flat at her knees. Corbett saw her lips moving and bent down to catch what she said. "Had the funniest dream . . . Dreamt my legs were cut off . . . Me and my husband . . . Us two without legs."

When he had seen the ambulance doors shut behind her, heard the importunate clang of its bell, he walked slowly back. On the wet cinders, beside the junk of the coach, a small body lay. A nude body. Without a head. A pink glistening torso, flung clear of the wreck. Tiny limbs rigid, yet oddly twisted as though their joints were of cloth. Ice ran through his veins before he bent down and picked up Joanie's doll.

He carried it back to Glen Argyle, drew himself up to the top step of the Pullman, sat there with his head in his hands and the broken doll in his lap, too spent, too utterly weary to move or to talk or even to cry.

Yet even that ended and he went into the car.

Joanie was on the settee in Nina's compartment, dressed in Nina's fur jacket, the sleeves long, making the end of her arms like seals' flippers. Nina's pancake hat was over one eye and her pigtails stuck out beneath it. Her thin legs were criss-crossed with band-aids.

She was playing a game with the grown-ups, commanding Elaine: "Now, you shut your eyes. Don't peek till I tell you." When she saw Corbett, she jumped up, poised for a leap, shrieked "Eeeeeeeee" and flung herself at him. The fur-swaddled arms encircled his throat, almost strangling. He gasped: "Take it easy . . . Such passion!"

As soon as he said it he remembered whose words they were. They belonged to the freckle-faced gunner's mate, to the guy in the whites who had come off the raft and gone back to sea. To her father.

Joanie snuggled her chin into his collar; the straw brim scratched his cheek. "My, my, my you're all wet," the child scolded. "You went out in the rain."

He released her arms, pressed her face against his for an instant, set her back on the sofa. She patted the cushion. "You sit here," she began. "Next to me," and then she saw what he held in his hand. "My dolly!" Her mouth and eyes gaped. "Why, you broke my dolly!" He laid the headless doll in her lap, saw her eyes fill with tears before he went out of the room.

Mrs. Weston came with him. In the narrow corridor, she breathed a few words: "Both mother and child?"

He nodded, averted his head.

She stood silent, absorbing his news. His nervous forefinger scratched across on the breath-frosted pane.

Then she asked: "Dr. Frankel? What happened to him?"

"The same."

She drew a deep sigh. "The poor man! He had only one wish. To live longer than Hitler." She halted a moment and somberly added: "You live through so much. You come to an end in this way. It's—it's almost a joke."

Again there was silence until Mrs. Weston was ready to speak. "Who gets the child now?"

"The child? . . . Why, why she has a family."

"Her father's at sea. You remember, her father's a sailor. He put them on the train."

He remembered. He remembered too well. "They'll have to notify him . . ."

"Oh!" Her hand went to her mouth. "They'll send him a telegram! Like they did us."

"He'll have to be notified. He'll have to say what he wants done with his child. There's a grandma somewhere. They were going to her mother's, you know." Talking details was good medicine. He felt his mind clearing, sharpening to practical matters. "Red Cross will locate them somehow."

"Oh, of course, the Red Cross." She seemed disappointed. She kept still again for a moment, then asked: "Do you think they could let Elaine keep her? For a while. It would help her so much. She has nothing. That's what's been killing her. Having nothing, nobody who needs her. You see, I have her. I always had someone."

He shook his head. "You and I can't decide that," and paused, knitting his brow. "She'll have to be told. How do you tell things like that to a kid?"

"We'll try . . . We'll tell her together."

He followed her back into the crowded cold room.

Joanie was hugging the headless doll, holding it tight on her beaver-wrapped breast. Elaine on the sofa beside her was starting a cat's cradle out of the paper ribbon from Nina's box. She seemed to have guessed what her mother-in-law and Corbett had been talking about, for she said tremulously: "Let me have the child."

He began, speaking softly: "There's a family somewhere. They were on their way to her mother's."

"I know. Let me keep her now."

Joanie was watching them both, her green eyes shifting from one to the other, dread dawning behind the bright pupils. " 'Laine." Her voice quivered. "Are we going to grandma's?"

"Not yet, darling. Not for a while."

"Where *are* we going?" Her eyes were like emeralds, polished by fear.

"We're going on a train. On another train."

"But mommy won't let me." She sent a terrified glance around the small room. "Where's mommy?" The emeralds spilled over. "I want my mommy," she bawled.

Elaine's arm encircled her. She cupped the small shaking chin. "Look at me, darling. Listen to me." Her voice was a soft, hoarse whisper. "Mommy and brother aren't coming with us. They had to go some place else."

The trembling stopped for an instant. "On a train?"

"On a different train."

The tiniest frown crept between the child's eyes. "To meet daddy?"

Elaine's arm tightened around the child's body. She shut her own eyes. "They'll meet daddy some day. Not now."

Joanie's nose puckered; her whole face screwed up. "Then where *did* they go?"

Elaine caught her lower lip between her teeth, delaying her answer while she steadied herself. "Far away, sweetheart." Her voice cracked. "Oh, it's a very nice place. So many good people are there."

"Then why didn't they take me? I want to go, too."

Elaine Weston's face worked. She opened her mouth to say something but no words came out. Mrs. Weston moved forward, put her arms around Elaine and the child. "Darling, they wanted you to stay here with us. We'll bring you to grandma's to wait until daddy comes home from the war."

"I can't stay without mommy." The child sounded panicky. She struggled in the woman's embrace, trying to get free. "Let me go," she screamed. "I have to go back to my mommy. I can't stay on trains without mommy. Daddy said I must stay with mommy." With one desperate push that took all of her strength, she broke free and jumped off the seat. She rushed toward the door.

Corbett barred her way. Her tiny fists flailed his legs. "Lemme go. Lemme go back to mommy."

He scooped her into his arms, held fast against her kicking and squirming. At last she grew tired and quiet. She sucked in big gulps of tears and saliva, burrowed her head on his shoulder. After a while, her tear-stained face turned up to his. She dug her eyes with her fists. "Is mommy dead?" she asked.

He knew he could stand it no longer and eased her arms from his neck, set her back on the sofa. "I'm going out, Joanie," he mumbled, not believing she would hear him or care. "I'll buy some crackers and stuff."

He felt Nina's hand on his arm, heard her voice. "You stay here. I'll go. You've done enough."

"I'll go," he said. "It's easier when you do something."

"Please wait for me. I have to go with you." She swooped down to a suitcase, whisked out a jacket and scarf, threw them around her.

They walked together as far as Glen Argyle's platform. Then his knees buckled. He swayed against her, steadied himself on her slender shoulder before he sat down on the step. "I'm tired," he muttered, ashamed of his weakness. "This takes it out of you. You don't realize—"

She sat down beside him, saying nothing, her thigh and her arm pressed to his. The rain swirled in their faces, dripped on their shoes. In their mutual silence, he knew comfort, greater comfort than words.

He broke it first. He said: "Sorry I caved. Too much all at once. Emotional. Physical. I told you we're not Superman."

She answered, stating, not asking: "You care a good deal for that kid. It's funny you should. You hardly know her." She sounded as if she was thinking out loud, yet with his mind rather than hers. "It's strange you should do so much for them all. With all your own problems."

He let her go on, not even trying to answer.

"Elaine Weston told me what happened last night—this morning."

He raised his brows.

"You're quite a person," she said.

Again he said nothing at all.

CHAPTER FOURTEEN

The hiatus of waiting stretched into hours. You squirmed through the crowd on the tracks, ran through the rain till you found a small grocery, bought what they had—packaged crackers and cup cakes and pies, a bagful of oranges—raced back in panic lest the train had decided to move in your absence. You sat in cramped corners, walked a few steps and returned. You tried to converse, to pretend that the chill of the heatless cars didn't ache in your bones. You had your girl, yet all you could do was anxiously watch her grow drawn with strain and fatigue, blue with cold.

Then a stranger popped into Nina's compartment, a man whom no one remembered seeing before, and he said: "I've got some Scotch. Anyone here need a drink?" and measured out modest doses of Dewar's for all of the women and Corbett. A quarter hour later, a woman stopped by, saying: "They have sandwiches and coffee out there. Some of the men went off and found food. Come out. Help yourselves."

Glen Argyle was making the best of disaster. A handsome brunette in Persian lamb was doling out cartons of coffee and wax paper wrapped sandwiches. A girl, swathed to the eyes in lush mink, bit into a sandwich. "Mmmm, dee-licious. I think Spam's dee-vine." She addressed herself to the long-eyelashed blonde in the silver fox jacket, but the blonde merely sniffled. "If you had the trouble I had, you couldn't think about food."

A matronly woman noticed that the two Westons looked almost frozen and asked them solicitously: "Why don't you put on your coats?" and when the elder explained that their coats had been up in the coach—in Sixteen that was wrecked—she cried, sincerely solicitous: "Why, we'll get you some things. Someone here must have a spare coat or jacket. Listen, you people, these women have lost all their clothes. Who has a coat to lend them?" The girl with the mink looked Elaine's figure over, said: "My sport coat should fit her," and the matron herself brought out a cloth coat. "You take it. I have my fur. I'll give you my address. Send it back in New York."

A man growled: "How long do you think they'll keep us sitting here?" and his wife shushed him quickly: "They got more important things to worry about."

One of the younger women cried: "Why don't we sing? Keep us warm. Help the blood circulate." Someone began *Mairzy Doats*.

Two men in overcoats, wearing gold badges, came into the car. They carried notebooks, looked harassed and tired. "F.B.I.," they said briefly. The singing instantly stopped; the car perked and a whisper raced from one end to the other. "They're looking for spies. Spies wrecked the train." One of the Federal men faintly smiled. "Just give us your names and addresses," he said.

When they reached Joanie, Elaine started to tell the child's name, but Joanie spoke up for herself. "I'm Joan Taylor. Four and a half. I live on this train."

"Who's the mother of this little girl?"

Joanie's lip trembled. "I'm Gunner's Mate William L. Taylor's *big* girl," she piped.

Elaine sidled up to the Federal man, touched his sleeve timidly. "Please, I want to ask you something." She framed her mouth with her hand. "Her mother was killed back there in the coach. Can I keep her until they hear from her father, connect with her family?" When she saw the man knitting his brows, she hurried to add: "Just temporarily. I'll take good care of her. Really, I will."

The man studied his notebook. "Which one are you?"

"Elaine Weston." Her voice shook with her eagerness. "You have my address . . . Oh, please."

"Make a note. Taylor's with Weston." The G-man nodded brusquely and moved up the car.

When they were back in the bedroom, Elaine's mother-in-law said thoughtfully: "It's funny how trouble makes friends. It warmed my heart. People so kind to each other. They give us food, bring us clothing. Don't ask who we are. Just say: 'You need a coat. Here, take mine.' You." She smiled sweetly at Nina. "You never saw us before in your life. Yet you take us in. You give us your room. You dress the child up in your furs. You share all you have, with absolute strangers."

"Don't!" Nina said. "I haven't done anything."

Mrs. Weston shook her head emphatically. "But you have. If people just understood how little it takes to make the world better. A kind word, the feeling of having a friend . . . Look, all over Europe my people are riding on trains. Not trains like this. In cattle cars, locked up like animals, riding to—" She remembered that Joanie was there and abruptly stopped. "That's the thing to remember," she began again. "The little kind actions. Not the big crazy hate." Again she suddenly halted, this time because Stengel had put his head in at the door.

The man's clothes were sopping; he was blackened with grime. "My, you got a crowd!" he exclaimed. "Nina, how are you? First chance I had to look in. I saw your friend. He said you were okay." He nodded at Corbett. "We were working together. In my stretcher crew. He ran out on us."

Nina bristled. Corbett saw her face changing, stiffening with resentment. Stengel swept off his hat, vigorously shook it. "Soaked through and through . . . Believe me, it's an experience. We'll have something to tell." The man glowed; he looked, pleased, excited. "Why, he's the kid!" Corbett said to himself. "The kid who thought it was sport to see Messerschmidts go up in flames. He's getting a kick out of this. I'll be damned."

"Nina," he heard Stengel say. "They're hooking a new engine on. An official just told me—a railroad official. They're pulling us back to the depot. I've got friends in Philly. If you want to stay over, rest up—"

She glanced at Corbett and he could see by her face that she hoped he'd say no. He said: "I'm going on home. As fast as I can."

"Thanks, Larry," she answered. "I'm going home. Straight on home."

Stengel raised his damp shoulders. "Well, no harm in offering. See you tomorrow in town. Talk over that business." He nodded at Corbett again, with his whole-hearted grin. "We'll make him a partner," he said.

Nina flushed; her eyes started to glitter. Stengel's brows rose. "Well," he said, after he had given her a curious stare. "Get yourselves packed. We start any minute." He turned to go, pivoted back on the threshold. "Look, one thing I want to remind you, don't sign any papers. Get a good lawyer. They'll pay for this. Clear case of negligence. Somebody forgot to grease up an axle. They'll pay through the nose. Won't let you sue."

"Sue?" The girl's voice was outraged. "Who's going to sue? And for what?"

Something new had entered the little compartment: surprise that had soured to resentment, hostility. Stengel seemed unaware that it had. "Be practical, Nina," he said blandly. "You're in an accident. You can be a rich woman out of something like this." He patted her cheek. "Now, now, little girl, don't say a word. You're nervous. Just a bundle of nerves. That's what they pay for, my friend."

When he had finally gone, and she stood with compressed lips, blazing eyes, Corbett squeezed her arm. "Take it easy, old kid. Take it easy."

Still seething, she opened her bags, brought out sweaters and scarves, said: "Come, kitten, we'll dress you better" to Joanie, and stood the child up on the sofa. She whisked off the fur coat and hat, eased the child's arms into a scarlet pullover that came to her knees, wrapped a soft woolen jacket around Joanie's shoulders, buttoned it over her chest, knotted a kerchief on her braids. Joanie stood stiff as a doll, bewilderment clouding her shiny green eyes. The train jerked. She fell forward, against Nina's bosom and started to cry.

The Palm Queen moved slowly, not sure that it could, wheezing and groaning. "We're going away! We're going away from my mommy!" The clash of the couplings rose over Joan's sobs.

At the depot, porters mysteriously appearing in time to corral their tips, swung down valises. The passengers eddied and clamored around them. "When's the next train? How do we get home from here?"

The Glen Argyle porter shrugged helplessly. "Ah don' really know. Ah'm on'y the pohtah. Nobuddy tol' me."

"That's a hell of a note," a woman complained. "Treat us like cattle after what we've been through."

A burly man in a raincoat wove through the crowd, calling out: "Palm Queen survivors, please follow me."

The depot was jammed with commuters, milling about, stamping their feet, muttering because scheduled trains hadn't come. They glanced at the Palm Queen travelers with mild curiosity, grudgingly squeezed into lanes to let them go through. The man in the raincoat kept shouting: "Palm Queen survivors this way," until he had shepherded fifty or more and their luggage alongside an exit and then he addressed them. "Those going on to New York, there's a train on the Reading in about twenty minutes. Don't count on taxis. It's just a short walk."

Corbett stopped at the newsstand to buy Joanie chocolate. A red-inked newspaper headline caught his eye. He bought the paper and carried it back. Nina glanced at it over his arm. She gasped: "Why, that's us!" He spread it open and they read it together. It was only a paragraph—the flash of disaster—under an eight column banner: "PALM QUEEN WRECKED: ONE HUNDRED FEARED DEAD."

Nina took a deep breath. "When you see it in print, you first realize—" Her teeth were chattering, with cold, he decided.

He played for a laugh. "Wait till you see my Brooklyn *Eagle*. If they learn I'm in this, know what they'll write? 'Brooklyn Man Escapes Death in Palm Queen Wreck. One Hundred Others Feared Dead.'"

He got his laugh, short and nervous. Stengel was right. The girl was on edge. Too much to expect that she'd keep her chin up all the time. He folded the paper, hoisted Joanie up to his shoulder, hefted Nina's large valise in his free hand. She protested: "You have the kid. You can't carry both."

"I can manage. The bag's big as you."

"Okay, thanks." Her quiet acquiescence was reassuring. Someone belonged to him, depended on him, took his help and his presence for granted. He looked back for the Westons. They were sticking close, directly in back. "My group," he said to himself. "My own family." Behind them he caught flashes of others he knew: the crest of green feathers on the grande dame with the dog, Mrs. Hastings' gray hair, without hat; Mrs. Forsythe's blue eyes, Rauchmeyer's square, soot-streaked jaw, Dr. Peck's tired, kind face, framed between collar and hat brim.

They strung out, a bedraggled, self-conscious procession, weighted with luggage, outlandish on staid city streets where people, dressed for the weather with slickers, galoshes, umbrellas, scudded by on their errands. One or two passers-by glanced at them fleetingly but didn't stop or ask questions. Once, at the end of a block, Corbett halted, set down the valise, flexed his numb fingers, shifted Joanie to his opposite shoulder. He hailed a man passing by. "How far to the Reading?"

The man gestured vaguely and continued to walk.

Corbett called after him. "Hey, mister!"

The man slowed and impatiently glanced at his wristwatch.

"How many more blocks?" Corbett asked.

"Two squares, I'd say."

"We get the New York train over there?"

"Might be." He looked bored.

Nina dozed a little, against his shoulder, as they sat close on her large valise in the jolting, jammed baggage car of a meandering local. At the end of two hours, they boarded a ferry.

"Let's go out on the deck," she suggested. "I've never been on a ferry. I'll leave my bags here."

The windswept deck was deserted. The skyline of lower Manhattan was shrouded in fog. He held fast to her arm and they stood in that silence that was better than speech, watching a trio of foolhardy gulls swoop, with rusty hinge creaks, down to the turbulent water. Rain sprayed their faces. The wind tore at her silly straw hat and he put the flat of his hand on the crown to keep it from spinning. The gale belled her skirt high above stocking tops. She freed her arm, pushed the skirt down, held it fast to her knees with both hands.

He asked: "Too windy. Do you want to go in?"

"Not unless you do." She glanced at his bloodied, soiled uniform. "Why, you must be freezing!"

"I'm used to the cold."

"That's all you have?"

"My coat and my bag were back in the coach."

She closed her eyes and he felt her arm's pressure against his side. "That kind of luck makes you humble."

Because her voice trembled, he tried to sound chipper. "Oh, I don't know. It makes me pretty cocky. Not every guy has the foresight to hire a good angel."

She smiled. "You're in your old form."

"And why not?"

"After what you've been through."

"Think nothing of it."

"It's the last lap. Almost home."

"About time." The skyline was a shadow, a broken-toothed line in the mist.

"You'll be glad?" she asked.

"Wouldn't you?" He stared at the gulls and the yellow white spume at the side of the ferry. He was aware of a lump in his throat, that knot made of fear and suspense and profound concentration that came up every time you were briefed for a mission. From head to toe he was tightening and he thought: "Am I scared? Am I frightened of coming home?" and to dismiss it, he craned his neck to try to see Bedloe's Island. "I can't find the old lady," he said.

"The old lady?" she repeated uncertainly.

"The French gal. Mrs. Liberty." He knew his voice shook and he made an effort to change it. "All my life I've been wishing I hadn't been born in New York, so I could get the big thrill of seeing the skyline for the first time. What do I get? Pea soup fog."

"Bad flying weather," she said.

He didn't reply yet he was aware and was proud that he hadn't drawn back from this lead to his immediate past. "I can take it or leave it," he thought.

"What are your plans?" Nina asked.

"Why—why I'll get a room at one of the hotels. Take a bath. Clean my clothes."

"Aren't you going to your father?"

"My father?" The thought startled him. "I'd forgotten I had one." She was compelling him to think of the end of this journey, to remember the lonely old man who was waiting for him. Not really waiting. Possibly hoping, but not really expecting. "I never wired him," he said. "He doesn't know I'm on my way home." That wasn't a home. It was a studio couch in a furnished room. "He'll be surprised. He won't believe all that's happened to me." Yet even as he said that to himself, he remembered he hadn't made plans to spend time with his father. Possibly dinner together, one evening off from the girls and the bars, drop in and see how the old man is doing. Yet the old man's was the name on his dog tags. That was the place to which the telegram might have been sent.

She saw how absorbed he was and stayed silent to let him complete what was in his mind. Then she said: "Don, come to my place. Call up your father. Let him come to us."

The "us" caught at his heart-strings and closed his throat, a concept so new, so overwhelming that he hadn't found words

with which to reply before someone touched his arm and said:
"I've been looking for you."

He turned. Dr. Peck stood at his elbow. "I've come for my
buck. Remember, I can't get home unless you lend me a dollar." The man's eyes were bloodshot, his skin gray as ashes,
sagging with fatigue, yet he sounded amazingly cheerful. "You
had just promised to pay for my breakfast, lend me a dollar.
Or have you forgotten? When they pulled out the diner from
under." He pocketed the bill Corbett gave him. "And where
shall I return it?"

Corbett shrugged. "Oh, Red Cross."

"Good enough. Well, it's been fine knowing you." He extended his hand as though he intended to shake a good-by,
and then let it drop at his side. "Well, we've been through a
good deal together." His color had risen somewhat, with wind
or confusion. "You know—" He seemed suddenly shy. "I
wonder if you'll get what I'm trying to say. Yesterday, when
we talked, you embarrassed me. Your presence, I mean.
Well"— He squared his shoulders— "I don't feel that way
any more." The March breeze plucked at his hat and he
reached up to anchor it.

Vaguely puzzled, Corbett started politely: "Oh, you didn't
need—"

Dr. Peck's upraised hand silenced him. "I'm the best judge.
I certainly did. When I saw men like you, I felt like—" He
smiled broadly. "Well, now I feel like a tired old man who
has done a day's work, and can look any other man straight in
the eye. Even you." He saw Nina veer swiftly around, as if
all of a sudden she had to see what was happening upstream.
"It's odd," he began, after a pause to make up his mind about
her. "You might say this wreck was class-conscious. Only
coach passengers were killed. Ordinary people. Almost sym-
bolic. The big shots got off. Hastings. He left us at Washington. His sort always gets off. God protects fools." He scowled
and then added. "Oh, don't give the wreck credit for Voorhees.
Did you get to know him? That man was scared of his shadow,

scared of his world. Ironic, wasn't it? He died in his sleep peacefully." His head slowly moved from side to side.

"Not peacefully." Voorhees' death was falling into its fateful design. The figure that skulked in the dark, slumbering Pullman. The dead man whose pockets held Voorhees' wallet. Benny Kalchis. Someone whom he knew, someone who had eaten with him, slept at his side. "The last thing that frightened that man was a thief. A common thief."

"Noooooo?" Dr. Peck took a step back. "Why, I'll wager that's when my—"

"Your watch and your wallet. The odd little horseplayer."

"Nooooo? . . . Did they catch him?"

Corbett's lips thinned. "Cold. Cold as a mackerel."

"I'll be damned."

Nina turned. "We're almost in. I'll go get my bags."

"Well, so long." Dr. Peck finally extended his hand. "Call me up, if you have a spare evening. Keep in touch. And good luck."

The Palm Queen survivors were all over the waiting room. You could sort them from commuters riding from Jersey by their tan and their hillocks of luggage. Just inside the door, Mrs. Forsythe stood. She had always looked fragile and helpless, yet now, as she stood by herself in the ferry doorway, she seemed almost pitiful. She brightened a little when she saw Corbett. "Are we nearly in?"

Nina murmured: "Don, I'll go get my luggage," and darted away from his side.

The ferry was easing into its slip. It jarred against pilings. He steadied Mrs. Forsythe with his arm. He said: "Watch yourself. Almost fell."

"I'm getting accustomed to danger." She smiled rather wanly. "Would you say it was time?"

"Time?"

"You must know what I mean. You sat at the table with Mr. Voorhees and me." Her color was rising. "You must have heard what I said—"

He didn't answer directly but asked: "Then you are going back?"

"As fast as I can. Whenever I can get passage."

"But the show isn't over. They're still taking hell, expecting more of it."

"I know." Her shoulders drew together. "It can't be much worse than what happened today."

His teeth clicked shut. "It can. This all day and all night. Every day."

Her chin came up slowly. "And if it is, I shall still be more safe." The flush had spread up her cheekbones. "I was mad, in a panic, afraid to go back, grasping at straws, anything I could cling to, to keep me here . . . Even an old—"

He cut in. "You don't have to tell me. I don't need to know."

"I'm sorry." She looked at the ferry floor. "I seem to forget that no one really cares what happens to anyone else." Her lips curved in a wry smile. "Well, it's high time I got back. I've become so un-British, confiding in strangers." She put out her hand, smiling courteously. "Perhaps we shall meet, if you come back to England."

"Good luck," he said and went into the waiting room.

Joanie stood on the wooden seat, looking out of the window. Elaine held her knees. When she saw him, she clutched the child tighter, as though she feared he had come to take Joanie away. Her slate eyes were sunken in hollows as purple as the bruise on her chin.

He said: "Take good care of my girl friend."

Elaine moistened her lips with her tongue. "I can keep her, can't I?"

"For the present, I guess. Contact the Red Cross. They'll have to locate her father."

"They'll send him a telegram?"

"Please! We've been through that before."

Her mother-in-law hooked her hand through his elbow, pulled him down, whispered: "She'll be all right." She looked almost as badly done in as Elaine. "Just getting home to our empty apartment, that's what I worried about. She'll be so busy with Joanie, she won't even notice. I can't thank you enough."

"Who? Me? Don't be silly."

She patted his arm. "We've been so lucky. If it isn't your time—"

He said: "So long, see you."

She plucked at his sleeve. "Lieutenant, if you could manage, while you are in New York, we'd like you for dinner. Friday night, maybe. A good home-cooked meal."

"I'd love it," he said. "Haven't had one in years. I'll call you. You're in the phone book?"

"Manhattan. West Eighty-seventh."

He put his arms around Joanie. "So long, kid, be good."

Joanie turned all the way inside his arms, hugged his neck. "Don't go away."

He loosened her arms to get his breath back. "I have to. I have to go home. Take a bath. Clean my clothes. Don't you see I'm all dirty?"

"I don't want you to go. Stay here with me. Right here on this seat."

He shook his head. "You're going home with Elaine, pussy-cat. I'll see you there. I'll come up for supper."

"Today?"

"Well, some day." The knot filled his throat. He hadn't guessed it would be so hard to say good-by to this kid. To all of them, even these women. It was like breaking a family up. He said, solemnly: "We mustn't lose touch with each other," and started away but turned back again. "Don't give Joanie ice-cream," he said. "Keep her away from the Good Humor man . . . Well, so long, take good care of my kid."

The ferry was clanging and grinding. He took one or two steps in the direction Nina had gone to assemble her luggage and was stopped by a nudge on his arm. It was the Hastings kid. The girl was carrying heavy valises and she glanced from the luggage to him significantly, with so plain an appeal that he found he was honestly sorry, for Pat looked bedraggled and poignantly helpless and tired.

He said: "Wish I could help you with those but I'm promised. If I'd just thought to bring my spare arm."

Pat set down one bag and brushed back the hair strings that trailed to her eyes. "It's all right. I'll get a porter or someone."

He said: "Well, so long ... Thanks for the Scotch."

She put her hand on his sleeve. "Will you give me a ring? We'll be at the Waldorf." She caught the involuntary curl of his lips. "Oh, don't let that scare you. Heavens, I'm not— Why, the way I feel now!" Again, she pushed her hair wearily back. "I feel as if I'd been through the war. Why!" Her eyes bugged, her mouth gaped. "Why, it's something like that, like that wreck, isn't it?"

"Something." His smile became full, almost pitying. "Only more so. All the time."

"Oh, no! ... But then how do they stand it?"

"Some do. Some don't," he said, rather sharply. "Depends on what kind of person you are. If you're one kind, you pull up your guts and do something to help. If you're another, you sit down and cry and say why did it happen to me?"

Her smudged forehead wrinkled; her juvenile, painted mouth stayed agape with the effort of thinking, until she said, quietly: "I catch."

He touched her shoulder and again smiled. "Facts of life, kid ... Well, so long. Take care of yourself." He saluted and squirmed through the going-off crowd to find Nina. She had said her good-bys. He picked up her luggage. They were caught in the swarm at the gates, pushed out to the shed, strode down the long, bilge-reeking ferryhouse tunnel, out to the raw, blustery streets of New York. A yellow cab idled in front of the ferry house and as they moved toward it, Rauchmeyer lunged past them, leaped into the cab, slammed the door.

For a quarter hour more, the Palm Queen survivors were all together again, scrambling and squealing and fighting for taxicabs. "You'd think," he heard Mrs. Hastings complain, "they'd take care of *us*. Pat, when we tell your father! What he'll do to that railroad!"

Pat Hastings's voice, ashamed and impatient, rose over her mother's. 'Oh, mother! Pu-leeze! Won't you believe there's a war?"

Corbett said: "You wait here," to Nina, ducked through the stream of truck traffic, flagged a cab as it came to the corner, jumped in, drove around, stopped not before Nina, but in front of the Westons and Joanie. "Get in." He lifted the child into the taxi. "So long, cookie, be good. See you some more." He re-crossed the street, wigwagged in the rain until he flagged another. He put in Nina's bags, climbed in beside her. She gave the driver an address in the Fifties and slid back in her corner.

He was busying himself with the waterfront fruit sheds, knowing the elation of seeing familiar scenes and so at first he failed to see that Nina was dabbing her eyes with a grayed linen square. When he finally turned, she had moved deep into her corner and was pretending to look at the piers. The droop of her back was betraying. He gripped her shoulders, turned her around.

The ridiculous hat was pushed back like a harridan's. Her hair straggled. She had just the one earring, on a lobe as black as a stoker's. Her tan was amber and tears had made streaks. He said: "Hey! What goes?"

She swallowed hard. "Nothing. I'm just a dope." She pulled out her compact, looked in its mirror. "Oh, good Lord, look at me!" She yanked off her hat, fumbled around in her bag for something with which to wipe off the dirt. "Women are the craziest people," she murmured: "Little things get them."

"Like what?"

She scrubbed at her face with a piece of cleansing tissue.

"Like what?" he repeated.

"Oh, like that nasty gorilla knocking down women and children to get the first taxi."

He drew her towards him. "Good God, women!"

She pulled back. She said, with a catch in her throat: "Now, I know what you meant when you said yesterday it all stinks and Chanel Number Five can't—"

He put his hand on her mouth. Very clearly, every syllable separate, distinct, he said: "I don't believe that any more."

Her eyes were large and round in the smudged heart of her face. "And why not?"

"Because I'm in it. I'm part of it."

He could see she didn't understand what he meant and he tried to explain. "Nina, life's very simple. You're in it. You do what you have to the best that you can."

"That's just words." She shook her head stubbornly. "I mean something else. It was so good for a while. People were kind to each other. Considerate, helpful. Trouble brought them together. They forgot, you forgot, they could be mean and selfish . . . Then Larry Stengel came in, talked about suing and lawyers—and—and I gagged."

The taxi swung into Fourteenth, began its crosstown snail's crawl. He studied the buildings a moment or two. No thought came of itself, by spontaneous combustion. You had to work it all out, word by word. He started again: "Dear, people don't change." He held her hand tightly. "There are no miracles. People aren't reborn with one hit on the head. They are what they are; they remain what they were. Even a small bit of bombing—"

She cried: "Oh please," and looked more deeply hurt than his words seemed to warrant.

"I'm sorry." The cab turned into Fifth, rolled slowly North. "There's the Flatiron!" he cried. "Hot damn! There's Madison Square! By God, I can almost see Empire State." Then he sighed. He wasn't yet free to enjoy his reunion with home. Something still had to be cleared for this girl. He said: "Honey, some people have stuff—stuff to grow on. When things happen to them they grow up. It has to *happen*, of course. You can't grow on second-hand experience. You might like to. You can't. You'd like to understand war, what it does to people, by reading newspapers and seeing the movies. Less painful that way. The sufferings of war in ten easy lessons. Well, it doesn't take." He shook his head and he smiled. "Yet even that, even the most harrowing experiences can leave people unchanged. For what we call better, I mean. Oh, they may get frightened, resentful, even bitter perhaps, but that's all . . . Now you take an extrovert like your friend Stengel. He did what was expected of him. He did the right things. But he stayed what he was. This was a picnic to him. Got a great kick out of carrying a stretcher. Made him feel like a hero. He'll be a social success for months with his story of what he saw and did . . . Now you take a tough son of a bitch like Rauchmeyer. To him it was nothing but personal inconvenience . . . You see, it's what's inside you that goes to work when there's trouble. The thing they used to call character. The thing we call guts. Now, take you—"

She moved closer, put her hand on his arm. "Don, let me for once do something important. Let me take care of a soldier." She wavered, as if the next words took more resolve than she had at that moment. "Let me take care of a soldier I love."

He moved back. "What did you say?"

"I said *love*." The trace of a smile came to her face. "I wanted to say it this morning . . . Ever hear it before?"

It was bewildering and startling and dazzling. A thing lay back in your mind, in the caves of your being, your most secret hope, longing, wish, but until it was spoken you could always deny it, push it back, push it down, to spare yourself disappointment or pain. Now that it was put into words—Nina's words—had become irrevocable, a great weight seemed to lift, a quiet contentment, warming, relaxing, seeping all through.

"It's an old-fashioned word," he found himself saying. "It doesn't belong in our world."

"If I prove that it does?"

He waited again before he said slowly: "I'll believe you, my darling." He picked up her hand, turned it over, held the palm to his lips.

He heard her say, softly: "Don, that was what you wanted, wasn't it, Don? Not with lust, not with pity. With love."

Her fingertips slid away from his mouth, down the groove in his cheek, gently, as if she hoped to smooth the crease out, and then more firmly, more purposefully, as though that was what she had meant to do all the time.

The taxi turned into a side-street. The driver cocked his head, asked: "Which number, ma'am?"

"Oh!" She seemed slightly startled, as if that simple question had moved her from one world to another. She peered through the window. "The house on the corner. The one with the canopy."

While he paid the fare, a doorman, six-foot of Ireland, dressed up like an Admiral, rushed out to the curb. "Miss Gilmore! Thank heaven! Switchboard's been crazy. Everybody calling about you." The doorman gave Corbett a critical stare, and touched Nina's elbow, held the umbrella over her head. "Here, you run right in. I'll bring up your bags."

Corbett followed her through a lobby of thick piled Turkish rugs, inlaid gilt-swabbed tables, high-backed red-cushioned chairs. The elevator man wrung her hand. "Gees, I'm glad to see you, Miss Gilmore. Your maid's upstairs, worried sick about you." When the car stopped, the white door of an apartment swung open and a wide-bosomed Negress in wine-colored poplin flung her arms around Nina. "Honey chile, I was almost skeered white. You feelin' good? You ain't hurt?"

He felt envy's pang. Old Home Week for Miss Gilmore. He shifted his mud-caked, scuffed shoes awkwardly on the rug of the foyer. She called: "Come in, Don. Come in, dear. We're home."

He went into her living room. It wasn't home, not any kind of a home he had ever known. It was something out of one of her magazines: sleek and dashing, original, costly: turquoise blue walls, thick, rough-textured oyster white rug, chairs cinnabar red. He said: "Hey! How'd we get here? Two dirty tramps."

She pulled off her hat and fur jacket, flung them down on a

chair. "Make yourself comfortable, Don. Take off your coat. Throw it down any place . . . Now the first thing we'll do is have a few good stiff drinks. Forget all the terrible things."

He stared at her and he laughed. Why, it happened to everyone. Fear, shock or strain did the same things to each sensitive person it caught. Made them want to run, hide, escape. The puzzle was clear, her swift changes of mood, her rasped edges. She had repeated his pattern precisely. The Sunday Don Corbett.

The maid brought in a tray. It had Scotch, small bottles of soda, an ice-pail, a big bowl of crackers. Nina started to pour. The telephone rang. She said: "Damn! Tend bar, Don," went to the hall and picked up the receiver.

"Hello," he heard her say. "Yes, it's Nina. In person. What?" Her voice rose. "*You* had a terrible time! *You* were upset!" She snorted into the phone. "My pet, what did *you* feel? What did *you* see? Your second-hand sufferings! You make me sick. *You* had a terrible time!" She banged the phone into its cradle, strode back to the living room. Her eyes flashed. "Imagine that! My best friend. My very best friend. Calling me up to let me know what a terrible time she's had worrying about me. Got a headache. Her stomach upset. Because she knew I'd be on the Palm Queen. Please be sorry for her. Poor darling, she suffered. Why, if she'd have had to go through just one half—"

She stopped because Don was laughing, laughing with head thrown back, from deep in his belly, until tears jumped from his eyes and streamed down the grooves in his cheeks.

THE END